QUILT CITY: PANIC IN PADUCAH

A HADLEY CARROLL MYSTERY
BOOK 2

BRUCE LEONARD

EYE-TIME PRESS

Quilt City: Panic in Paducah

A Hadley Carroll Mystery, Book 2

By Bruce Leonard

Published by Eye-Time Press

Cover designed by Getcovers.com

Cover photos by Bruce Leonard

This is a novel, meaning I made up the story but set it in Paducah, Kentucky, a real and impressive small city where I lived for two years and still visit frequently. The characters came from my imagination, so they're not based on anyone, living or dead. If one of the characters reminds you of your Uncle Ned, well, that's just coincidence. However, a young woman I didn't know when I wrote *Quilt City Murders* named Hadley Carroll is from Paducah. I met her at my first book signing. I took this highly improbable coincidence as a sign that I was meant to write *Quilt City Murders*, the first novel in the Hadley Carroll Mystery series, when and where I did. The real Hadley hasn't sued me yet. I take that as a good sign, too. If you'd like to reproduce part or all of this book, you are not legally allowed to do so, in any format. Doing so would violate the copyright, and then lawyers would have to get involved. Although many of my friends are lawyers, I'd rather not involve them because I probably owe them money.

Cover Design: GetCovers.com

Cover Photos: Bruce Leonard

Second Edition

Printed in the United States of America

Paperback ISBN: 979-8-9868235-0-8

ebook ISBN: 979-8-9868235-1-5

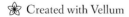 Created with Vellum

I dedicate Quilt City: Panic in Paducah to my parents, to my brother and sister, and to Sedonia Sipes, the most impressive spouse anyone has ever loved.

ALSO BY BRUCE LEONARD

Quilt City Murders

A Hadley Carroll Mystery

Book 1

Named Best Mystery of 2022 by the National Indie Excellence Awards

Quilt City: Measure Once, Cut Twice

Book 3

Quilt City: Proving a Negative

Book 4

Quilt City Cookbook

A companion book, narrated by Hadley at her funniest and most vulnerable, that contains dozens of sweet and savory recipes, anecdotes, characters' backstories, and plenty of laughs.

And soon:

Hard Exit

A Jack Drake Private-Eye Mystery

Book 1

ONE

A WHISPERED CLUE

"Be careful. Quilting's addictive," I said to Janet Loy as she ran her hand across a piece of paisley fabric in the sewing section of Walmart.

"Hi, Hadley," Janet said. "You caught me. I need more fabric like I need another wheelchair, but here I am debating whether to add this sandpaper to my stash."

"Hey, I won't judge you. I'm supposed to be buying office supplies to replace my campaign signs that someone tore down, but I couldn't make it through the store without seeing if a certain fabric would jump into my hands."

Janet's rheumatoid arthritis had become so bad that she'd gone from using a cane to a walker to a power wheelchair as her joints progressively betrayed her. She was only sixty, but the pain in her fingers was so extreme some days that she couldn't quilt with us on Sundays during our weekly Paducah Quilters Quorum sessions—which we called PQQ. No matter which of our houses PQQ was held at, she attended our sessions because missing out on gossip was almost as bad as missing a stitch. She was a talented quilter and a world-class gossip.

She said, "I was in here the other day buying the mess kit I just returned—my grand nephew let me know I bought the wrong kind—and I saw your creepy opponent buying ammo. If Nick Stoddard is elected mayor, I should run for Miss Teen USA because anything can happen."

I laughed and said, "I agree about the creepy part, but the Stoddards usually get what they want."

"Then they must want to be hated," she said. "Everyone in Paducah could tell a Stoddard story that crime writers could use as source material."

Because she was usually cold, she often draped a small quilt across her lap, careful not to let it snag in the wheels of her motorized chair. That Friday afternoon, the crazy quilt that the other PQQ members had created secretly on consecutive Saturdays with her eighteen-year-old granddaughter, Ashley Pope, sat across her lap. The words *Ashley loves Grammie J*, and *Grammie J loves Ashley* were overlaid. When she was three, Ashley gave Grammie J the nickname she cherished. We gave Janet the quilt on her sixtieth birthday.

"You're the best, Janet. I have to run, but we'll see you Sunday, right?"

"Of course. You don't mind if I run over a few of his campaign signs, do you? The battery on this beauty is fully charged."

I laughed, then bent over and hugged her.

Six minutes later, while I was gathering office supplies, I jumped at the sound of a rifle shot. The explosions that followed made me spring into action. I turned toward the loud bangs coming from the sporting goods section and saw a billow of rising black smoke.

Ten men dressed in black from head-to-toe, including face masks, dragged large, heavy duffel bags that impeded their strides as they rushed toward the exit. In case a customer needed help, I sprinted toward the wall of flames racing across a top shelf in the camping section.

A deafening alarm blared, and a husky voice over the P.A. system said, "Attention Walmart shoppers: Exit through the front entrance immediately. Leave your merchandise. Again, drop your merchandise and exit through the front doors."

The smoke triggered the overhead sprinklers. As I ran toward the flames, I slowed on the wet floor because I couldn't help anyone if I broke a tibia. I hurried but set my Asics down carefully. I followed the last of the robbers with my eyes as he lumbered toward the back exit. He appeared to weigh more than four hundred pounds. He saw me looking at him, then drew his right index finger slowly across his throat. I'd received numerous death threats after I'd sued Paducah and its police department—and I was still alive that day in Walmart— so I wouldn't be scared into silence by a mountain of a criminal slogging away while hiding behind a mask.

I rounded a corner to find a Walmart employee, a young Black man of about twenty wearing a blue vest, huddled on the floor, gagged with a bandana and bound with zip ties at his wrists and ankles. He tried to wriggle away from the flames that burned toward him. They incinerated the camo clothes and other hunting supplies on the racks and shelves and danced toward the ammo that the robbers hadn't stolen.

Every rifle and shotgun that had stood upright in their locked racks minutes before had been dragged out the back door in the duffels. Only two BB guns and about twenty boxes of ammo remained. The drawers and glass cabinet behind the counter were open, without having been jimmied or smashed. The horrible chemical smell emitted by the burning synthetics and the melting plastic camping coolers made me gag, and I thought I'd be sick. I managed to control my stomach, but the smoke burned my eyes and made me cough repeatedly. The extreme heat drenched my body in sweat within seconds.

I ducked as low as I could without crawling to avoid the smoke and made a decision. I took four steps to the ammunition, and tossed one box after another underhand down the aisle. In the thirty seconds it took me to remove the ammunition, two employees in blue vests arrived and carried their fellow employee away from the flames.

Over the screams of fleeing customers and between bleats of the ear-piercing alarm, I heard a woman yell, "Help."

I grabbed a bandana from a shelf and held it against my mouth and nose. The flames raged, and water covered the floor. The smell of propane assaulted my nostrils, and I realized the blasts were camping-sized canisters exploding. My eyes burned and shed rivulets of tears. Customers fled and firefighters and police officers arrived, but my focus was on finding the source of the cry for help because I feared the worst. I rounded a corner and saw Janet in obvious pain, slapping at the flames on her blouse and the quilt.

I ran to her, grabbed the burning quilt in her lap, threw it to the ground, and stomped the flames out along one of its borders.

"Hadley," she whispered. Her lavender blouse was scorched through in four places, and there were burns on her chest, arms, and palms. Sweat bathed her face, her eyes seemed too large for their sockets, and her exposed skin was bright red. She said something, but I couldn't hear her.

I coughed again and again and couldn't stop. The display of propane canisters that had blown up near us had turned into an inferno that the water falling from the sprinklers couldn't extinguish. About half of the fifty or so canisters had not exploded yet, so I had to hustle us away from them before they detonated. The fire had spread to the toy department and to the section on the far side of it. Flames shot toward the ceiling between us and the exit at the front of the store.

I picked up the quilt, set it in her lap, and tied the bandana around my head and across my nose, bandit-style. I pushed the toggle on the wheelchair to go forward. Nothing happened. I looked down and saw a melted wire that connected to the battery. Next to a back wheel sat a packaged mess kit in a half-inch of water.

I tilted the chair onto its back wheels, struggled to balance it, made sure I had a good grip, and pulled her backward toward the exit that the robbers had used. I figured we weren't in danger from the robbers because they were long gone. Flames burned between us and the front exit, so I headed for what I hoped was the safest escape route.

I coughed hard as I pulled the chair backward, then realized I'd go faster if I pushed her. I stopped so I could rotate the chair, and Janet reached up, grabbed the back of my head, and pulled it toward her mouth.

What I heard her say was, "Whaaaaf."

She grabbed the left side of her chest with her right hand, and fear shot across her face. Beads of sweat burst onto her face and neck, both turning brighter red than they had been. She opened her mouth, but I only heard a weak squawk. I leveled the chair, stepped in front of it, and looked into her eyes. Despite her fear and pain, she summoned the strength to say, "Woooo."

"Again," I said.

"Woof." She grabbed her chest with both hands and gasped for breath.

"Like a dog?"

She nodded. Did I hear her right? Was she referring to Chica, her Chihuahua?

I maneuvered Janet out the door and into fresh air and lowered the front wheels to the ground. I pulled the bandana down and inhaled deeply. Big mistake. I doubled over coughing. I put my hands on my knees, looked at the ground, and tried not to be sick. Sirens wailed, and I heard cops, paramedics, and firefighters running past us. I couldn't stop coughing. My hacks and gasps for breath took my attention away from Janet.

When I finally straightened, I saw frustration in her eyes as she desperately waved the quilt with her right arm, hoping I would see it in my peripheral vision. Her face was racked with distress. Waving the quilt appeared to worsen her anguish. I took the quilt from her.

"I'm sorry, Janet. I couldn't clear my lungs." My voice sounded pickled. "You have my attention."

"A ... A ..."

"Ashley?"

She nodded.

"Of course. But you can give it to her. You'll get through this."

A paramedic hurried toward us. Her name tag said Ruth Green-
blatt. Nearby, her partner tended to another woman who had been
injured inside. Ruth reached to feel Janet's pulse, and I stepped out
of the way. Janet looked at me, her eyes pleading for me to compre-
hend her.

"Woof," she whispered. Her eyes asked if I understood.

"Woof, like a dog. I understand."

She closed her eyes, and her head tilted to her right.

I didn't think she was telling me about Chica, and the last
sentence I spoke to her was a lie. I understood what "woof" meant
but not what she meant.

I stood three feet from Janet, numb, hoping Ruth would resusci-
tate my friend. I couldn't believe this was happening. Not again. I'd
suffered a series of traumas about a year and a half earlier. On most
days, I thought I'd moved on. Occasionally, however, my body let me
know that being dumped by my fiancé, Matt Ackerman, who was
later murdered, finding his body, and being beaten by Officer Josh
Williams were still with me. I hoped these traumas wouldn't always
bunch my shoulders and give me headaches, a racing heart, nightmares, and panic attacks that drenched me in sweat. However, the
abuse and neglect I'd suffered as a girl had embedded those symp-
toms in me. I'd worked hard with my therapist, Dr. Elaine Bourget, to
overcome my various traumas, but some days the past got the better
of me—and occasionally still does.

Ruth pulled a defibrillator from her truck, but when she applied
the paddles to Janet's chest, I hyperventilated, which caused another
coughing fit. I walked away.

I felt overwhelmed by sadness and couldn't form a coherent
thought. A bunch of incongruent ideas ran together: How could I
help Ruth save Janet? Where was Chica, and had she eaten recently?
If Janet died, what was I supposed to do? Call Ash, then the morgue?
I looked at Ruth, who applied the paddles four more times. She used

a stethoscope to listen for Janet's heartbeat. She shook her head, turned to me, and said, "She didn't make it. I hate this job."

She put the defibrillator in the truck, and I made the mistake of looking at Janet's limp body sitting in the wheelchair.

My decades as a journalist kicked in, and I knew that after I called Ashley to let her know Grammie J had passed, I had to report the story. The assailants had to be caught. As far as I was concerned, they'd just killed my friend.

So, I did what I do—I got to work. I would grieve later.

TWO
ANOTHER LOSS

I didn't possess superpowers or the ability to round up a posse to track down the criminals. But I did have *Paducah Pulse*, the free weekly newspaper I'd started five months prior with part of the settlement money I'd received from the city.

Paducah wanted no part of the publicity that a civil trial would bring, so it settled with me out of court. With the settlement money, I'd created *Paducah Pulse* and purchased a fixer-upper (faller-down-er?) Arts & Crafts house in Lower Town, Paducah's arts district. If I spent my money cautiously, and if *Paducah Pulse* continued to grow at the rate it was growing, I could possibly scrimp together enough to restore the 1962 MGA that Matt had left to me.

That afternoon at Walmart, I had resources at my disposal: five journalists and the power of the pen. I'd seen the crime occur, so I would be interviewed by police, and I would interview anyone who would enable me to write the best stories possible. My friend had just been killed, so I had no choice but to help capture the killers. After all, I'd done that before.

During the commotion, I'd set my purse down in the store. Two officers were talking fifty feet from me. Firefighters continued to arrive and run into the back exit. Before the cops cordoned off the perimeter, I walked toward the door, holding my arms up in front of my face as if to ward off smoke. But I was trying to prevent the officers from recognizing me.

I suspected Officer Kramer—the one who'd watched as Officer Williams pummeled me—of tearing down my campaign flyers and posters and ripping out my yard signs. He'd received a significant suspension but no jail time. Based on the late-night calls I received from a blocked number and the vandalism of my home, I believed he held a grudge. I didn't know which of Kramer's fellow officers sided with him, so I thought it wise to try to conceal my presence from them.

Inside, I maneuvered my way through the pandemonium until I found my purse. My damaged airway caused me to cough repeatedly. I left the office supplies where they were and headed outside.

I walked around the edge of the building, hoping to lessen the sound of the blaring sirens contributing to the headache that felt like a vice on my temples. I called Ashley Pope but got her voicemail.

"Hello, Ash. It's Hadley. Please call me when you get this."

I put the phone in my purse and pulled out a reporter's notebook, a pen, and a voice recorder. I preferred it to the app on my phone. I rounded the corner in the other direction and approached Ruth, who was tending to the young Walmart employee I'd seen tied up. I made a point not to look in Janet's direction. I didn't want to see her still sitting there, and I didn't want to see that she was on her way to the morgue.

"I promise you," the employee said, "I was scared, and my throat hurts. Getting bounced off the floor and being kicked don't feel good, but I'm not badly injured."

"Okay," Ruth said. "Your vitals are fine. Nothing appears to be broken. I'd rather you get some X-rays, but that's up to you. Keep an eye on your abraded wrists and ankles. The ointment should prevent it, but they could get infected."

"Sounds good. Can I go?"

"Yup."

I stepped toward Ruth and said, "Thank you for helping Janet. I appreciate your efforts." She nodded and turned away, trying not to cry, it seemed.

"Excuse me, please," I said to the young man as he walked away.

"Yeah?"

"I'm Hadley Carroll, a reporter for *Paducah Pulse*." It was technically a true statement. People were more cooperative when I bumped myself down the masthead, instead of revealing that I edited and owned the paper, as well.

"I'd like to ask you a few questions," I said.

"Okay, but make it quick, please. Just want this day to end." I pressed the "record" button and held the recorder under my notebook.

"I understand. First, what's your name, with spelling?"

"David Robie, R-O-B-I-E."

"Thanks."

"You're the one who threw the ammo."

"Yes."

"That was smart. Coulda been worse."

"Maybe. What can you tell me about the guys who tied you up?"

"One grabbed me from behind, arm tight around my throat, other hand over my mouth. He said, 'Don't wanna kill you but will in a heartbeat, you play hero.' That's it, word for word. Took the keys and unlocked the mounted guns and cabinets. Just bad timing, really."

"What's that mean?"

"Wasn't supposed to be there. I work in automotive. Just covering Buddy's lunch."

"Got it. Know Buddy's last name?"

"Mc-something. Not McNugget, but something like that."

"Thanks. I'll find it. Did anything about them or what they did stick out?"

"Never been grabbed like that or tied up, so that sticks out, but you mean something that could identify them. They were rough tying me up and gagging me, then threw me to the floor. Landed hard on the concrete. Then the dude kicked me in the ribs. Guess I was lucky he only did it once wearing sneakers. Boots would've been worse. Don't know if this helps."

"You're doing great. We never know what will help when writing a story. Or, in this case, trying to catch these guys."

"Cool. You saw Carl and Eddie carry me down the aisle, but what sticks out is what the guy who told me he'd kill me said when I was on the floor: 'Ain't right, none a this.' Then he kicked me."

"I'm sorry. I'm glad you remembered that."

Cops were stringing yellow crime-scene tape around the far edge of the asphalt. I saw three officers looking at me. One of them started to walk toward us.

David said, "Only other thing could mean something is one dude had a dog tag around his neck. But before you ask, no, I didn't see anything written on it."

"Any clue why someone fired the rifle?"

"All I heard was some dude say, 'Woof, watch this,' then the shot. Sorry, guess I shoulda mentioned that."

"It's fine. You just mentioned it. You're doing great."

Before I could ask him for his contact info and how long he'd worked for Walmart, a voice over my left shoulder said in a sarcastic tone: "Better beat it, kid, 'fore she puts stink on you, too. It's a talent she got."

"What's your phone number, David, in case—"

"You're done here," the officer said to me, stepping into my personal space. He was blond and short, and his breath smelled like deep-fried failure. He held his left hand over his badge, concealing his name. "This is a crime scene, and you're impeding our investigation."

David stepped back but spoke his number slowly as I took two steps away and wrote it down. I never relied only on my recorder. Well, almost never.

"Thank you, David." I tried to hand a business card to him, but the officer slapped it out of my hand.

"Pick that up or I'll cite you for littering. By the way, Officer Kramer sends his best."

I weighed my options. I could crack wise—my natural inclination —and hope I'd still be alive to regret my smart mouth, or I could crack wise and not live long enough to regret my smart mouth. I didn't see a third option. To my surprise, David picked up my business card.

"You got to the count of three to be gone," the officer said, still covering his badge.

My natural inclination kicked in, and I said, "Let me know if you need help counting that high."

His face flushed with rage, and he said, "I'm warning you!"

I shook my head and put the notebook, recorder, and pen in my purse but didn't turn off the recorder. I realized I'd forgotten to pick up Janet's quilt. I looked to my left. The quilt was on the blacktop, beside Janet's empty wheelchair. The EMT or the coroner must have taken her away. I walked to the quilt and picked it up.

With Janet's quilt under my arm, I walked toward David Robie and Officer No Name, thanked David, and headed toward my truck.

From behind me I heard the officer yell, "Watch your back!"

My natural inclination put a cutting retort on my tongue, but I suppressed the urge to express myself. Doing so was harder than saying no to a free bolt of Prairie Cloth Red Rose by Moda Fabrics, but I kept my mouth shut.

THREE

A TOUGH CALL

Ashley called an hour later while I was at my desk in the *Paducah Pulse* building. I was writing the article about the Walmart robbery, explosions, and fire so I could post it to our website and beat the *Chronicle* to the story. Of course, the race was only in my head and was inspired by the nearly universal journalistic belief that publishing news quickly matters. We were a weekly newspaper but updated our website many times each day as reporters filed their stories and when news broke. The *Chronicle*, a daily, didn't post live to its website when breaking news happened. It posted only once a day, at midnight, even if America had been attacked by aliens eight hours earlier. It was easy to understand why many locals called the newspaper the *Paducah Comical*.

"It's Grammie J, right?" Ashley asked when I answered.

"I'm afraid it is. Are you driving?"

"No. She didn't answer. I called five times."

"Yes. She and I were both in Walmart when a robbery occurred—"

"On, no, no, no—"

"There was a fire, and the commotion was too much for her."

"This can't be happening. She died in a fire?"

"No. She suffered minor burns, but I think her heart gave out."

Ashley broke into a wail that sounded similar to the one I'd emitted when I found Matt's body in the Ohio River. I knew that "hush now" and "you'll be okay" and "she's in a better place" were not what she needed. Short of her grandmother being alive, what she needed was to wail, so I listened and cried silently.

Eventually, she said, "I'm sorry. It's just ..."

"No need to apologize. This is tragic. She was nowhere near old. No one should die at her age, especially not the way she did. Because the authorities aren't likely to find your mom, they'll probably contact you. Whenever you feel up to it, you should probably call the coroner."

"Might be ready when I'm thirty. Sorry. Shouldn't've said that."

"It's fine. Say whatever you need to say. You're angry and sad and grieving and confused. Take whatever time you need. If you want me to, I'll take you to identify her. If you can't do it, I'll see what I can do. And if you want PQQ to plan the funeral, we'll take care of it. In fact, we'll take care of everything, unless you want to help."

"Right now, I want to cry and sleep."

"That's a good plan. If you want to, call me when you wake up. I'll bring you a meal."

"Whatever. Sorry. I mean, sure, that sounds nice but probably won't want to eat."

"I'll bring Mellow Mushroom pizza."

"I'll want to eat." We said goodbye and hung up.

As the sole editor of *Paducah Pulse*, I made most of the decisions about which stories we would cover and how to cover them, although I encouraged the reporters to show initiative and pursue stories they deemed worthy. After I filed this article, I'd think about which other story angles *Pulse* would pursue about the robbery.

I thought about calling Dakota to let her know what had happened. I decided to wait until I'd finished writing the story.

My cell rang. It was Officer Brandon Green. We'd run into each other around town three times in the seventeen months since the Quilt City Murders—as the local and national media invariably referred to them. Brandon and I had spoken about what was going on in our lives, and the conversations had flowed easily. He'd ended each of them by saying, "Let me know when. Or if."

"Definitely yes, but I don't know when," I'd said the last time, about three months earlier.

"When you do, you know how to reach me. My Craftsman tools and mechanic's creeper are ready."

After pretty much solving the murders together, he and I had discussed restoring the MGA. I was certain Brandon wasn't calling about the car that evening.

"Are you okay?" he asked.

"I'm fine now. Couldn't stop coughing for a while, but now I'm just sad at the loss of Janet and furious at the idiots who killed her."

"I'm really sorry, Hadley. You knew the deceased?"

"Yes. Very well. She was a good friend and a member of PQQ."

"I'm sorry. I just heard two of my less-than-esteemed colleagues saying less-than-flattering things about you. We almost came to blows."

"Why, Officer Green, you defended my honor. How chivalrous!" I ladled a triple serving of Western Kentucky accent over those sentences.

"Just did what any male who isn't a jackass would've done."

"I heard tell those males had gone extinct. The last Southern Gentlemen."

"Only if Southern Illinois counts. I'm from Murphysboro."

"I know. You told me in Mellow Mushroom. But I'm a reporter, so I also know that you finished second in a pass-punt-and-kick competition in the sixth grade."

"Keith Hoffman cheated. His dad was one of the judges. Fudged the distances. But I'm not bitter."

I laughed.

"Your reporter files need updating, though, because I'm Detective Green now."

"Congratulations, and I apologize for not stalking you properly."

We exchanged a few more pleasantries, but I hadn't filed my story, so the tragedy at Walmart elbowed its way back into my thoughts.

I said, "How much do you know about what happened?" He told me what he knew, then I said, "That's almost all of it. Two additions, though. Janet's last word to me was 'woof,' as in a dog's bark. And David Robie, the Walmart employee who was tied up, told me at least one of the robbers, assailants, murderers—whatever we're calling them—wore a single dog tag and said to him, 'Ain't right, none a this.'"

"Any idea what wasn't right?"

"You're the trained law enforcement officer. I was hoping you'd hazard a guess."

"We learned not to guess in the academy, but if I were to speculate, based on my years of investigative experience, I'd say: Not a clue."

"Thank you for your honesty. I met a colleague of yours in the Walmart parking lot. Blond, five-six, maybe 135 in his boots. Bit of a Napoleon complex. Hid his badge."

"Didn't I bend the rules enough for you on the last case? You want me to do your homework again?"

"Just so we're clear, *Detective* Green: Were you under the impression that it was my job, a much-maligned female journalist with a quilting addiction and a mutt named Trapunto, to solve the Quilt City Murders? Is that the homework assignment to which you refer?"

"Phil Shannon."

"I'll take that as an acknowledgment that my previous statement eviscerated your argument, so you acquiesced to my request."

"Do you quilt as well as you speak?"

"No. But your question popped a Eugene O'Neill quote into my head: 'Stammering is the native eloquence of us fog people.'"

"You've been reading while I've been watching reality TV."

"Oh, I watch some, too, especially baking shows and house-rehab shows. *Restored* with Brett Waterman. He's kind of a dolt, but he does wonders with old houses. And I now own an old house. And by old, I mean barely standing."

"Congratulations, if that's what's warranted. If not, my condolences."

"Both, probably, and thank you. But I have to finish my story. I'm glad you called, Brandon. I hope you have a great weekend."

"You, too. Are you going to Barbecue on the River?"

"Was thinking about it, but that was before this day turned ugly."

"I understand. If you change your mind and would like an escort—"

"Your Craftsman tools and mechanic's creeper are ready."

"Exactly. Take care."

"You, too."

I finished my story, posted it to our website, and added it to the content-management system so it would run in Wednesday's print edition. I called Dan Eidie, the reporter I'd hired away from the *Chronicle* to cover the cops and courts beat for *Paducah Pulse.*

"You sure you're okay?" he asked, after I told him I'd been in Walmart.

"I'm not physically hurt, and I've lived through worse many times, so I'll be fine."

"I hear you, and I'm sorry. What do you need me to do?"

"Try to get quotes from Walmart corporate, from the manager of the store, and the assistant managers on duty. You won't succeed because no one could get a quote from any of them under these circumstances, but you should try. Someone there may accidentally act like a human being."

"Got it. How about a post on Facebook to see if any of the customers who were there will go on record?"

"Great idea but be sure to verify that anyone who gives you a quote was really there. Kooks love this kind of stuff."

"Got it. Want me to look into whether other stores or gun shops have been hit?"

"Good idea. You got this. You don't need to run your stories by me anymore. You've proven you have great instincts. If you're on the fence, or you think a story could do more than ruffle feathers, run it by me. If not, keep meeting deadlines, writing solid copy, and providing good art."

"Thank you. Get some rest."

"I'll do my best." That was all I could promise because I battled anxiety and insomnia. "Good luck."

I ordered office supplies and scanned the slate of ads scheduled for Wednesday's issue. I would worry tomorrow about revamping the editorial lineup to include extended coverage of the Walmart robbery.

While I refilled my water bottle in the break room, I heard my cell on my desk ring. I returned to my office and saw that the incoming call was from the Paducah Police Department. I didn't pick up because I'd had more than enough turmoil for one day. My desk phone rang, and I knew I had no right to attempt to avoid more turmoil, not with Janet dead. I picked up and said, *"Paducah Pulse* newsroom."

"Is this Hadley Carroll?" asked a male voice I didn't recognize.

"Yes."

"You were at Walmart. We'd like you to come in to answer a few questions."

"Who are you, officer?"

"Officer Kevin Kane. I don't have anything against you, but Kramer's not happy about your editorials. Trying to get the department to sue you."

"If your legal counsel thought you had a case, I would've been served already. I'll answer your questions now, on the phone."

"Tell me what you saw at the scene. We've interviewed employees and other witnesses."

I told him what I'd experienced, including the robber dragging his index finger across his throat, threatening me.

"The threat seemed showy," I said. "Like something he'd seen in a movie and thought was cool. I wasn't about to chase them. An unarmed woman wouldn't impede the escape of ten large men loaded for bear. Instead, I helped my friend, Janet Loy, who was stuck in her wheelchair and had been burned. I pulled her outside. By then they were gone. The shots and explosions and fire caused her to have a heart attack. She didn't make it. They killed her, as far as I'm concerned."

"Not sure the law would agree, but if you think of anything else, you know how to reach us."

"Absolutely."

I locked the office and walked to my truck. After receiving the settlement from the city, I briefly considered buying a new vehicle, but I liked my old, blue Nissan Frontier. Trapunto liked lying in the back of it, inside the camper shell with the side windows open. The truck had no significant problems, so why spend money on a newer one? In addition, increasingly larger slices of the settlement money went toward keeping my century-old house upright, so I didn't want to spend money I didn't have to spend.

I drove home, and Ash called while I was walking Trapunto near the river. She sounded foggy, as though she didn't know how to proceed. She was a freshman at Murray State University who didn't know what she wanted to major in and lived with her grandmother because her mother had fallen into the bottomless void of OxyContin. Ash commuted about fifty minutes to campus in her beaten-up Ford Focus. Considering that her grandmother had died a few hours before, leaving Ash alone in the modest, water-logged, three-bedroom, one-bath house that Janet had neglected, Ash's fogginess was understandable.

She was beautiful in an understated way, the kind of woman who didn't feel comfortable slathered in makeup. She usually pulled her long blond hair into a ponytail and let her luminous skin, high cheekbones, and large blue eyes with extra-long lashes work their magic. Jeans and a tee were fine by her, but if she felt she needed to kick her fashion game up a notch, she'd tie a scarf around her neck. I'd never seen her in that look, but Janet had told us at PQQ that she'd given Ash a scarf every year on her birthday since Ash was ten.

After Trapunto and I got home, I called in an order for a large pizza, drove to Mellow Mushroom, then to Janet's house with Trapunto.

I was glad to see Ash eat two large slices of Holy Shiitake, the best of the many great pizzas that Mellow Mushroom sells. As I ate, she communicated as she saw fit. She was silent for four minutes but eventually said, "Grammie J told me she gave the house to me in her will, but I thought that would be, like, when I was forty or something. I don't even know where her will is. It could be here or in a safe deposit box. It's probably in her stash room, but good luck finding it, right?"

"I'm here for you in any way you need, Ash. People say that, but I hope you know I mean it. In fact, if you'd like to move in with me for a while, in case you don't want to be alone, or even just for a change of pace, I have plenty of room. And Trapunto obviously likes you and Chica."

My lovable mutt was nestled at Ash's feet—well, reclining *on* her feet—and Chica was nestled against his chest, in the C made by his legs and body.

I sat on the old couch with squashed cushions, and Ash sat across from me in an armchair that was newer than the couch. Draped over the back of it were at least four quilts that Ash leaned against.

"That's a great offer," she said, "and I know you mean it. But I don't even know what I'm supposed to do in the next hour. Plus, I have a ton of homework. College is way harder than I thought. Way harder than Tilghman. The reading is non-stop, and I'm not even an English or history major. And I have a paper due Tuesday in my psych class. I haven't started or even thought about it, and it's Friday."

"One step at a time," I said. "I always break daunting tasks into the smallest possible units. That way, I know what I have to do for the next ten minutes, and I don't worry about the fact that I have fifty or one hundred ten-minute sessions ahead of me. I know that sounds reductionistic, maybe even condescending, but it works."

"Might help. But it'll be a while before I can think about homework."

"I was going to ask if you want to go to Barbecue on the River, as a distraction, or maybe because you don't want to be alone."

"That's my favorite event in Paducah. I love the desserts, even though they're bad for you."

"True, but a fair's a fair, not a health convention."

"I know, right?" she said. "But I'm not up for that—seeing people I know, trying to have fun. I mean, Grammie J is in the morgue. They called, and I'm supposed to go identify her. But they have her purse. They know who she is. That's how they knew to call me. I mean ..."

She started to cry. I stood, crossed to the armchair, sat on the arm, gently pulled her toward me, and hugged her. She sobbed for two minutes.

We ended up playing Scrabble. Ashley won but said, "I know you let me win, so thank you. I mean, something has to go right, right?"

I excused myself to go buy funnel cakes, deep-fried Twinkies, and whatever other desserts that Barbecue on the River offered. I walked the few blocks. When I got back, I brought the desserts inside. I'd decided to leave Janet's singed quilt in the truck. Ash would probably debate whether to keep it or to set it in Janet's coffin. She didn't need to make that decision then. She couldn't choose among the four desserts, so she ate some of each.

As I was trying to coax Trapunto away from Chica so we could head home after realizing it was already 9:32, Ash's cell rang. She stood, looked at the caller ID, picked up her phone, and said, "What's up, Kelly?"

Ash listened for five seconds, then said, "No, no, no, no, no." She collapsed onto the couch, and I could hear Kelly crying through the phone.

FOUR
EXTRACURRICULAR

I guided Ash to the couch. We sat and I put my arm around her as she cried, gasping for breath. Eventually, she said, "Someone killed Baahir Ali, Kelly's boyfriend. Murdered him. We were friends. I introduced her to him. Thought they might, like, get along, and they did, right off. They've been together every minute they can be. Now he's gone. This is awful. Grammie J and Baahir, both dead the same day."

I couldn't say anything that would eliminate or even lessen her pain, so I pulled her tighter and let her cry. After a minute, she leaned away, pushed herself to her feet, and said, "I'll take you up on your offer. Well, Chica and me will. Give me a sec to pack."

As she put clothes, books, and beauty products in an overnight bag, I called Dan Eidie.

"Sorry to call you so late, Dan—"

"Just heard the scanner. I'm getting dressed now." He listened to police scanners less obsessively than the previous cops and courts reporter at the *Chronicle* used to, but Dan frequently had an online scanner playing quietly while he read novels. He liked his day job and was good at it, but he wanted to write historical romances.

"What do they know?" I asked.

"Young male, twenty-one, student at Murray State. Stabbed twice. The dispatcher called him, quote, 'Some kinda foreigner.'"

"His name's Baahir Ali," I said. "He was a friend of Ashley Pope, whose grandmother was killed at Walmart today. Ashley got a call from Baahir's girlfriend, Kelly Sprague, Ash's best friend. Getting this?"

"Yes. On my way."

"Good. Call me when you're done, no matter how late."

"Will do."

Ash and Chica settled onto the bed in the guest room downstairs on a quilt that my sister, Jenny, my mother, Ellen, and I had cobbled together when I was eight or nine. At the time, I was impressed with our efforts—a pieced quilt in our three favorite colors: hot pink for Jenny; yellow ochre (mustard) for my mom; and cornflower blue for me. The combination was ghastly. We would be arrested for creating that in Paducah today. I hid the quilt when it was my turn to host Paducah Quilters Quorum, and I replaced it with one that did not appear to be the result of Trapunto throwing up a five-year-old girl's birthday cake.

But that night, with Ash and Chica sprawled atop that quilt on the four-poster bed that the house's previous owner had left behind because she didn't want to pay to have it disassembled and hauled away, I saw the quilt as one of the few mementos I'd kept from my childhood—the only one that had anything to do with my mother.

Single, violent, alcoholic narcissists rarely raise happy, well-adjusted offspring, but they occasionally inspire some of those offspring to disavow them and their chaos, resulting in resilient, independent adults. But some of those offspring become needy, alcoholic basket-cases who cling to anyone who smiles at them—so dire is their need for acceptance, love, and a sense of self. My mother, bless her heart, managed to create one daughter of each type.

That night, Ashley, the two dogs, and I settled in to sleep, or at least I pretended to because I knew I wouldn't nod off until I heard from Dan.

He called at 3:08. I picked up on the first ring.

"What did you find out?" I said as I sat up in bed.

"Were you really awake?"

"Of course. If I start to sleep well, call an ambulance."

"Okay. Baahir Ali was a twenty-one-year-old senior at Murray, majoring in computer science. Transferred in as a junior from a university in Egypt, according to Kelly Sprague, who was onsite crying non-stop, asking Murray PD over and over who did this. Although I didn't want to for humane reasons, I corralled her for a few questions. She didn't know which university he'd transferred from, and she said she didn't have his parents' contact information in her phone. Said she'd find the info and get it to me tomorrow. Don't expect to hear from her."

"What about the scene?"

"No evidence of a break in or robbery. By the time I got to Hart Hall, the place was swarming with cops, but I've worked with Sergeant Vazquez before, and he gave us what he could. Said he'd give me whatever else he got if I'd bring him some barbecue tomorrow. He said it was just a standard second-floor dorm room, nothing unusual, except maybe the Egyptian flag on the wall, but nothing else stood out. Books, posters, sweaty socks. Baahir's roommate, Peter Rivers, wasn't in tonight, having gone to Louisville to visit his parents for the weekend, according to a student in the next room. I'll try to follow up with Peter. Techs are doing their thing in the dorm now. The assailant probably grabbed a closing door in the back of the building when somebody went out because the front desk has someone asking students to show ID twenty-four-seven. Cops have probably secured surveillance video, if the camera was working, which, based on the general decrepitude of Hart Hall, I wouldn't bet on. Or it could have been a student who lives in the dorm. Two students in rooms nearby, including"—I heard pages in his reporter's notebook flipping—"Harding Phillips, the one who told me Peter went home, said they thought they might have heard grunts and screaming but thought it was just a couple having sex."

"A homicide in a dorm without useful witnesses. Bad on many levels."

"Wait, it gets better. By which I mean weirder."

"Of course."

"Most stabbing victims are found with the knife still in them. Perp panics, forgets to take the weapon. Or he planned the attack, unlike most stabbings, which are spontaneous, so he wears gloves, then leaves the knife in the vic. No prints. But this perp removed the knife and left it outside, stuck in a tree."

"Odd. Definitely the same weapon?"

"Wouldn't bet my life on it, but I also wouldn't bet my life that any of us really exists."

"Keep it on this plane, space cadet."

"Whatever you say, you dull pragmatist. I was interviewing Vazquez outside, kind of out of the way, in the dark, near the corner of the building because you know how most cops are about media. Vazquez has been around so long, the others kind of give him a pass, but who likes getting hassled? So, he steered me out of the way. The new *Chronicle* cops reporter, Benny Washington, was pacing slowly nearby, eavesdropping on my interview. After Vazquez gave me a look, I said, 'Do you mind?' to Benny, so she walked a few steps away.

"A cop car turned into the lot with its lights on, and I saw Benny whip her head sideways, then walk toward a pine about ten feet away. She got close to the tree, ran back to us, and said, 'I think the knife's over here.' She was right. She saw the headlights glint off the blade. The point was in the tree, but the perp had taken the time to carve four twenty into the bark, in deep cuts, not just scratches. Had to take a while."

"Four twenty, meaning code for marijuana?"

"A dealer sending a message to others not to double-cross him, I'd guess."

"Probably. This is ugly. But good job, Dan. Post the story in the morning."

"It's already up."

"You're kidding. Wait, you wrote the story before calling me, knowing I was waiting?"

"Hmmm, let me think. There's a journalistic adage I can't quite remember. How does it go? Oh, yeah: The readers come first."

"Yeah, the two of them who are awake perusing our site at 3 a.m. But great job. I hope you and your adage get some sleep."

"More than you will, I bet."

FIVE

PAIR OF DEUCES

After only two hours of sleep, during which I dreamed about a dozen of my quilts burning in a fire, I did what everyone on the verge of total collapse does: I drank too much coffee.

How did I know I drank too much? Because my thoughts raced around like a bleeding rabbit being chased by a cougar down three flights of stairs.

Of course, my synapses could have been short-circuiting because I'd slept only two hours and because my good friend had just died (had been murdered, according to the Laws of Hadley). Or because a twenty-one-year-old university student had been stabbed to death. Or because I was running for mayor (and half of Paducahans hated me for having the gall to run for mayor while being a woman). Or because I didn't know which section of my house was going to collapse next.

I finally fell asleep about 4:30, only to be awakened at 6:30 by Trapunto's tongue alarm. I loved him. I really did, but there's a reason no company sells slobber clocks that rouse consumers by application of a wet tongue that only minutes before had lapped toilet water. Or worse.

Yet my day began with just such an alarm, replete with halitosis that made my nostrils threaten to go on strike. I fobbed off Trapunto's walk on Ash, who said she wanted to introduce Chica to the neighborhood, so why not let Trapunto tag along?

I went to the *Pulse* website and reread Dan's article about Baahir Ali's murder. I'd groggily read it after we'd ended our conversation, so I thought I should read it once after caffeine had jump-started my mind.

Dan was very-good-approaching-great at his job. During his job interview, when I was trying to lure him from the *Chronicle,* he'd said, "We all know that anyone with talent is wasted over there. I've been thinking of leaving to open a bakery or a pottery studio because both of those are closer to journalism than what Greg is overseeing at the *Chronicle.* This town is starved for fact-based journalism and opinion pages that don't appear to be reprinted from the 1950s. Last week we actually ran yet another editorial that used the phrase 'sexual preference,' a term that fell out of favor long before I was born. So, yes, I accept your offer. I appreciate the raise, and I look forward to having a real journalist as my boss."

He started his job at *Paducah Pulse* a few days later. He didn't bother to give notice. He just left a note pinned to Greg Wurt's office door that said, "I'm out of here, you clown." He was referring both to the fact that Greg's office was filled with frightening, awful clown photos that Greg had conceived of and shot, and to the fact that Greg Wurt was, at his core, a clown.

However, Greg looked more like a troll doll, with a short, squat body and long straight blond hair that always draped over a sweater. I'd never seen Greg wear anything but a sweater, even in the swampy inferno that is a Paducah summer. His sweaters were fodder for conversation in the office, as were the clown photos. When I'd worked there, the other reporters and I would commiserate over how badly he did his job. In fact, Trapunto was a better trumpet player than Greg was an editor.

Before I went for a jog, and before Ash walked Chica and

Trapunto, I logged onto the *Chronicle* website. Benny Washington hadn't managed to file her story about Baahir's murder before the *Chronicle*'s 11 p.m. deadline, which didn't surprise me. I'd worked for that rag, so I understood that the reporters were on their own, each one foundering through every assignment without input from the higher-ups. Although, in truth, Greg was more of a lower-down, despite his title.

I plugged my tablet in to charge and jogged next to the river, along the grass median on Jefferson, then back down it to the river again. Well, I set out to jog that route, but my smoke-damaged lungs told me I was making a mistake within the first block. They shouted, "WALK NOW" just short of the one-mile mark.

I walked quickly and thought about *Paducah Pulse*, my campaign, and my opponent, Nick Stoddard—the one who'd grabbed my butt at the *Chronicle* Christmas party, ultimately resulting in the sweet, used, bribery truck I'd received. I walked along the river. I'd had to work hard in therapy to be able to see the river's beauty again, to see its commercial relevance and its bounty as a replenishing life force, instead of as the place where I'd found Matt's body. I'd eventually managed to see the river's positives, at least on most days.

I thought about my decision to buy in Lower Town, the arts district that had been dramatically revitalized by the Artist Relocation Program, which provided nearly free houses to artists willing to move into them and fix them up. The house I'd moved into only six weeks before was not part of the program. Although I loved living in Lower Town, my house, built in 1924, had been a money pit since the day escrow had closed.

The previous morning, when I'd tried to open the front door to walk Trapunto, the doorknob dropped into my hand. The week before, I had to have the rickety stairs to the basement replaced and the basement rewired because somehow the antiquated knob-and-tube wiring hadn't ignited in the house's hundred years of falling apart. Within days of me moving in, the Orangeburg sewer pipe surrendered to time in a disgusting display, costing more to replace than a decent used car. While removing the backyard fence so he could replace the sewer line, the plumber destroyed three-quarters of the retaining wall that kept the backyard from spilling onto public property. Replacing the retaining wall had cost somewhere in the ballpark of what I could expect to pay to have the sputtering steam-heat system fixed, but I had about another month before I had to worry about that expense, I hoped.

When I returned home, Ash sat at the bottom of the front stairs with both dogs leashed at her feet. When I opened the wrought-iron gate in front of the house, she looked up, and I could see an unusual look on her face. I didn't see pain or sadness, but her expression was familiar. It took me a second to recognize it: revulsion.

"What's wrong?" I asked. She gestured with her right arm toward the front door, four steps above her, across the porch. I looked and saw what I didn't think I really saw, then stepped onto the bottom step and acknowledged that I was looking at two human turds sitting side-by-side on my *Quilters Rule!* welcome mat.

"I didn't know what to do," Ash said. "I mean, I knew I should clean it up, but then you wouldn't see it, and I thought maybe you should see it, you know, like for the impact. So, I just sat here, feeling stupid."

"You shouldn't feel stupid," I said. "Unless those gifts are yours."

She laughed. "That's not funny."

"You laughed, so credit where credit's due. And speaking of doo, which of my enemies left us these porch presents? Do you think they squatted here or transported them from elsewhere? My bet's on the Stoddard crime family. With them, any of thirteen brothers, cousins, or otherwise related felons could've been Nick's poo-poo accomplice. Of course, it could have been Greg Wurt. If his bowels are as crappy as his editorials, they could both be his."

"Gross. Who's Greg Wurt?"

"Editor of the *Chronicle*. My former boss. A major nincompoop, pun intended."

"You're enjoying this more than you should. After all, the situation stinks." She laughed.

"That's the spirit."

"I'm going in the backdoor," she said. "It's not my house."

"Mi caca es su caca," I said. Ash shook her head, stood, and walked around the house to the backyard, with the dogs in tow. Whether we were handling the stress well was debatable, but at least we had distracted ourselves for a few minutes.

However, after carefully disposing of the welcome mat and its contents, and ordering a new welcome mat online, I received a call from Unknown Caller. I almost never answer those, but Kelly Sprague, Baahir Ali's girlfriend, could have been calling after she'd failed to reach Dan. Or it could have been whichever miscreants had besmirched my doorstep wanting to brag about their childish vandalism. I answered, and an artificially deep voice, as if the speaker were trying to disguise it, said: "Hope you got plenty a ink. You gonna need it."

SIX

RESOLVE

After I showered, I checked my phone. Dan had texted: *Heard from Kelly Sprague. Baahir transferred from American University in Cairo. She gave me his parents' email. Swears he didn't drink or do drugs.*

Ashley didn't want to accompany me to Walmart to buy the supplies that the shooting had prevented me from buying, but Dakota Crowley, my best friend, texted: *Be there in ten.*

Unlike nearly all of us, Dakota didn't need time to get ready. She could roll out of bed with a hangover, wrap herself in a muddy burlap sack, step into one orange Croc and one tattered Ugg boot, and slather her lips with grape jelly, and she'd still outshine the rest of us. Everyone who knew Dakota wondered why she wasn't making millions as a model (she couldn't act a lick, so making it in Hollywood was out, Pamela Anderson notwithstanding). Because she was a successful lawyer, because her parents were rich enough to make Midas seem only well-off, and because they gave generously to their two daughters—Dakota, and her younger sister, Cathy—Dakota didn't need to become a spokesmodel for a beauty line to keep herself in designer clothes, expensive shoes, and delivered meals at least twice a day. She had recently traded in her third vehicle, a Nissan

Murano with twelve thousand miles on it, because she'd chosen the wrong color. The orange Murano "didn't look right" in her four-car garage next to her black Range Rover and black Porsche, so she'd traded it in for a black one.

In someone else, such entitlement and extreme consumption would frustrate me, if not anger me. But Dakota did a significant amount of pro bono work, as well as being kind, inclusive, and generous. Most people would likely jump at the chance to live as she did, if they could afford to do so. I loved her, and she'd always been there for me, so I chalked her Murano episode up to progress. She had an undiagnosed color fetish: Nearly every outfit featured orange. So, I didn't begrudge her vehicles' newfound chromatic consistency. I considered it a sign of health.

Her sensitivity about her looks was less healthy. The last time I was in her presence when someone asked her if she was a model, she'd said: "I can't help my looks. I did nothing to earn them. However, I've done a tremendous amount of work on my mind, spent countless hours in the law library trying to prove I'm more than what people see. Apparently, I've failed."

She was almost never that rude. We'd been at the birthday party of our friend and PQQ member Cindy Baron, and three of Cindy's granddaughters had independently asked Dakota that question, and a great niece had asked, "Are you a princess?" So, when a young twenty-something woman whom neither of us knew asked Dakota essentially the same question that she'd already answered four times, she responded with: "I can't help my looks."

Despite the travails that go with exquisite beauty, most women would love to be burdened with such stunning looks. Sure, people tended to dismiss or discount her other assets, but women not blessed with a cascade of auburn hair, sultry blue eyes, and a five-nine statuesque frame had had their intellects and talents dismissed by others, as she had. So, most women would have traded places with Dakota.

But I was fine as me.

I was broken in many ways, but I'd worked hard for everything I had. The successes I'd achieved—being high school valedictorian, earning various scholarships to UCLA, landing reporter jobs at four newspapers, never missing a deadline, loving and being loved by Matt, enduring various forms of abuse and loss, and starting *Paducah Pulse* from scratch—I'd achieved despite my mother, not because of her. I never knew my father, and my mother never told me who he was. My younger sister, Jenny, is sweet, but she has never assisted me in any way, unless regularly having to bail her out of one emotional or financial crisis after another has benefited me in a way I can't identify. I've been known to turn a head or two when my hair is behaving, and my athletic five-eight stature doesn't repulse me on most days, so I wouldn't trade the lessons my life has taught me—the resilience and resolve it instilled in me—for the ability to turn every head everywhere I went.

However, when Dakota pulled up in her black Range Rover, looking as though she'd just conquered a continent while curing cancer, I momentarily reconsidered my desire to remain in my own skin. But then I remembered I am not a fan of ostentation, and black does my complexion no favors, so, as if I had a choice, I decided not to trade places with Dakota.

She stepped out of her regal ride and gave me a hug. She wore an orange Adidas running jacket over a white form-fitting running tee, black tights with three white stripes down each leg, and Adidas running shoes with orange stripes. A white scrunchy held her auburn mane in a ponytail. Although she claimed not to like being defined by her looks, she didn't go out of her way to downplay them. If her tights were any tighter, they would have been a tourniquet.

"Ashley's staying with me," I said after we exchanged hellos and Dakota pulled out of Lower Town. "She's going through far too much. You know about Janet, but last night her bestie, Kelly Sprague, called to say her boyfriend had just been murdered. Baahir was Ash's friend. She introduced the two of them."

"That's awful. How old?"

"Twenty-one, a student at Murray. Baahir Ali."

"And it's definitely murder?"

"Yes. The knife used to kill him was stuck in a tree, on which was carved four twenty, the universal abbreviation for marijuana."

"Weird. Was he a dealer?"

"Dan, our cops reporter, spoke to Kelly, who insisted Baahir didn't touch alcohol, let alone drugs."

"Another stabbing. Just what the region needs."

"I know, right? Let's hope this was a college kid hopped up on something, trying to prove he was tough, or he was just dumped by his girlfriend, or..."

"Anything to make this a one-off," she said. She parked in the crowded Walmart lot, and we walked toward the entrance.

"I received a weird, maybe threatening, call," I said, "not to mention two human turds on my doorstep."

She stopped, reached out, and turned me toward her. "What?"

"It's probably time I spring for security cameras."

"Definitely. I turn mine on every time I leave the house now, after Brandon let me know how foolish I was not to use them. What did the caller say?"

"'Hope you got plenty a ink. You gonna need it.'"

"Meaning something's gonna happen *Pulse* will write about?"

"I think so."

"Have you told the police?"

I grabbed a buggy, and we walked into the store, which still smelled of smoke. I saw crime-scene tape to the right, stretched across the aisle that led to the sporting goods section. We walked toward the office supplies.

"What would I say? 'Officer, someone called me and said something I didn't understand.' That's not worth much."

"No, but if something happens, you'll feel awful."

"True, but what that could be, we don't have a clue." I grabbed Scotch tape, construction paper, a ream of copy paper, and a package of Sharpies, and set each in the buggy as we spoke.

"Wait, I think I know what it could be," I said. "Maybe one of

PPD's lawyers thinks he has a libel case against me and *Pulse* for articles I wrote. He would be wrong, but the officer I spoke to last night suggested the department might sue me. The call could've been some blowhard's way of saying I'll fill column inches with a story about a libel suit."

"If so, you'll have to be served. Can't be served if you can't be found."

"Are you suggesting I flee, Dakota Crowley? Run from a piece of paper?"

"I'm saying my family's house in Nashville is unoccupied and well-appointed, and I could tell the neighbor who waters the plants I won't need her for the next week or two. You can run *Pulse* remotely. That is, if you insist on working during your Nashville interlude."

"I'll take you up on it when I choose to get away, preferably during a slow news stretch, not after the murder of a college student and a major gun heist that led to the death of Janet. Thank you, though. Keep shopping, and I'll find you. I need a few minutes."

She nodded and said, "Take your time. I'll be in the magazine section."

I left the buggy next to her and walked to the service desk. After waiting for three customers to complete their transactions, I said to the pretty, young Latina behind the counter, "Hello, I was here yesterday during the robbery, and I'm trying to reach one of your employees for personal reasons, but I only know his first name: Buddy. Any chance you can tell me his last name? It's important." She hesitated but said, "Sure." She scrolled through screens on the computer and gave me his last name. I thanked her and walked down the main aisle toward the yellow crime-scene tape.

Every aisle but one in the sporting goods department was taped off. I could've purchased a bike if I'd wanted to, but the camping, hunting, fishing, and boating sections were off limits. Four white, male employees in blue vests stood outside the tape, talking. I nodded as I approached, and the two younger males, in their early twenties, gave me big smiles, which I took to mean they didn't consider me physically repugnant. The two older males—the one on my left in his early thirties, and the one on my right in his early fifties—either considered me repugnant or did not like women, because they looked at me as I had looked at my porch presents.

"Hello, gentlemen," I said, scanning their nametags. "Were y'all here during the excitement yesterday?"

The two younger guys shook their heads. The one in his fifties said, "My day off." The one in his thirties didn't respond. His nametag read: Buddy.

"Where were you, Buddy?" I asked.

"Lunch." He appeared to have spent most of his life on a couch scooping ice cream with Cheetos. He was more droopy than fat, as though gravity had twice the effect on him than on others, causing the corners of his mouth and eyes to sag downward. His skin drooped like a Bloodhound's, and his shoulders sloped at a steep angle, making him look like a collapsing tent. His dark-brown, tattered flannel shirt looked like an item a thrift-store had rejected, and his brown eyes didn't look at me but at the floor between us.

"Did you go to lunch at your usual time?"

"Ain't said who you is, lady," Buddy said, "and ain't gotta answer even if you done."

"Sorry. I'm Hadley Carroll. I work for *Paducah Pulse*. I was shopping yesterday when the robbery occurred. I'm working now, and I wonder if any employees can provide relevant information."

The two younger guys shook their heads. The guy in his fifties—Mitch, according to his nametag—said, "Like I said, my day off. Ain't heard nothin' 'bout it in the breakroom."

"Thanks, Mitch. Anything else?" The two younger guys shook their heads again, joined this time by Mitch.

"Anything else, Buddy?" He continued to look away, but this time he turned his head from me, not just his eyes. "Buddy, will you please look at me?" He hesitated for two seconds, turned toward me, then forced his eyes to meet mine.

"Did you go to lunch at your usual time?"

"Assistant manager told me to go early."

"Does that happen often?"

"Sometimes." He looked away again.

"I have to say something else to you, so please look at me." He forced his eyes to meet mine.

"Woof," I said.

His eyes showed surprise, not confusion. I glanced at the others. They looked confused, but not Buddy. His eyes also had fear in them.

After three seconds, he said, "Waitin' for me to say somethin'?"

"Already said plenty."

"Ain't said squat. You lying, you say otherwise."

"If you say so. You could tell me now, or I could look up your criminal record. It's McNaught—M-lower-case-c-capital N-lower-case-a-u-g-h-t, right?"

"Damn media. Think you know it all. Wrecking this country."

"Thank you, gentlemen—and Buddy—for your cooperation. Save Money—Live Better."

When I got back to Dakota, she looked worried.

"Are you okay? Was that about the robbery?"

"I'm fine. I have no proof, but I think it was an inside job. I saw surprise on one of their faces when I said 'woof' to him, as Janet and the employee I interviewed said the thieves did."

"Okay, but what does that mean?"

"No idea, other than to say the thieves didn't randomly decide to rob this Walmart, as opposed to the South Side one. And it could have something to do with the comment one of the robbers said to David Robie, the employee who was bound and gagged: 'Ain't right, none a this.' Maybe he meant the plan was going awry."

"Awry. Good word. Can things other than plans go awry?"

"A toupee could go awry, I suppose, but I'd go with askew."

A woman in her fifties wearing a yellow vest approached.

"Excuse me," I said.

"Yeah?"

"Can you please tell me which assistant manager oversees sporting goods?"

She appeared to have put on a pound of makeup while doing a headstand in the dark. I am a fan of abstract art, so her haphazard application intrigued me. But I'm also a fashion-conscious woman who takes care with my appearance, so the word "Yikes" popped into my head. I could smell the reek of cigarettes from five feet away.

"This about the fire?"

"Yes."

"Then we ain't allowed to talk about it."

"What if I want to know which camp stove is best?"

"Walmart.com." She smiled in a manner that told me where I could stick my camp stove. She walked away.

I pulled out my cell, looked up the phone number for the store, called it, was put on hold for four minutes, got disconnected, redialed, got put on hold for two minutes, and was connected to the sporting goods department. After twenty-two rings, someone picked up and said, "Sporting Goods. This is Buddy."

"Woof," I said, and hung up.

SEVEN
THE CAMPAIGN TRAIL

Dakota and I brought the supplies for my mayoral campaign to my house, where Ash helped us create posters and flyers. Most campaigning takes place online these days via social media, but yard signs, billboards, posters, and flyers increase name recognition, although neither Nick Stoddard nor I needed much name recognition.

He was Nick Stoddard, the eldest brother of the six Stoddard siblings who comprised the Stoddard crime family—I mean, the entrepreneurial pillars of Paducah. Generation after generation of Stoddards had fleeced Paducahans—um, bolstered the local economy by running shipping companies, car dealerships, and fast-food joints, among other less-legal endeavors. I suspected that the Stoddards' criminal operations brought in the lion's share of their millions.

The name Stoddard was widely recognized in the Jackson Purchase region in Western Kentucky—similar to the level of name recognition the Capone family received in and around Chicago. The difference between the two families, however, was that Al Capone was eventually arrested and sentenced, then spent four and a half years in prison. Nick Stoddard, however, had never been convicted of a crime. The Stoddards regularly lost lawsuits but evaded jail time. Yes, his family gave me a used truck as part of the settlement my lawyer negotiated after Nick grabbed my butt at a *Paducah Chronicle* Christmas party a few years ago, but I'm sure Nick wrote the truck off as a business expense. So, coughing up such a pittance of a penalty is a long way from suffering true consequences.

I have a different kind of name recognition. According to then-Officer Brandon Green of the Paducah Police Department, I had been instrumental in solving the Quilt City Murders that terrorized Paducah about a year and a half earlier.

But many people in Paducah and the surrounding area know the name Hadley Carroll because the *Paducah Chronicle* wrote five editorials excoriating me for having the audacity to sue the city and the police department. The editorials, all of them written by Greg Wurt, the sweater-wearing troll who knew as much about journalism as I know about growing a beard, said that my lawsuit would deprive school children of knowledge, senior citizens of liberty, puppies of love, and plants of much-needed oxygen (I never claimed that Greg knew anything about botany; I'm just revealing what his editorials said). In the editorial I considered to be the most hilarious, Greg wrote:

The city is under a financial strain, burdened by debt because people expect to be paid for everything they do, including getting pensions, although we at the Chronicle are pro police pensions because their work is dangerous. If they need to blow off steam every now and again, well, sometimes people get hurt by that steam.

What we shouldn't have to pay for is a woman's pain and suffering, especially

when that woman deserved what she got,
at least if our interactions in the
newsroom are any indication. She could
be, how shall we say this: bossy,
demanding, and, let's face it, bitchy.
And she was incompetent at her job.
Worst employee I ever worked with. She
got lucky solving those so-called
murders. Probably just women's intu-
ition, so how can she take credit for
something God granted to her? And
imagine asking your male boss to treat
you the same as his male colleagues.
What world does Hadley Carroll live in?

Should I have sued for libel? Perhaps, but I figured the best way for me to make a difference in a world dominated by men—and, truth be told, messed up by them—was to become the mayor of Paducah. I knew I would have to overcome millennia of entrenched ignorance to win the election, but I have never run from a challenge. And, despite Greg's inane editorials stating the contrary, I was great at my job and good with people. So, I thought I could win, even though I expected Nick to fight dirty, if not to cheat outright. One advantage I had over Nick, however, was that I owned and operated *Paducah Pulse*, and I wrote the weekly editorials.

An adage exists in politics: Never pick a fight with someone who buys ink by the barrel. As a daily, the *Paducah Chronicle* bought more ink than I did, but a drunk chimp with a head wound and broken thumbs could bang out better editorials than Greg Wurt wrote, so I suspected that my insightful editorials could lead me to victory.

The Stoddards were the *Chronicle*'s largest advertiser, so Greg felt obligated to help Nick in his mayoral battle. However, Greg was so out of touch that he didn't realize that his editorials promoting Nick amounted to free advertising for me, at least to readers who lived in the twenty-first century.

I wanted to avoid cutesy slogans on my yard signs and other campaign advertisements, but Dakota persuaded me to choose whichever slogan stuck. The slogan didn't need to be intellectually stimulating. It didn't have to capture my platform in a phrase or enumerate my agenda in three bullet points.

"What it has to be," Dakota had said when I'd told her I intended to run for mayor, "is memorable. The only point of a campaign slogan is to get people to remember your name when they're in the voting booth or filling out their mail-in ballots. If you inspire people who wouldn't otherwise vote, great. But the point of a campaign slogan is to be memorable."

Which is why my yard signs read: "We're voting for Hadley, gladly!" Most of the other campaign literature read: "Vote Hadley, gladly."

You aren't alone. I hated those slogans, too. But the focus group that Dakota convinced me to pull together preferred those slogans in a landslide over the second choice: "Let a Woman Fix This Mess. Vote Hadley Carroll."

My younger sister, Jenny, unwittingly came up with the slogan when she started calling me Hadley Gladly when she was six. I'd disliked the nickname the first time I heard it, and as I aged, my dislike intensified. But when Dakota and I decided to go with the slogan, I had called Jenny to thank her for my nickname.

"I get a royalty or something?" she asked. I had sent her money monthly since I graduated from college, and I tripled the amount I sent her after I received the settlement. But her response to the campaign news momentarily reminded me of our deceased mother, who didn't know the meaning of the verb "to give." I knew my assessment was unfair to Jenny because I understood that Jenny's neediness resulted from our mother's total lack of mothering skills and her tendency to throw punches or Jim Beam bottles. So, I responded: "I'll buy you a plane ticket so you can attend my swearing in, or any other time you'd like to visit."

"Cool, I guess, but I was kinda thinking of, like, a Ferrari, you know?"

A $350,000 sports car for coming up with Hadley Gladly, my name modified by an adverb? The slogan sounded like a rejected Ben & Jerry's flavor, or the last line of a song kindergartners were too embarrassed to sing.

Or the nickname bestowed by a younger sister upon her beloved older sister.

So, I said, "A Ferrari's a bit steep, but if I win the election, how about you fly here first class?"

"Really? You'd do that. Like with Champagne, celebrities, and everything?"

"I will make it happen because you are my little sister, and if I win, your slogan will have proven to be effective."

"With Evan, right? Or whoever I'm dating then?"

"Jenny, please. I think you have a warped idea of the settlement I received, as nearly everyone else does. I put a down-payment on a house that is as structurally sound as a Swiss-cheese boat. And starting a newspaper has proven to be far more expensive than I had planned—and I budgeted very conservatively. Businesses don't want to advertise in a start-up, and *Paducah Pulse* is free, so it doesn't generate income from subscribers. My total assets are worth far less than the contents of Dakota's clothes closets, and maybe less than only her shoes. But, if I win, I'll see what I can do. How long have you been dating Evan? You haven't mentioned him."

"Oh, we ain't dating. He's a dishwasher at my Cracker Barrel, you know, and he's really cute, and I heard he's got connections, you know, for drugs, and I'm kinda thinking of, like, letting him know I'm interested."

Because I couldn't go down that rabbit hole, I said, "Okay. Good luck, Jenny. I have to go. Love you."

As Dakota, Ash, and I completed, organized, and gathered the finished posters and flyers so we could distribute them around town, Dakota said, "You know my history, Hads, so you'll understand why I hesitate to tell you what I'm about to tell you, but I had an excellent first date last night."

"Fantastic," I said.

"With everything that's going on, I didn't think it was appropriate to bring it up sooner."

"Well, you've brought it up now, so spill. Who is he, is he funny, does he like his job, is he kind, does he treat servers well, and does he know who Bella Abzug was?"

"His name is Paul Ward. We were born exactly one week apart. He's originally from a St. Louis suburb, but he wanted to try a small town, so he looked for somewhere with an arts scene—he's a realtor with an appreciation for the arts. He and his son, Paulie, arrived in Paducah a couple years ago. I'm surprised neither of us had run into him before."

"I'm so happy the date went well. How did you meet?"

"As you know, I appreciate a man with confidence, gumption."

"Who doesn't?" Ash asked.

We laughed, and Dakota said, "I was leaving the Quilt Museum as he and his son were entering. He and I made eye contact. He bent down to his son—who's really cute, with a mop of dark hair and big brown eyes—said something, and walked over to me. He said, 'I don't know you, but I feel I should. I *know* I should, in fact. My name is Paul Ward, and if you happen to be single and inclined to accept my invitation, I'd like to take you to dinner soon.'"

"That's some serious smooth," Ash said.

"That's what I thought," Dakota said. "I am rarely tongue-tied, but I stood there like a panting dog, unable even to say my name. He took a business card out of his wallet and handed it to me. I finally managed to say my name and tell him I'd love to accept his offer.

That first encounter was awkward, but the first date was magical. We laughed hard and revealed various aspects of ourselves at dinner at Jasmine, some of them fairly personal. Then, to my surprise, we shot pool at Cardinal Lanes. The yin-yang of it was perfect. When he hugged me goodnight, it was my turn to be bold. I kissed him, and I'm smitten, to put it mildly."

"I'm jealous," Ash said. "What's he look like?"

"No complaints, that's for sure. A well-built six-foot-one, dark, curly hair, and eyes that seemed to understand me, however insane that sounds."

"Not insane at all, D. 'Understanding Eyes' will be the title of my next country song," I said. "I'm happy for you. No one deserves a satisfying, healthy love life more than you do. Being swept off our feet can be wonderful, but so can building a relationship slowly. Take your time."

"I hear you. With my history, I definitely hear you."

A few minutes later as Dakota drove Ash and me toward Noble Park, Dan called my cell.

"Sorry to bother you on the weekend," he said.

"Please stop saying that, Dan. I run a newspaper, and the news never sleeps. I should be telling you to pull back, so you don't miss out on your life while you pursue your career. I couldn't be happier with the job you're doing, so relax a little. That said, what do you have?"

"Not a lot. Just thought I'd let you know what's going on. I pulled together a feature on Baahir, after getting a lot of info from Kelly and his parents via email and phone. Obviously, they're crushed. I actually had to break the news to them because Kelly couldn't bring herself to do it. After they cried themselves out, they told me about Baahir and put me in touch with a childhood friend of his in Cairo. Kelly gave me the numbers of four friends of theirs at Murray. I posted the story. I think it works."

"I'm sure it does. I'll read it when I'm finished running errands. Great job. Anything else?"

"The usual assortment of petty crimes, impaired driving, bar fights, and domestic disputes. Two car thefts, an armed robbery in Lone Oak, a two-car wreck on I-24, and a large U-Haul truck stolen from a residential street near WKCTC."

"Okay, write up the ones you think carry the most weight, and I'll see you on Monday. But only if you promise not to work tomorrow."

"Promise. See you Monday."

When I hung up, Ashley looked even more sad than she'd looked since she learned of her grandmother's death.

"What's wrong, Ash?" Dakota asked. "Other than the obvious, I mean."

"I've never even attended a funeral, but now I have to—"

"Hold on, Ash," I said. "You don't have to do anything, including attend your grammie's funeral. You're grieving, not only for your grammie, but also for your friend. One thing I feel confident saying is: Don't let anyone tell you how to grieve. The process is personal and unique for everyone. We all lose people, and how we respond is up to us. If you want to feel angry or cheated or anxious or depressed or any other way, do so. But what you can't do is worry about planning Grammie J's funeral because I told you I would enlist the help of the other PQQers—and I do what I say I will."

"Okay, thank you both. I'm fine. Just sad. Guess it will take a while."

"I lost my grandma six years ago," Dakota said, "and she still pops into my head and makes me sad. But then I try to remember something fun we did together—mostly quilting—and I feel better, grateful she visited me."

"If you're really okay," I said, "and I have to trust that you would tell me if you weren't, we're going to make a lap around town, posting this Hadley Gladly nonsense."

Ash smiled and said, "I'm okay. Or okay enough. And it's only nonsense if you lose. You don't seem like someone who loses a lot."

"No, I lose frequently, but I don't quit. I keep competing until I win. Then I recognize that any win is temporary, so I get back to work."

"You know how to reach us, Ash," Dakota said, patting Trapunto on the head. She reached farther down to scratch Chica under her chin.

The slathering of Paducah with words about me and a picture of me I almost didn't hate went smoothly. We handed flyers to many of the 300,000 people who would attend Barbecue on the River and affixed flyers to whichever telephone poles already had Nick Stoddard's propaganda stapled to them. We stopped at the National Quilt Museum and swung by the fine-dining establishment on Madison, Café de Fae. We hit the Paducah School of Art & Design and walked the downtown streets asking employees in every open business whether we could post a flyer in their windows or on their bulletin boards. Most of the employees couldn't have cared less, although one woman said, "Last vote I cast was for Nixon, and look how that turned out." I almost told her she was being too hard on herself because I was nearly certain she didn't bring on Nixon's problems. Instead, I considered her response a "no," nodded to her, and moved on.

We headed to Noble Park to hand out flyers to people enjoying their Saturday outdoors, then to the Coke Plant, which was abuzz, as it nearly always was, with people ingesting their favorite caffeinated beverages at Pipers Tea & Coffee or their favorite alcoholic beverages at Dry Ground Brewing Company. Or they were eating quite possibly the best pizza in the world at Mellow Mushroom. We swung by Bike World and the True North Yoga studio, hit Midtown Market, then drove to the South Side and posted flyers in most of the businesses there.

I noticed throughout the afternoon that about half as many of my lawn signs were posted in front yards and in front of businesses as were present a few days before. Of course, I couldn't prove who had stolen the signs. Many of the houses that I *knew* had featured one of my signs now sported one of Nick Stoddard's, so figuring out who was responsible was even easier than buying too much fabric.

Potential voters were able to pick up a free yard sign of mine at various locations, including, of course, the *Paducah Pulse* office. Because I am who I am and believe that turning out the vote benefits every community and America as a whole, I also provided free Nick Stoddard signs at the office. Did Nick provide free Hadley Carroll signs? Of course not. I was aiding my competition to highlight how different the two mayoral candidates truly were.

Dakota and I were tired and thirsty, so we pulled into the Kroger on Park, and I went in to buy her a green tea and me an orange Gatorade Zero. While waiting in line, holding the bottles, I heard Nick Stoddard ask from behind me, "Why you the only one don't realize I'm running unopposed?"

EIGHT
THE NEMESIS

I was tempted not to give him the satisfaction of a response. I could just ignore him, and he would look like an idiot hassling a woman in the market. But I don't do silence well—or at all—and I'd told Ashley a few hours earlier that I didn't run from challenges. Nick Stoddard was certainly challenging me in Kroger.

He was in the lane next to mine. I turned to him and said, "Unopposed? That's a three-syllable word, Nicky-boy. Soon you'll impress your friends and relatives on Cellblock D."

My retort wasn't award-winning, but it was good enough to elicit laughs from the three women in front of me in line. Over Nick's shoulder I saw a Black male teenager pull out his phone and start to shoot video. Beside Nick stood Rachelle Hunt, the granddaughter of private investigator Garrett Hunt, who'd been instrumental in solving the Quilt City Murders. Rachelle was wearing more clothing than the last time I'd seen her with Nick, but it would have been difficult to have worn less in public without getting arrested. This time, she had on a fashionably tattered (probably expensive) T-shirt that had *Why Me?* scripted across her ample chest. Well, her chest might have been no more ample than average, but her shirt was two sizes too small. Her jeans were either painted on or her feet were detachable. The flip-flops she wore were calico and featured cat's whiskers rising from the straps and a short tail protruding from the heels. Her footwear didn't prove whether Rachelle's feet screwed on and off but did make me wonder whether we were all doomed.

Nick had his right arm draped across her shoulder, his hand dangling down to cover the W in *Why*. Under his left arm, he held a box of Cheerios, and his left hand held a plastic half gallon of orange juice. I saw the teenager who was filming us step out of line and move to his right so he could get a better angle on Nick, the woman who was nearly forty years his junior, and me. I've never been slow on the uptake, so I recognized my opportunity—and made the most of it.

"Still got that smart mouth on you, you cow," Stoddard said.

"Better than your dumb one, Nick. But with the amount of stupidity that comes out of yours, you may as well have two."

I heard four distinct laughs. I couldn't tell if Nick had seen the guy filming, but I had to assume he hadn't because Nick said, "You're hated by half this town and unknown by the other half. I'm a Stoddard. We own this town. The election's pointless. I already won."

It didn't seem possible that one person could personify ignorance and arrogance so well. I said, "Is that a confession, Mr. Stoddard? Have the uncast votes already been counted? I know that you and your family are more than familiar with District Attorney Suzanne Bigelow, and she'd love to hear about the in-the-bag election, as I'm sure the voters of McCracken County would."

He took his arm from around Rachelle, who looked scared and embarrassed. He stepped to his left, closer to me, and I could tell from his sudden look of surprise that he now saw the phone filming us. The teenager was holding it out to the side, and Nick, who was not a tall man, had had his view of the teenager obstructed by the checker and the register.

Nick did his best to backpedal, which didn't come naturally to Stoddards. They usually bullied, steamrolled, intimidated, threatened, bribed, or eliminated whatever or whomever stood in their way.

He said, "I meant that the people of McCracken have known the Stoddard name for seven generations, and my family has been widely respected"—someone started to boo loudly—"and loved"—someone else started to boo—"and we've done a ton for this county"—the chorus of boos started to drown Nick out—"so all I'm saying is, the election's a done deal."

A chant of "Vote Hadley—Gladly" started and sprang from nearly everyone's mouth after two repetitions. I laughed. Nick went from flustered to frustrated to angry in three seconds. He dropped the cereal and orange juice and headed toward the exit with Rachelle in tow. The filming teenager maneuvered deftly around the other customers so he could continue to record Stoddard's retreat.

Next to the entrance, I saw Dakota shouting "Vote Hadley—Gladly" with everyone else. I smiled at her and raised my hand to get the teenager's attention.

He smiled as he approached me. He was rail thin, had short hair, and wore jeans and a blue sweatshirt from the local community college, WKCTC. Before I could speak, he said, "You were great, Hadley. You got my vote."

"You're old enough to vote?"

"Will be by November."

"That's great. What's your name?"

"Shawn Chambliss."

"With an ea, u, or w?"

"W."

"Great to meet you, Shawn."

"Gonna send this"—he lifted his phone—"to WKYC and anywhere else I can think of."

"Do whatever you think is right or whatever you want to do. It's not my place to influence you."

"See, right there's why you got my vote. Stoddards, all they do is bully. Couple years ago, my momma was four days late on rent, and a Stoddard brother threw us out. Big, ugly dude just kept throwing things out front. No respect for us or our property. We couldn't do a thing. The sons think they've accomplished something, but their granddad and great-granddad made their name and money. These guys just act like fools."

I handed the tea and Gatorade to the checker, who rang them up. I paid, said, "Thank you," and turned to Shawn. Dakota crossed over to us, and as we walked to the exit, I said, "Because the Stoddards are powerful, they think that's enough, that love, or even likability, doesn't matter. Machiavelli said, 'It is better to be feared than loved, if you cannot be both.' The Stoddards are in no danger of being loved, so they rely on fear, bullying, extortion, and violence. But Machiavelli wrote those words five hundred years ago, and I'd like to believe we've progressed since then."

"At least men no longer wear codpieces," Dakota said as we stepped into the sunlight.

"See? Progress," I said. "Shawn Chambliss, this is Dakota Crowley. Dakota, Shawn."

"Nice to meet you, Shawn. Thanks for filming that exchange."

"My pleasure. Recognized Hadley when she walked in, from the stories about the killings and the campaign for mayor. When I heard Stoddard mouth off, figured I better do what we young folks do: Use our phones."

"Thank you, Shawn. Take care of yourself, and if you find yourself in a position to encourage other young voters to head to the polls...."

"Got my word, Hadley. We got you."

NINE
INEVITABLE

"You're famous," Brandon said instead of hello when I answered my cell after Dakota drove me home. I finished chewing a cold piece of pizza (still delicious) before I spoke, but I finally said, "I'm guessing you mean you and fourteen other Paducahans saw my exchange with Stoddard?"

"Fifteen, probably, but, yes, on Facebook."

"Well, there's famous, infamous, and Facebook famous. I'm not sure which is worse."

"You made him look like the entitled, corrupt moron he is. Perhaps some of the fifteen people who watched the video—at least until it plays on the news to a much larger local audience—will change their votes, or they'll decide to vote for you if they didn't plan to vote."

"I can hope."

"Well, that's kind of why I'm calling."

"For the second time in two days, I'll remind you. If I were suspicious by nature, Detective Green, I would suspect that you're acting outside your capacity as an officer of the law because you have an interest in my welfare."

"If that supposition proved to be accurate, would that be wrong of me?"

"Despite laws that decree otherwise, right and wrong can be subjective. It is *always* wrong to wear a checked blouse with striped pants, although no laws forbid such a fashion train wreck. But if a certain gentleman respectfully bides his time while allowing a certain woman to grieve and heal, letting her arrive at a conclusion that seemed inevitable from the beginning, then a certain mayoral candidate would deem said gentleman's actions and intentions right and proper."

"Great, but do we have to speak in stilted and veiled hypotheticals?"

"No, we do not."

"Then, would you care to accompany me to closing night of Barbecue on the River?"

"Definitely. What time would you like to pick me up?"

"When can you be ready?"

"One hour." I gave him my address.

"I'll see you there and then," he said.

"I'll try not to let my house crumble on you while you're here."

"I'm willing to take my chances, but I have to ask: Will this be a date?"

"I'll show you the aforementioned and dilapidated MGA while you're here. Isn't that what you're truly after?"

"Am I that transparent? Darn. Thought I had a better poker face."

"For the record, I'm glad you aren't a good liar, and, yes, this will be a date."

"Great. I look forward to it."

"Me, too. See you soon, Brandon."

Even though a date doesn't usually include a third wheel, I asked Ashley if she wanted to join us. If she wanted to tag along, I'd explain her situation to Brandon, and if he didn't understand, then perhaps he and I would attend the festival as friends, only as friends, and never to be more than friends. Any man not willing to help someone in obvious pain would never be my man.

Ash said she appreciated the invitation but passed, saying: "The more fun people are having around me, the worse I'll feel. I'm about to head to Kelly's. She's in a really bad place. Baahir was amazing, the nicest person I've ever known, and a good friend. As sad as I am, Kelly's much worse."

"I understand. Be safe. Call me if you need anything, no matter the hour. Text me the address, and I'll be on my way in minutes." She nodded and turned to walk toward the door. She stopped, came back, gave me a long hug, turned, and left.

I showered and debated which dress to wear, hoping to find one that said, "Hello, Brandon," not "Looking for a good time, Detective?" I decided on my white Stradivarius sleeveless smock dress. It left my shoulders exposed, and it draped nearly to my ankles, which would not allow my legs—my best feature—to distract him from the purpose of the evening: To continue to get to know each other, slowly, carefully, and to see if I was ready to date. I slipped on my Sketchers cream ballet flats, fed Trapunto, let him into the backyard, then called him inside. I was about to send a text to Dan to see if he needed anything from me when I heard a knock at the front door.

While talking with Brandon in Mellow Mushroom seventeen months earlier, a week after PPD had made the Quilt City Murders arrests, I'd alternated between feeling relaxed and feeling guilty. Our conversation had flowed, we'd laughed easily and often, and I'd thought we found each other attractive—which is why guilt kept popping into my head. Matt had recently been murdered, and we'd been engaged until he'd broken off our engagement—on a technicality—a week before he was killed. In Mellow Mushroom that day, I'd only been talking to a police officer who had listened to my theories about the murder cases, who had taken me seriously. He'd helped to bring the killers to justice. So, why did I feel awkward during our conversation, as though I were doing something illicit?

But seventeen months had passed. Although I still thought of

Matt frequently, he didn't haunt my thoughts or invade what little sleep I usually got. Because he was no longer around to satisfy my neediness and lessen my insecurities, I was able to see that our relationship had been significantly flawed, built as it was on salving each other's wounds, instead of bringing out the best in each other. As a couple, we should have aspired to collective greatness, but our troubled pasts were like invisible anchors we hauled behind us, limiting our aspirations and our sense of ourselves.

We had both been broken by our childhoods, but he was never comfortable enough with me—never believed in us or trusted me enough—to let me know just how awful his childhood trauma had been. In fact, he never even hinted at it, except to say that his childhood home had been "wallpapered with lies." I understood that people have secrets and that couples don't need to share everything about their lives, especially their pasts, but if one partner can't reveal the most defining aspect of his or her life to the other—effectively lying by omission day after day, night after night—how strong and healthy is that relationship?

In the intervening months, I'd forgiven myself for having believed that my relationship with Matt had been wonderful, or even good enough. I'd decided not to settle for another relationship that was riddled with omissions and was held together by insecurities, neediness, loneliness, and desperation. That Saturday night, I was stronger than I'd been when Matt and I had met, and I believed in myself more.

In the note Matt had left me in his journal, he'd written: "I hope you choose better next time because I'm sure you'll be able to choose nearly anyone you want."

The man I wanted was Brandon Green. I gave myself credit for admitting this and tried not to wonder if Matt would approve.

I put Trapunto in my office, told him not to bark, closed the door, and opened the front door to see Brandon standing on the porch, the one without a welcome mat at the moment. He wore a navy-blue, well-pressed, long-sleeved dress shirt tucked into Levi 501 button-fly jeans, without a belt, and slip-on brown boots. His dark-brown hair was a little longer than it had been the last time we'd bumped into each other, and I preferred it as it was that night. The right edge of his mouth rose into what I chose to categorize as a smirk, and his blue eyes seemed to have a question they wanted to ask me.

In his right hand he held a mixed bouquet of flowers, and in his left hand he held a huge bar of Belgian dark chocolate from Trader Joe's. I looked up at him (I'm five-eight; he's six-two) and smiled, then hugged him. He gingerly returned the hug because his hands were full.

"Hello, Brandon," I said.

"Hello, Hadley."

I let go, stepped back, and smiled.

"If my gifts are too old-school, or if they paint me as a sexist dinosaur, I—"

"Hush. They're wonderful. Thank you very much. And thank you for tucking in your shirt. Would've been a rocky start otherwise. How'd you know I prefer dark chocolate?"

"You mentioned it in Mellow Mushroom. I bought it in Nashville a couple weeks ago."

I showed him in and closed the door behind us. "How'd you know we'd have a date soon?"

"Honestly? Your home is amazing, by the way." Amazing was a bit much. It had good bones, the way a skeleton might, but no one ever says of a skeleton, "He looks robust, so let's ask him to haul the sofa upstairs."

"Thank you, but I look at my home as having potential. You said 'honestly.' Honestly, what?"

"Don't take this the wrong way, but this is the third bar I purchased, in anticipation." I laughed. "I can vouch for their deliciousness."

"I'm glad you didn't let them go to waste. I'm sorry it's taken so long. I'm nervous, and I feel kind of—"

"No, I'm sorry. If you're not ready and I pushed you into this—"

"You didn't, and I'm ready. I think the trappings of a date are messing me up a little. I haven't been on a first date for ... more than six and a half years."

"What if I take the pressure off?" His smirk came back, and his eyes seemed on the verge of asking another question.

"Okay, how?"

"As we walk through the festival, sample the barbecue, eat horrible-for-us-but-delicious desserts, you won't have to worry whether I'll give you a goodnight kiss. I won't. In fact, I don't find you even vaguely attractive. As you may recall, I prefer the women I date to be..." He paused to let me deliver the punchline. If he was trying to keep me at arm's length, he was failing miserably.

"Short, fat, ugly, mean, and stupid," I said. "That's a big relief, because what kind of woman would I be if I wanted a tall, dark, handsome man with a mischievous smirk on his face to kiss me good-night at the end of a pleasant date?"

"Pleasant? That's all you're anticipating? Pleasant? I didn't realize you were such a pessimist."

I laughed and went to the kitchen to put the flowers in a vase and to put the chocolate away, out of the reach of Trapunto. I walked back to the living room. Brandon was looking at the books in one of the two built-in cabinets that separate the dining room from the living room. He crossed to the other cabinet, tilted his head to the right, and perused the books. He either heard or saw me enter because while he was still tilted to the right he said, "I'll hit Amazon when I get home. You and I have many of the same novels. But I haven't read Jess Walter or Douglas Kennedy or Liz Moore. I obviously should."

"My reading tastes are eclectic, but I always avoid horror and fantasy. They're just not for me." I walked to him, opened the glass doors, pulled out Walter's *Citizen Vince*, Kennedy's *The Pursuit of Happiness*, and Moore's *Long Bright River*, and handed them to him. "Start with these. And, of course, you're free to borrow any of the others, provided you don't kiss me tonight." I smiled.

His smile, the one I remembered from our previous interactions, lit up his face, and his eyes smiled, too. I put my hands on his shoulders and kissed him on the cheek. I looked into his eyes and said: "That's for being patient and understanding. I figure I'm safe because I'm not your type."

"Not even close." His smirk returned. I liked it. A little too much.

I said, "Mind if I show you the MG and the rest of the house another time? I feel an urgent need to clog my arteries."

"Let's go."

Barbecue on the River annually fills the Lower Town section of Paducah with approximately 300,000 fans of pork, fried desserts, crafts of every stripe, and music, making the three-day festival ten times larger than QuiltWeek, the annual event that gave Paducah its world-wide reputation, at least among quilters. About three dozen pit-masters barbecue 90,000 pounds of meat while competing for the Grand Champions trophy.

The best way for visitors to arrive in Lower Town during the annual festival that had been taking place for more than twenty-five years at that point is by bike or on foot because the parking lots downtown and the street parking are filled long before the event is in full swing each day. Many people, therefore, have to park umpteen blocks away and walk.

Brandon put the books I'd loaned him on the seat of his black Ford Ranger parked in my driveway, in front of my detached, rickety one-car garage, and we walked a few blocks to Barbecue on the River. We negotiated our way between the multitude of booths, slowly maneuvering down each aisle, careful not to bump into anyone brandishing a plate of pulled pork, a tri-colored snow cone, a funnel cake coated in confectioner's sugar, or a skewered corn on the cob slathered in butter. The air was filled with commingled scents and the sounds of various bands.

Our progress down each aisle was slow because even though I was on a date, I was also a candidate for mayor, so I said hello to what seemed like half of Paducah's population, waving to many more as we passed slowly through the human obstacle course.

After considering our options, Brandon ordered a plate of pulled pork from the previous year's Grand Champions, The Pork Dorks, and I gnawed on a salted-and-buttered corn on the cob because I'd eaten pizza before our date. Brandon politely (or chivalrously) looked away while I picked a sliver of corn from between my teeth (with a toothpick—I'm not a heathen.) Then we shared a funnel cake, and he chivalrously (or politely) allowed me to eat the last bite. He daubed some sugar from my cheek with a napkin.

We admired the artistic creations in a few of the booths, but most of the crafts were uninspired at best. A sad display of thirteen multi-hued pipe-cleaner animals made me wonder about the long-term damage done to the country by the decimation of arts funding in schools. When we were out of earshot of the creator of the lackluster animals, Brandon said, "My youngest sister, Connie, once had a cat whose furballs were more artistic."

"It's hard not to like you," I said.

"You were hoping to dislike me? Sorry to disappoint. If it would help, I could tell you I love Justin Bieber."

"You could tell me that, but you don't, right?"

"Of course not." I laughed.

As the evening progressed, I wondered if I was simply swept up in the novelty of being on a first date for the first time in many years or if Brandon and I really were as comfortable around each other as we seemed. Matt had been so awkward on our first date that I'd threatened to walk away if he didn't stop trying to be someone who he thought I'd like, rather than being himself. He eventually settled down, and we became a couple. But on his best day, after years of us being together, Matt was not as comfortable in his skin, as relaxed, or as confident as Brandon was on this first date.

Because I do my best to face issues head on, I asked Brandon if he'd like to sit by the river. He said yes. We walked through the opening in Paducah's famous Wall to Wall, a blocks-long floodwall painted with elaborate panels of the city's and region's history. After I made the suggestion, I realized we were heading to a location that could trigger trauma in me because of its role in the Quilt City Murders and how Matt played into all of it. And I wondered if I was subconsciously sabotaging this date by introducing Matt into it.

But I cut myself some slack. Matt would always be with me in some way. We'd spent five years together, and he'd died suddenly and tragically, so his loss lived in me. But I'd worked hard in therapy to process that loss, so as Brandon and I sat on a concrete step, facing the water, I admitted that perhaps I only wanted to talk to my date in a romantic setting.

The loop by the river known as the Foot of Broadway was mostly dark, but there was enough light for me to see Brandon's eyes. I looked into them and said, "I wear my emotions on my sleeve, but I'm not flighty. Just expressive. And I want to tell you that I feel disconcerted by how comfortable I feel in your presence. I recognize the contradiction in that statement. My comfort with you frightens me a little, because maybe I'm letting newness and the prospect of hope lower my defenses."

If I'd said similar sentences to Matt on our first date, or, even later in our relationship, he would have launched into a comical bit that would have made me laugh. And even though laughter can be therapeutic and is essential in a supportive, healthy relationship, Matt would have tried to elicit laughter as a defense mechanism, as a way to avoid the issues I'd just presented.

Brandon, however, said nothing and nodded, indicating that I should go on. He knew I had more to say. I said, "I'm not nutty, or a stalker, or like my sister, Jenny, who convinces herself she's in love with any man who says hello to her. But I do feel as though this isn't anywhere near a first date. I know we've spoken to each other—what, eight, ten times? Some of those were long conversations, but my comfort level seems disproportionate to the time we've spent together. I'm afraid I'm overreacting to Matt hiding his biggest secret from me throughout our relationship. I'm not that way—I'll never hide anything from you, how I feel, what I'm thinking. I know I must sound batty, and I'd understand if you excused yourself. Politely, I'm sure. But if you don't, I hope you understand I'm demonstrating that I'll be who I really am around you, or at least who I believe myself to be. I'm really not trying to scare you off. I swear. I'll be very upset with myself if I have, but I don't want you to like who I present myself as. I want you to like who I really am, so I thought you should know what I'm thinking and feeling."

TEN
MISDIRECTION

He waited a century before he spoke, and I learned to hate myself amid the silence in three new ways. He eventually took my right hand in his left, and said, "Hadley, you have not come anywhere close to scaring me off. In fact, if you don't mind me throwing out our goofy routine about you not being my type, I felt a little of what you just described the first night we met in Noble Park. I was on duty at a murder scene but was overpowered by your presence—your willingness to interact with officers, despite one of them having broken your cheek, your willingness to treat me objectively despite me being Williams' coworker, your professionalism, your determination, your intelligence, your beauty. I almost couldn't do my job.

"I thought, 'Her fiancé has just been murdered, she found his body, and she was beaten by a cop. Why are you trying to charm her, you moron? What's wrong with you?' Since then, I've hoped this day would come, even believed it would. I've been on a few dates since, including with Dakota, but I didn't give any of those perfectly date-able women a chance because I needed to have my first date with you so I could get you out of my system or try to get you into my life.

"But, complete disclosure, you've been in my life since that night, just not in the way I'd hoped. I haven't done anything creepy—stalked you, tapped your phone—but I've followed your progress, hoping to run into you. I've admired your gumption and resolve. It takes a very strong, capable person to launch a newspaper while journalists are being called the enemies of the people. You're truly impressive, not the least of which is your forthrightness. So, if you're asking me if I feel as comfortable tonight as you do, the answer is, 'Yes, at least as comfortable.' Despite how we feel, however, we *are* actually on our first date, so maybe we should continue to have a good time, be grateful for our comfort with each other, and we'll see how things—"

A barrage of gunfire interrupted him from the other side of the painted red and white sign on the floodwall that says PORT OF PADUCAH, KY—WELCOME. Shotgun blasts and rifle shots roared in rapid succession from above and behind us. Brandon slid me from the concrete step we were on to the next one down, then rotated toward me and covered my body with his.

At first, I registered the sounds as celebratory fireworks, part of the event we were attending. Every Fourth of July, those steps and every section on the bluff were filled with McCracken County residents watching fireworks explode high above them, so maybe I was conditioned to hear explosions there as fireworks. But Brandon recognized the sounds as what they were within two seconds, so he took action.

The weapons sounded as though they were being fired from above street level, maybe from the rooftops on the other side of the floodwall. The shouts, screams, and shrieks of thousands of people mixed with the gunfire, which didn't let up. To my horror, I suspected that the ten or so guys who had stolen guns and ammo from Walmart were slaughtering festivalgoers at random in a terrorist attack similar to those that had devastated far too many cities and towns around the world.

I could hear the crowd panicking—booths being knocked over and people being trampled while running into each other trying to figure out which way to escape. Children yelled for their parents, and vice versa. I counted what sounded like four different alarms going off. Most of the gunfire seemed to be coming from the other side of the wall atop the River Discovery Center, the museum that tells the stories of the Ohio River and of Paducah. The weapons kept firing, but the screaming got quieter as the crowd dispersed, fleeing the area.

About two dozen people ran through the opening in the flood-wall, joining us on the large, sloped concrete apron by the river. Most of them stood down near the water, as far as they could go in that direction without getting wet. A few of the people who'd fled through the entrance must have seen us sprawled behind a step, or they had the same idea Brandon had, because I looked up to see two other couples assuming similar positions in our row, with the men draping themselves over the women.

Brandon didn't say anything obvious such as "stay down," "be calm," or "this isn't good." In fact, he didn't say anything. When he finally spoke, he said, "Where are they?" I thought he meant the shooters, but within fifteen seconds I heard distant sirens heading toward us. I'd seen about a dozen officers walking throughout the festival, and Brandon had nodded to most of them. Those officers had likely done what they were trained to do: Protect the public and attempt to subdue the attackers. But because they had been walking through the crowd, they weren't likely to fire their weapons at the shooters, even if they saw them and thought they could hit them, for fear that retaliatory fire from the shooters would kill bystanders.

Brandon's torso was covering mine. His gesture was brave and noble, but if the shooters walked through that entrance and decided to shoot us, Brandon's body would do little more than die a split-second before mine would.

"Do you swim well?" I asked.

"Yes. That's the play. If a shooter comes through the entrance, bolt for the river, and we'll meet at your place."

I wanted to dive into the river then. Why wait for a shooter to force us to run? Sure, the river was filthy with diesel fuel, dead Asian carp, and who knew what else? But all Brandon and I had to do was to swim downstream, make our way around the point, climb up a ladder on the dock, then wash the river gunk off us when we got to my house. When I factored in those elements, my escape plan didn't sound all that simple. But it sounded better than hoping a shooter didn't decide to search for potential victims by the river.

I didn't want to imagine how many festivalgoers lay dead or dying on the other side of the floodwall, and I didn't want to become a statistic on this side. I'd rather fail while attempting to escape than fail by not making an attempt. Because escaping could be a matter of life or death, the decision was simple.

I opened my mouth to say, "See you at my place," when the gunshots stopped. As the booms of the last shots died away, blaring sirens joined the ear-splitting alarms. Car tires skidded on the black-top. Car doors slammed, men shouted, and footfalls sounded as officers ran in various directions.

I didn't know how long it had been since the first shot. Two minutes? Four? The din was still significant, but the lack of gunshots settled me a little. When two uniformed officers with guns drawn walked through the gap in the wall onto the Foot of Broadway, Brandon sat up and raised his empty left hand. The officer nearest to us said, "Got you, Detective," and continued scanning the area for the perps. Brandon stood, helped me to my feet, and walked over to the officer who'd spoken to him, as the officer scanned the area, panning across the river with his gun. As they spoke to each other, I pulled out my phone, called Dan, then Teresa Land, the city reporter, then Sheila Hatcher, the A&E reporter.

None of them answered. I left messages with each. They were probably driving to the scene or conducting interviews and taking photos on the other side of the floodwall.

"You okay?" Brandon asked me when he returned. He'd been all business when the attack was happening, but his tone and the concerned expression on his face let me know he was asking not as a police detective but as my date.

"I'm fine but anxious about what we're going to find up there."

"It sounded like a massacre, but Officer Brown said he only saw what appeared to be one casualty. They expected dozens, at least. The scene's still active. They're detaining anyone who hasn't fled while they search for the perps. Easy to disappear into a large crowd. I should join them. I'm sorry."

"No need to apologize for doing your job. I have to get to work, too. But there's something you should know."

"What's that?"

"I never said *I* wouldn't kiss *you* at the end of our date." He smirked, and I kissed the smirk off his face. I intended the kiss to be just a peck—on the lips, but not long and lingering. My intention proved to be naïve as soon as our lips touched. I don't know if the extreme danger we'd just experienced, the seventeen months of anticipation, our obvious chemistry, or the position of the moon that night added to the magic of our exploratory, delicious kiss. Whatever it was, I'd be a zillionaire if I could bottle it and sell it to the lonely, the distraught, the romantic, and everyone who has lips.

I reluctantly extracted myself from Brandon's embrace, looked into his eyes, and turned to see Chris Knudsen, a press-operator at the *Paducah Chronicle*, filming us with his phone from fifteen feet away. He was about thirty-five, five-ten, muscled but not absurdly so, with a dark-brown mullet and a goatee that had gone gray at the bottom. He lowered the phone and smiled at me.

Great. Just what I needed. My first kiss with Brandon would now be used against me. I'd been waiting for some kind of corporate sabotage by the press operators because I rented the press from the *Chronicle*, and the two papers were competitors, or perhaps enemies. The press operators could introduce any number of errors or falsehoods to our copy, headlines, cutlines, or graphics if they were vindictive enough—or if they were ordered to do so by the *Chronicle*'s editor, Greg Wurt, or by its publisher, Ed Colapinto.

I'd written four editorials criticizing the *Chronicle's* editorials and its coverage of local topics, especially of sports. Girls and women didn't receive the coverage they deserved, and they almost never saw their pictures in the paper. Greg had responded to one of my editorials with an editorial of his own that included this line: "Women exerting themselves while wearing skimpy athletic uniforms, perspiring, breathing heavily and inciting lust in certain readers shall not be encouraged in these pages." I couldn't leave that alone. I responded with an editorial that included this passage: "I'm amazed that home subscribers of the other Paducah newspaper ever receive their editions on time. Based on the antiquated and otherwise ill-informed editorial positions espoused by the publication's putative editor, I would guess that carrier pigeons or the Pony Express delivered the Comical."

"What are you doing?" I asked Chris Knudsen. I'd only interacted with him a few times during my more than five years at the *Chronicle*. He'd been friendly each time.

"Helping your campaign."

"Why?"

He walked closer to us and stuck out his hand to Brandon.

"Chris Knudsen."

"Detective Brandon Green."

"Nice to meet you, but I know who you are. My cousin's a cop, guy you just talked to."

"Brown."

"Yup. Says you ain't bent."

"Brown's not bent."

"That's what I'm saying. You and him, some a the good ones."

"Nearly all of us are. But a few bad officers can destroy the reputation of a force. We still have a lot of work to do."

"You haven't explained why you filmed us," I said.

"When I post this, the whole 'she hates cops' argument goes up in flames, don't it?" He glanced over his shoulder toward two men and a woman standing at the top of the ramp, watching our interactions.

"Maybe," I said, "but I'd prefer you didn't post it. And I wouldn't have guessed you'd want me to win because you work for the *Chronicle*."

"That's only my job. Got many mouths to feed. But let's just say —and I ain't got nothin' against you—I'm voting *against* Nick Stoddard, the snake, and other slimy folks associated with the *Chronicle*. Saw on Facebook you made him look like the corrupt moron he is. Anyone running against him, I'd vote for him—or her."

"Fair enough. But it's dark. The quality of the footage can't be good."

"You familiar with social media? Quality ain't got nothin' to do with nothin'.'"

"Can't argue with that," I said, "but I wish you wouldn't post the video."

"Respect that, but, trust me, you need all the help you can get. Lotta people still mad about the settlement, think you're anti-cop, anti-Paducah, anti-democracy."

"I'm running in an election that will be won by the candidate who receives the most votes, but people think I'm anti-democracy?"

"Talkin' 'bout the internet. Don't have to make sense for dimwits to believe it."

"Guess not."

"Plus, Stoddard admitted at Kroger he's gonna cheat. Saw the video."

"He did, didn't he? Then do what you have to do, I guess, and I appreciate your vote. Truly." He nodded and walked up the ramp, heading for the nightmare on the other side of the wall. The woman at the top of the ramp, maybe in her mid-twenties, nodded at him.

"Our first kiss, captured for posterity," Brandon said.

"True, but it would've been better if it had only been etched forever in our memories."

"It will be in mine, but right now I have to get out there." He looked up the ramp.

"Me, too. Despite being caught in what appears to have been a terrorist attack, Brandon, our first date was magical."

"It was, wasn't it? Would it be needy or inappropriate to ask you to call or text to say you got home safely?"

"No. In fact, I was about to ask you to do the same."

"Then we'll talk later. Be careful."

ELEVEN

THE TARGET

When we reached the intersection of Water Street and Broadway at the top of the ramp, it looked as though the entire Paducah Police Department was scouring downtown, searching for the shooters. A heavily fortified PPD SWAT vehicle skidded to a stop, and four armed-to-the-teeth officers jumped into what was left of the action. Three Kentucky State Police cars roared in with sirens blaring, and six troopers insinuated themselves into the investigation. The officers walked Broadway, Maiden Alley, Market House Square, Marine Way, Third Street, Kentucky Avenue, and Jefferson Street with their guns drawn as the shrieking alarms were turned off one after another. The cops probably knew that the shooters had gotten away.

All but one of them.

At the base of the River Discovery Center on South Water Street, a man dressed in street clothes—jeans, a plaid flannel shirt, despite the warmth of the September night, and blue New Balance running shoes—was sprawled in an unnatural heap. He lay only about thirty yards from the entrance to the boat ramp on the Foot of Broadway. Although I couldn't see his face because officers were gathered around him, I knew he was one of the men I'd seen robbing

Walmart. My gut told me that, and my gut is almost never wrong. My head, frequently—but my gut, almost never.

He didn't wear black from head to toe as he had in Walmart, but I'd bet my life the rifle sticking out from beneath him would prove to be one of those stolen on Friday afternoon. He'd bet his life that the attackers' plan would succeed, and he would survive the evening, whatever their objectives had been. He lost that bet. I stared at his twisted body but couldn't guess at their objectives.

I surveyed the scene and assessed the damage. The significant destruction I'd expected didn't exist. Yes, a few windows were broken, the wares in many of the booths were scattered, and two booths had collapsed, probably because festivalgoers had damaged the support poles while fleeing. Despite that minimal damage, I was mystified by the near lack of casualties, considering the amount of gunfire we'd heard.

Because the dead assailant had obviously fallen from the roof of the River Discovery Center, and because he appeared to be the only casualty, I deduced that the shooters must have been shooting above the people toward the confluence of the Tennessee and Ohio rivers, in the direction of the sliver of land that separates the two for a short distance called Owens Island. If the shooters had wanted to kill people, they would have shot into the crowd as festivalgoers fled down South Water, Maiden Alley, and Marine Way. I suspected then, and confirmed later, that the shooters had been posted on the roofs of buildings on those streets, too. The shooters had probably broken the windows to set off the alarms.

I saw Brandon talking to five officers surrounding the body. He pointed south toward Kentucky Avenue, and one of the officers headed in that direction. Another peeled off toward Jefferson.

Brandon turned and looked for me. I raised my hand to indicate I saw him looking. I'd been about to shout to Dan, who was walking toward me but was being stopped by an officer farther up Broadway. I waited to hear what Brandon wanted to tell me. He approached and said, "We're about to clear everyone but law enforcement from the area. The fatality is Basil Hayden, thirty-two, wearing a dog tag that has nothing but the capital letters BP on it. If you need to quote me, quote me."

"Thank you. I understand the awkwardness of your position and the flak you're subjecting yourself to by consorting and cooperating with the press. Basil Hayden probably isn't his name. This is Kentucky, so his parents could easily have been fans of bourbon, or maybe he was conceived under the influence of it, but Basil Hayden is the name of a Kentucky bourbon."

"You astound me. How do you know that?"

"My mom was a drunk, remember? Jim Beam killed her, but she was his co-conspirator. I spent countless hours in the library reading about this beloved commonwealth and its deadly and most popular creation, bourbon whiskey. If I had to, I could probably whip up a batch of sour mash while blindfolded. His ID is fake. My guess is when you find the other perps, they'll have IDs that say they are Elijah Craig, Evan Williams, Old Granddad, etc."

"If you're right, I should deputize you."

"Sure, that would go over well with your colleagues. It could be his name, but I'll bet you a dinner at Cynthia's it's a pseudonym, or, in his sad case, a *nom de guerre*."

"You're on."

"Any thoughts on what the BP on the tag means?"

"No. You?"

"British Petroleum? Blood Pressure? Boiling Point?"

"Batting Practice? Bullet Proof? Border Patrol?"

"Bills Payable? Breaking Point? We'll figure it out," I said, "but for now, let's go with Beyond Pointless."

"Okay, but if you come up with that answer, too, I'll buy us one dinner at Cynthia's and another at freight house."

"Getting ahead of yourself, aren't you, Detective? What if I suddenly find you repulsive, or I run off with a fireman before then?"

"Good point. They do have cool uniforms. Gotta go." We said "Stay safe" at the same time.

I walked up Broadway toward where Dan begged a state trooper to let him move closer to the body. But the Statie wasn't budging. Dan saw me approach, raised his upturned hands and shrugged, pantomiming, "What am I supposed to do?"

One news-copter approached from the west, another from the east, from across the river, adding to the thwack-thwack of the police helicopter that was bouncing a cone of light around downtown. I was relieved to hear the last of the alarms finally stop clanking because the night had been far too loud, according to my headache. My pulse had slowed, but the shock of the attack had bunched my shoulders, turned my palms clammy, and caused the anxiety hounds to nip at my heels. Adrenaline had kicked in while the bullets had flown above our heads, but now I took deep breaths to prevent those hounds from overtaking me.

I said, "Hi, Dan," but my phone rang. I answered, made a "wait a sec" gesture to Dan with my hand, and heard arts and entertainment reporter Sheila Hatcher say, "It was a diversion. Get to the Quilt Museum."

The National Quilt Museum is on Jefferson, between Second and Third, a few blocks away.

"Follow me," I said to Dan. I took off as quickly as my ballet flats would let me run. He was about ten years younger, three inches taller, and was wearing running shoes, so he had no trouble keeping up. We arrived at the museum a few minutes later. Sheila, forty-two, a few months older than I was, stood outside the front entrance looking worried.

After placing a job listing on journalismjobs.com, I'd lured her away from a weekly called the *Los Feliz Ledger* located in a ritzy part of Los Angeles. She lived "south of Pico," she'd told me on the phone. That meant she lived a long way from Los Feliz, not in miles but in driving minutes, causing her to commute many hours a week, factoring in traffic. As I learned while I attended UCLA, Angelenos should always factor in traffic.

Sheila had hated her bumper-to-bumper commutes, the

extremely high housing costs, and the dangers and temptations that gangs presented to her sixteen-year-old son, Aaron. She'd lost her husband, Aaron's father, to a fatal stroke two years earlier. She'd said during the phone interview, "a new location would do us good." I'd scheduled her visit to Paducah so she could watch shows at both the Carson Center—the impressive entertainment hall that hosts Broadway shows and concerts by major performers—and Market House Theatre, the community theater that features a surprisingly talented group of locals. While Sheila and I ate at Doe's Eat Place, she said, "If you're offering, I accept."

Two squad cars were parked in front of the entrance to the National Quilt Museum next to the large lawn. Robby Golden, fifty-seven, the CEO of the museum, was pacing back and forth very quickly across the entrance, onto the grass, then back onto the concrete walkway, looking as if he was about to start pulling his hair out.

Sheila said to Dan and me, "The shooting was a distraction. They wanted to get everyone running south, set alarms off to create chaos, make people panic and think they were going to die, focusing all attention away from the museum so the shooters could steal quilts. The chaos and the other alarms created cover for the museum's alarm and the theft taking place out the back door, away from the crowd."

"Wow, that's elaborate," I said. "Of course, the quilts are irreplaceable. You got the info from Robby?"

"Yes. I'm afraid he's going to have a heart attack, stroke, or both." She looked at her notebook and said, "Quoting Robby, 'Yeah, we're insured, but that's like saying it's okay your spouse died because you get the life insurance payout. In what world is that okay? If the quilts are gone forever or are damaged, I'm done, the museum's in trouble, Paducah's in trouble. This is so much worse than horrible: It's catastrophic.'"

"Great job getting that out of him," I said. "That couldn't have been an easy interview."

"Looks like he could use something to calm down," Dan said.

I asked, "Does he know how many they stole?"

"He said he's too frantic to count," Sheila said. "A member of his staff told him she thinks more than twenty are gone. When she realized more than a few were missing, she started to do a complete inventory. It could take a while. In total, the museum has something like nine-hundred quilts in its possession, but not all in this building, if I remember correctly. I didn't ask Robby because I figured it could wait, but were specific quilts taken? Or did they just grab the first ones they found so they could escape quickly? He was visibly shaking, so I backed off."

"You did great," I said. "Anything else?"

"They took them out the back. I got a call a few minutes ago from a blocked number. The caller said a U-Haul truck that wasn't there an hour ago was at a used car lot across from his house on Jefferson. He'd seen on our website a U-Haul had been stolen."

"We got lucky, then," Dan said, "by including that blurb in the crime write-ups."

"Probably transferred the quilts to different vehicles at the lot," I said, "and split up in case one of them was pulled over."

"That sounds right," Dan said. "I assume the cops made sure the building was clear before they let staff in?" He gestured toward the museum.

"Yes," Sheila said, "but it was obvious no one was in there. Looks like they used one of those battering-rams that cops use to destroy the back door. Then they ripped it off its hinges, probably so they could get the quilts out as fast as they could. Or maybe destroying the door made it hard to get past, so they had to remove it. They were gone by the time anyone gave a second thought to the alarm. All the chaos by the river did the trick."

"Not likely a grudge against the museum," Dan said. "They would've just set the place on fire if destruction was the motive. Someone will get a ransom demand soon."

"Yes. We'll probably be included, based on the call I received telling me to stock up on ink."

"Wait, what?" Sheila said. "When was that?"

"Yesterday, after they stole the guns from Walmart. I don't know what I should have done with the threat, but now it seems I should have done something."

"How could anyone know this was going to happen?" Dan asked. "Now it's happened, and yet we don't have any idea why, so this is definitely not on you."

"Thank you," I said. "We have a ton of work to do." I looked at my phone. 10:02. "Dan, get what you can on the assailant who was killed, whose ID said his name was Basil Hayden. But I'm almost certain that's an alias. He was wearing a dog tag that said BP on it. I don't know what it stands for or its significance. BP could be his real initials, or the tag could be a tribute to a relative or friend. At this point, we know close to nothing, so be open to any possibilities. Search BP to see if anything comes up that could make sense. The Walmart employee I interviewed said he saw an assailant wearing a dog tag. Whether that was this assailant, we don't know. Sheila, stay with the quilts. I don't see anyone from the *Chronicle* or WKYC here yet, so this is all yours for now. Do what you do. Post blurbs now, then pull more substantial pieces together and get them up when you can."

They nodded, then went to do their jobs. I called Brandon.

"Hello. What do you have?" he asked.

"Hi. An anonymous call saying the stolen U-Haul that almost certainly hauled the stolen quilts away from the museum was dumped at a used-car lot on Jefferson. Probably so they could easily hide their trucks or vans in the lot, load the quilts into them, and take off in different directions."

"Great job. I'll send two squads. Officer Donner called in the museum robbery. I'm heading over now, and many of the rest of us will as soon as we've completed the sweep here. It was a heck of a diversion—well thought out and well executed."

"Except for Basil Hayden."

"True, but my gut tells me 'executed' may be the right word.

Obviously, anyone firing a weapon on a roof could lose balance from recoil, or trip and fall. The perps on the other roofs managed to fire their weapons, climb down, and escape. Faux Basil could've slipped, but my gut tells me otherwise."

"Did they teach you how to use your gut in the academy?"

"No, but that's how I became a detective. That, and the Quilt City Murders."

"What's your gut telling you now?"

"That they'll issue a ransom demand soon. And yours?"

"It's going to be a long night. I should have told someone about the call I received yesterday that was, in hindsight, almost certainly from one of the attackers."

"What did he say?"

"That I was going to need more ink."

"You are incredibly impressive, Hadley, but is clairvoyance among your talents?"

"Are you teasing me, Detective Green?"

"Actually, no. I'm saying now that you've told me what the caller said, I wouldn't have known what to do with that info, either. It was more likely to be a crank than to mean anything, and nobody could've known what he meant until this shooting, heist, ransom play, whatever we're calling this."

"I should have known."

"These guys appear to have planned this well, so the phone he used will turn out to be a burner. They'll make their demands soon, and we'll act accordingly. But if I owned *Pulse* and received that call, I would have rolled my eyes and gotten back to work. You're far too hard on yourself, Hadley."

"So I've been told."

TWELVE

THE DEMAND

On my walk home, I was glad Ash was staying with me because Trapunto would have launched a terrorist attack of his own had she not been there to let him out. When I arrived I petted him, let him out just in case, and looked in on Ash, who was asleep, as was Chica, on top of the quilt that covered Ash. While Trapunto patrolled the backyard, I checked the *Pulse* website on my phone. Dan and Sheila had posted blurbs that journalism schools could use to teach how to cover breaking news effectively. A photo of law enforcement officers gathered around the body of the dead man whose ID said was Basil Hayden accompanied Dan's brief, and a photo of the damaged door-frame of the National Quilt Museum accompanied Sheila's brief.

I checked to see if Dan and Sheila remembered to post their stories to the *Pulse* Facebook page. They had. I didn't want to look at Facebook posts about the Barbecue on the River attack because I didn't want to be influenced by what might be in them, as opposed to what I saw and heard while on scene. I made the mistake of checking my personal page, and I'd been tagged by Brian Cairns, whom I used to work with at the *Chronicle*: I clicked the link, and the video played of Brandon and me kissing. As I'd predicted, the lighting wasn't good, but I was identifiable, especially when I looked into Brandon's eyes after our kiss ended. Chris Knudsen, who'd shot the video, had captioned it: Hadley Kisses Her Mayor Chances Goodbye.

Darn it. He'd lied to me, and he'd done it well. I'd been suspicious of his motives but had believed his explanation about why he'd filmed Brandon and me. The *Chronicle* put food on the table for Chris's family, and he said he had many mouths to feed, so I was correct to be suspicious. I didn't want to look at the comments, but I couldn't help myself.

The first one read: "Who would kiss that hag?" The second read: "Ain't that the wench stole the city's money?" The third said: "Best and brightest? Yeah, right. Two groups that deserve each other, cops and fake news idiots." I skimmed about fifteen more comments to see if any positive ones were in the string. I was pleased to learn that more than half of the first twenty comments (I went back and counted) were either positive—"You got my vote, honey. You're obviously doing something right"— or neutral—"What's this got to do with her qualifications? You'd rather vote for someone who doesn't seek love?"

My favorite comment read: "Least she ain't dating jailbait," which was a reference to the married Nick Stoddard, who was dating Rachelle Hunt, the granddaughter of P.I. Garrett Hunt. Rachelle wasn't technically underage, but because she was two generations younger than Nick, I appreciated the commenter's poetic license.

My mood had lifted by the time I finished reading the thirty-three comments. I hit play on a link in my feed that showed both of the videos I'd starred in recently side by side: Stoddard being chastised by me in Kroger as he stood next to his twenty-year-old mistress, and hunky, forty-five-year-old Detective Green kissing me by the river. The comments were nearly all positive, my favorite of which read: "Vote Hadley, Gladly, not Stoddard, Sadly."

It was 11:40 p.m. I ate a banana and a handful of almonds, drank some water, and went to my home office. I opened a Word doc on the desktop computer, gave it the slug (journalism lingo for title) "Shooting," added that day's date, and stared at the page.

I almost never have trouble starting a story, but that night I was bombarded with unrelated thoughts. Had Janet specified what kind of funeral service she wanted, and did she care who attended the service? I'd forgotten to ask Dan if he'd learned of any developments in the murder of Baahir Ali. Had I really misread Chris Knudsen's intentions, or had someone demanded that he put a negative spin on the video of Brandon and me kissing? If so, that someone would likely have been associated with the *Chronicle* because the Stoddards were the *Chronicle*'s largest advertiser. So, had Chris originally posted the video accompanied by a caption that encouraged voters to vote for me, only to be told by a *Chronicle* mucky-muck to change the caption? If so, would that command have come from Greg Wurt, the editor; Ed Colapinto, the publisher; or Nick Stoddard, the snake, to use Chris's slithery description? These thoughts and others about tomorrow's Paducah Quilters Quorum session and about Brandon and about chocolate (What was I doing? Brandon had given me a HUGE bar of dark chocolate, and I was being downright rude by not sampling it) didn't help me fill the blank screen in front of me.

I decided to rectify my bad manners by indulging in a square or four of chocolate. I went to the kitchen, took the bar from the cupboard, unwrapped it, and snapped off a chunk consisting of four squares. I broke that hunk in half, bit one square off, and heard from behind me, "Mind sharing?"

I turned to see Ash wearing what appeared to be an XXL men's Murray State sweatshirt and purple socks. Because my mouth was full, I handed her the piece with two squares. She said, "Thank you" and bit one of the squares off.

When my mouth was empty, I asked, "How are you feeling?" She pointed to her mouth, indicating she was savoring the square of chocolate, so I waited ten seconds and asked, "Did Grammie J mention any preferences for her funeral?"

After swallowing, she said, "No. Think that's why I woke up

anxious. Took me a long time to get to sleep, even though I'm totally drained. I normally go early. Grammie J made fun of me for how early I go. If I lived in the dorms, I'd probably get teased about it a lot."

I made sure I didn't have chocolate on my hands before hugging her. She returned the hug, and said quietly, "How did you do it? How did you survive losing Matt, 'cause I don't think I'm gonna make it, and I only lost Grammie J and a friend?"

"I'm not going to sugarcoat it: I didn't think I'd survive." I stepped out of the embrace and looked at her. "I had many horrible nights and many horrible days. I started seeing a therapist and taking antidepressants. I think growing up with an abusive, neglectful mother gave me an advantage processing my grief because I was so used to disappointment, failure, and absence. But it was still extremely difficult. With your mom being similar to mine, I believe you have the tools you need to get through this—and anything else that life throws at you—so long as you acknowledge that your progress will not be linear and that you possess the tools and strength to prevail, however long it takes."

Tears streamed down her cheeks. She stepped back into my arms and said, "But right now I can't do anything but cry."

"That's all anyone can do immediately after a major loss, and you've just lost Grammie J and Baahir. Allow yourself to feel whatever pain you're feeling. There is no right way to grieve, but there is a wrong way: To pretend nothing has changed and your world will continue to function as it did before your loss."

We talked for a few minutes and downed four squares each. She said, "Grammie J didn't like red, if that helps."

"Okay, no red at the funeral. Eat as much of this as you want but please keep it away from Trapunto. If he can't reach it, neither can Chica."

I sat at my desk, changed the article's slug to that day's date (midnight had come and gone), stared at the page for four seconds, and dialed Brandon.

"Hello, Hadley. Please tell me you're not back at the scene."

"No. I forgot to call to tell you I made it home. I always try to do what I say I will. Any news you can share with the woman you recently kissed?"

"You used the definite article. How do you know you're not one of many?"

"Because, to paraphrase a famous song, it's in your kiss. If you're kissing other women that way, you're a world-class actor."

"I played the Pirate King in *The Pirates of Penzance* in high school, so who says I'm not?"

"I do. Listen, Casanova, I understand that you're all atwitter, your world sweetly discombobulated because you recently kissed an incomparable woman with a penchant for sarcasm. But we both have work to do, so please only think of me every other breath." He laughed.

"You got it."

Because the crowd had fled while the shooting took place, I hadn't interviewed festivalgoers. The investigation was ongoing, so I didn't have enough information to write even a mediocre news story. So, I dashed off a first-person account of what this festivalgoer experienced during the commotion that resulted in the destruction of property, theft of quilts, and one death. The story would not win any awards, but any journalist who enters the business in order to receive accolades or riches is in the wrong business.

After I showered, brushed my teeth, and slipped into my pajamas —the blue pair with the sewing machine on the chest—I checked to see if Dan or Sheila had texted (they hadn't). I turned out the light and soon heard the text chime. The text said: *Goodnight, Hadley. (From the man who thinks of you even between breaths).*

I responded: *You're an intrepid, kind, generous, funny, attractive, intelligent man. Sleep well.*

Our great date (excluding the mayhem) and his goodnight text should have allowed me to sleep soundly. But did I? Of course not. I tried not to wonder what my next move with him should be, how wrong that move would turn out, and how negatively he would respond to that inevitably wrong next move. Would I mess things up so badly that he would change his name and move to Uzbekistan?

As I did my best to claw my way out of that rabbit hole, I received a text that read: *Fifteen million dollars by Monday at 5 p.m. We'll tell you where and when. Our advice? Don't fail.*

I forwarded the text to Brandon, who called me a few seconds later.

"I got it, too. Texted to your cell?" he asked.

"Yes, and the call telling me to stock up on ink came there too. That shouldn't worry you. My cell's on my business cards, which I've handed out all over town. My guess is the sender used one of many text-masking apps. I researched them a while ago for a story about a stalker."

"Okay. They're soliciting publicity and inducing panic, which will give the insurer incentive to meet their deadline. I'm sure they sent the same text or email to other media outlets, the city, and law enforcement."

"Which is why I have to post a blurb quickly. The *Chronicle* is out of the mix because it doesn't post breaking news in real time, but I should try to beat WKYC to the punch."

"Because at 1:42 you have plenty of online readers?"

"It's the principle of being both right and first. A tenet of my profession. But perhaps we should stop chatting because bad guys are wreaking havoc, and it may be in the best interests of the Jackson Purchase Region to capture said ruffians before they further terrorize its citizenry and render moot its civic institutions."

"You are not normal."

"Thank you for noticing. Considering what's going on, perhaps we should postpone our second date."

"A shame, but that gives me more incentive to solve this quickly."

"Sure, if you feel comfortable using me only to save lives and invaluable quilts."

"I do. Gotta go."

"Okay, but if you solve this soon, you may receive another kiss."

"Consider it solved."

THIRTEEN

OVERSIGHT

Even though I respected Dan's ability to do research and had told him to look into BP, I couldn't suppress my curiosity or my decades of scratching whichever intellectual itch needed to be scratched. I searched using Google, Google Scholar, and LexisNexis. I came up with only six BPs that could—if I squinted at the words while in child's pose—be used by a terrorist group: Blowpipe; Battle Planning; Breaching Point; Battlefield Position; Boundary Point; and Black Power. Because the so-called Basil Hayden appeared to be white, I ruled out the last option. I then dismissed the exercise as meaningless because the BP on Basil's dog tag could simply be his real initials, or the initials of his significant other, or his kid. Or maybe his first name really was Basil. A search for Basil Hayden delivered various methods by which I could buy that bourbon if I so desired. If Paducah's circumstances continued to deteriorate at anywhere near the rate they had in the last couple of days, I could probably be persuaded to imbibe some of Kentucky's primary contribution to alcoholic spirits, but I'd go with Maker's Mark, if I decided to reintroduce bourbon to my life.

I knew myself well enough to know I had no chance to sleep that night, so I quietly made a pot of coffee, careful not to wake Ash. I sat in the dark in the living room in the comfortable, upholstered chair I usually sat in while reading novels, mostly mysteries. But instead of turning on the reading light over my left shoulder, I drank a cup of coffee, and another, then closed my eyes to facilitate thought. As the caffeine coursed through my system, I wondered if the prints on the knife that killed Baahir Ali had been matched to anyone whose prints were in the Violent Crime Apprehension Program database? Was Brandon awake wrestling with this mess, and what did he wear to bed, if anything? Did Chris Knudsen shoot the video of Brandon and me kissing because he wanted to hurt my campaign? Was it time for me to check on Jenny, my troubled little sister? What should I eat for breakfast? Did the videos help my campaign or hurt it? Could an insurance company really pay out so quickly? Did the terrorists behind the mayhem know how long it took for such a payment to be made, or were they only hoping the National Quilt Museum's insurance company would be able to pay out by Monday? And would the museum's insurance cover a $15 million loss?

Then it hit me: I'd heard a term while I toured the Kentucky Bourbon Trail, just after I quit working at the *Chronicle*, that the terrorists could be using as their name. It was a longshot, but the man identified as Basil Hayden was likely using the name of a bourbon as a pseudonym, so it was a shot worth considering. Along the Bourbon Trail, I hadn't drunk a sip of any of the samples offered to me, but I'd been fascinated by how Kentucky's signature spirit was produced. For the resulting product legally to be called bourbon, a minimum of fifty-one percent of the grain had to be corn. The term "Kentucky bourbon" is almost redundant because ninety-five percent of the world's bourbon is produced in the state (technically a commonwealth, a distinction almost without a difference).

But what was the term I thought I remembered having heard? I did a search of bourbon terms on my phone. I scanned the list until I found Barrel Proof. *Eureka!* I couldn't remember which tour guide at which distillery had explained the term, but I remembered hearing it.

I looked it up. According to Ruling 79-9, established in 1979 by the Federal Bureau of Alcohol, Tobacco, and Firearms, the definition of barrel proof is: "The proof of the spirits entered into the barrel and the proof of the bottled spirits are the same." This means that a bottle that contains a label on which is written "Original Proof," "Original Barrel Proof," "Entry Proof," or "Barrel Proof" has not had water added to it by the distilleries that produce each product. In layman's terms, such bourbons have not been watered down, adulterated, or diminished.

I knew I hadn't proven that BP stood for Barrel Proof, but if my supposition was correct, then the terrorists' demands or their ideology would have something to do with purity—probably racial purity, as if that concept was anthropologically sound. If I was correct, then the terrorists had slept through the history classes that taught the concept of America as a melting pot in which generations of immigrants have melded their cultures and genes to create American society. And the adopters of the BP moniker likely failed biology, specifically the lessons on genetics. I hoped I was wrong about Barrel Proof, for various reasons.

It was still too early to call anyone, so I researched ransoms, how often they are paid, how often kidnappers escape with the ransom, and how the "drops" are usually made. The lack of sleep, the jolts of caffeine, the thanklessness of the research, and the stress of what Paducah found itself in the middle of were causing anxiety to flood my cranium, so I decided to quilt.

Paducah Quilters Quorum was supposed to take place at 2 p.m., as it had nearly every Sunday for years. It would be at Dakota's house (okay, house is an understatement: gigantic Italianate mansion bordering Paducah Country Club), but only if we didn't decide to cancel because of Janet's death and the tumult Paducah was undergoing.

Despite losing one member about seventeen months ago, PQQ had added two others within the last year, only to have Janet Loy be killed in Walmart on Friday. So, we were back to seven members:

Dakota Crowley, Vivian Franey, Cindy Baron, Donna Ackerman (mother of Matt, my former fiancé), Evelyn Lewy (one of the two new members and the sister of the current mayor, Richard Lewy), Tasha Wilson (the other new member), and me. It took a lot for us to cancel because most of us deemed the camaraderie we shared at PQQ to be essential to our emotional wellbeing. But I suspected that the death of Janet and the theft of the quilts would put a major damper on that day's event, if not cancel it.

However, we had to organize Janet's funeral, so we could do that while we worked on our current project: a Celtic Log Cabin in seafoam green and coral that was too busy for my tastes. I, however, had chosen the last quilt we'd created, a Lancaster Rose, and Tasha had liked it the least, or, more accurately, she'd hated it. So, per tradition, she got to choose our next pattern, and she'd chosen the Celtic Log Cabin.

I needed to get my mind off of the turmoil for a little while, at least until I had to leap into it headfirst when morning officially arrived. But the first thought I had upon entering the Stash Hash, the name of my quilting room, was that I should quilt a pristine, unburned version of the quilt we'd made with Ash's help for her Grammie J, replacing the burned one. Of course, that thought immersed me in the turmoil, instead of distracting me from it. So, I closed my eyes, reached into the mound (mountain?) of bolts stacked against a wall, braced with my left hand the bolt above the one I was going to yank out with my right hand—as though pulling a tablecloth without toppling the china and cutlery on it—then whipped my right hand toward me in a manner similar to pulling the cord on a lawn-mower, but level instead of upward. I was prepared for a fabric tsunami to wash over me (was I hoping for that result by undertaking this pointless, precarious, closed-eyed selection process?). All that happened, however, was that I held a bolt of lovely dusty-rose broad-cloth. I hadn't suffered an injury, and the resulting fabric was more than satisfactory, so I vowed to use this technique again (although for legal reasons I can't recommend you try it at home).

I must have awakened Trapunto because as I cleared my workspace, he wandered in and lay at my feet. Even though I didn't know what I wanted to create, I unrolled the bolt and was considering how much to cut off when my cell rang. It was 6:02.

"I'm sorry to wake you, Hadley," Dan said.

"You didn't. I haven't slept."

"I hardly did. I have news. Big news. Sergeant Vazquez from Murray PD texted me about two hours ago, I think from a burner phone because his number's in my phone, but his name didn't come up. I woke up and saw his text. It said the prints on the knife that killed Baahir Ali belong to the dead shooter on Water Street."

"Wow! That's huge. And his real name is?"

"Durrell Mahan, thirty-two, from Mayfield. A big family. Most of them crooks, from the small amount of research I just did. Durrell's been popped for assault and battery twice, resisting arrest, possession of stolen property, possession of methamphetamine, DWI twice. Did time for a few of those."

"Murder is a big jump up."

"Up, as in escalation, yes, but down in terms of morality. Durrell's the oldest of four brothers and two sisters. Probably the dumbest based on the Facebook post I saw. In it, he wrote ... hold on, let me find the quote. Okay, got it. He wrote: Fightin—no apostrophe, no g—made this county. I assume he meant country, but who knows? Fightin—same spelling—gone—g-o-n-e—save it."

"Tell me he hasn't reproduced."

"Not that I could tell. According to stories in the *Mayfield Messenger* about the family's numerous arrests, they all live in what the paper called a ... let me find it ... 'a would-be compound made up of trailers in a rough circle, with as many broken cars in the front yard as chained-up pit bulls.' End quote."

"They're probably good neighbors, though. Friendly, generous of spirit. I would've sent the article back to the reporter."

"Knew you'd say that. Could be zero cars and pit bulls."

"Or a thousand. You've done an incredible job, Dan. Really.

When we hire our next cub, please remind me to have you explain to her or him the importance of cultivating relationships with sources. Sergeant Vazquez came through in a big way for us, probably at some risk. Any thoughts on why he'd risk being caught cooperating with the dreaded media?"

"Best guess, I'd say he's dealt with the Mahans before. Murray and Mayfield are about a half hour apart. He'd have to be more broken than bent to let someone get away with murder."

"Probably. But Durrell didn't get away with anything. Baahir's murderer has been brought to justice, however eye-for-an-eye it may be."

"Meaning you don't think he fell off the roof?"

"Correct. Detective Green said his gut told him that Basil Hayden, as he was known at the time, had been pushed."

"Possible, but why not just shoot him while you're shooting up everything else? No guarantee he'd die in the fall."

"True, but you're assuming the fall killed him. Maybe someone broke his neck, made sure he was dead or dying, then shoved him."

"Hadn't thought of that. That's why you're the boss."

"That, and I'm a better quilter."

"No debate there, but how's that relevant?"

"Quilting is always relevant."

"If you say so. But do you mind if I ask you something kind of personal?"

"Of course not."

"I was wondering, you know, if you're, uh ... if you are—"

"Seeing Brandon? Yes."

"Okay, that's what I thought. Saw the video. Wanted to make sure it wasn't a deep fake, you know, put out by Stoddard so you'd lose."

"Who knows what the effect will be? The response has been pretty even, pro and con. Apparently, romance still resonates with some folks."

"Well, I'm really happy for you. I've been hoping you'd meet someone, not as much as I've been hoping for me to, of course, but close."

"Well, if your hoping played a role, I'm grateful to you, and I'll hope just as hard for you to meet the right someone. Brandon and I have only been on one date, but it was by far the best first date I've had, and yet we had bullets whizzing over our heads. So, that should tell you something."

"It does, but I have to write this up."

"Of course. Again, great job. I just remembered I have some information to add. I could be wrong, but I think the BP on the dog tag around Mahan's neck refers to Barrel Proof. It's a term from bourbon distilling that refers to distillers maintaining a certain purity. If I'm correct about BP, then I think we're dealing with lizards who believe racial purity exists, meaning white supremacists."

"Then let's hope you're wrong."

"Yes. We'll see how the ransom plays out. If the insurance company pays in full and on time, maybe these imbeciles will get away with it, but the tenuous peace will be maintained."

"Let's hope. Gotta go. Take care, Hadley, and congratulations on finding Brandon."

"Thank you. You're a champion cops reporter, and when you move to a bigger market, I won't be surprised when you win a Pulitzer."

"No plans to leave—but thank you."

I gave up on quilting, ate two pieces of wheat toast with raspberry jam, downed another cup of coffee, and called Brandon.

"Did you get any sleep?" he asked.

"Didn't even try."

"I tried but got nowhere."

"Dan Eidie, our cops reporter, has made progress. The knife that killed an Egyptian student at Murray named Baahir Ali had the prints of the pseudonymous Basil Hayden on it."

"Really. That's significant. How good's his intel?"

"A source in Murray PD who's been solid for years. The murderer's and vic's name is Durrell Mahan, from Mayfield, thirty-two, a long rap sheet that includes assault and battery, resisting, possession, DWI."

"Not going to give me the PD contact, are you?"

"Now, Detective Green, our kiss was magical, but a source is a source."

"Fair enough."

"In case this cross-jurisdictional nightmare hasn't ratcheted up your blood pressure enough to alarm your phrenologist—"

He laughed. "What's wrong with you?"

"Well, there's this boy, see, and he has these dreamy blue eyes and a smirk at the right side of his mouth that does things to me—and, well, I better stop there."

"That's a shame. Sounded like a story even my phrenologist, Dr. Lumpyhead, would enjoy."

"Pretty sure I caught his TED talk. It didn't go smoothly."

I told him about my BP theory.

"Meaning you think we're dealing with racist halfwits?"

"Less than half, but yes."

"No one said this job would be easy."

"No sane person would," I said. "Let's keep each other posted."

"Sounds good. Dinner?"

"Doesn't seem appropriate with all this going on, does it?"

"People have to eat, Hadley. Basic biology. No one can solve crimes, or, I'm guessing, write about crimes or anything else on an empty stomach."

"There's a donut joke in there somewhere."

"I'll let that pass. We won't dine in public. We will, while we discuss what comes next in this fiasco, partake of clams and linguine at my house."

"Wow, you cook, too?"

"Yes, but boiling water, mincing garlic, chopping parsley, and heating clams don't constitute culinary expertise."

"True. I'll bring my famous peanut butter cookies."

"Great. How's seven?"

"Assuming nothing else blows up, crashes down, or dies, that should be great." He gave me his address, which I put in my phone. We said goodbye.

I hoped a shower would revitalize me because I was already feeling the effects of my sleepless night and my trough of coffee, and I had a busy day ahead of me. I showered, got dressed, ate a bowl of oatmeal with walnuts and dried cranberries in it, and was about to let Trapunto out when Sheila Hatcher called.

"You're not going to believe this," she said.

"That sounds ominous."

"Worse."

"Worse than ominous?"

"Yes. I just got off the phone with Robby Golden. He sounds like he might kill himself."

"He said something to that effect?"

"No, but I don't think I've ever heard anyone that distraught. He was frantic last night, but he was so low-energy and morose just now I could hardly hear him. He said they know how many quilts were stolen. Twenty-six."

"That's a lot. Any significance to the number?"

"Not that he or his staff could tell. They're trying to make sense of which ones were taken, looking for patterns or groupings or something. He didn't want to tell me—he said because they weren't sure yet, but I think my being Black influenced his reticence. It looks like they chose the quilts they chose because they were created by people of color."

"Really?"

"Which means they didn't just grab the first quilts they got to. They'd done enough research to know where to look. Their search was made easier because an exhibit of quilts from the Gee's Bend Quilters Collective in Alabama was about to go up. The fifteen quilts in the show hadn't been unrolled, and they were all in a storage room, so they only had to carry them out, not find them or roll them up.

When Robby and his staff finished their inventory and realized which other quilts were missing, they were kind of forced to admit what should probably have been obvious: The other eleven quilts were created by people of color, as the Gee's Bend quilts were. Four Latinas, four East Asians, and three Native Americans."

"Great work, Sheila. Stealing those quilts seems to support a theory I have: The perps are using the abbreviation BP, for Barrel Proof, denoting the purity of bourbon. Seems like they must've worked with someone on the inside, doesn't it?"

"Or they did a lot of homework," she said. "The website lists the upcoming Gee's Bend show, so that wouldn't take an insider to know those quilts were there, but the others? I mean, would they risk taking the time to search through all the quilts, probably hundreds of them, then, what, do a Google search and compare the results to the notes about each quilt in some file cabinet? No way. Had to be an insider, someone who let them know which quilts to grab."

"I agree. But why twenty-six? Were those all of the quilts by people of color?"

"No. Robby said a dozen quilts had just arrived from Africa for the exhibit that would follow the Gee's Bend exhibit. They were in the room next to the one they hit. They could've grabbed the fifteen from Gee's and eleven of twelve from the next room, all still pack aged, if the number twenty-six means something."

"If the ones from Africa just arrived, maybe the inside person didn't know about them or didn't have time to tell the thieves. Or maybe we've jumped to a conclusion we shouldn't have. Maybe the stolen quilts were stolen for a particular reason, one we don't know yet. But if the reason they were stolen isn't because their creators are people of color, then that seems like too big a coincidence, doesn't it?"

"Absolutely. When we combine your Barrel Proof theory with the fact that all twenty-six quilts were made by people who aren't white, the odds are too long for coincidence. This is really weird. Not exactly another day at the office."

"That's for sure. But that's one of the many aspects of journalism

I like: Although I've written hundreds of stories that contain similar elements, I've never written the same story twice. Working in a newsroom is never like working in a factory. I know. I worked in a zipper factory in L.A.'s garment district for exactly four days. I told myself I quit because commuting from Westwood to downtown L.A. to make minimum wage made no sense. But I think I really quit because after sewing on zippers for seven minutes, every zipper became identical, meaningless, just one more widget, and every minute I spent there probably shortened my life by an hour. I landed a job three days later writing for a local paper, and I already wrote for the *Daily Bruin*."

"I know what you mean. Even covering any boring civic meeting is better than being a greeter, which I did in college: 'Hello, welcome to Applebee's.' By the fifth hour every shift, I wanted to send them to the TGI Friday's across the street just so I could say something different."

"Sounds tedious. The one bit of good news here so far is that the dead shooter has been identified. He's Durrell Mahan, and his prints were on the knife that almost certainly killed a student at Murray."

"That's awful, but it's progress. Oh, I haven't told you the worse-than-ominous part."

"Seriously?"

"You sitting down?"

"I am now."

"The museum was only covered for fire, flood, tornados, earthquakes, and hurricanes—acts of God. Robby said he let the theft rider lapse."

"You've got to be kidding," I said. "The thieves did their homework well enough to know which quilts to steal but not well enough to know the current insurance policy doesn't cover theft?"

"The world's mostly made up of C students."

"And mostly run by them."

FOURTEEN
CONTRADICTIONS

On Sundays, I usually went for an early run or bike ride, showered, attended the 11 a.m. mass at St. Francis de Sales Catholic Church, wandered aimlessly around downtown, then attended PQQ at 2 p.m. But that Sunday was unusual, to say the least.

I looked in on Ashley, who was asleep. Chica stirred when I opened the door, jumped from the bed to the shorter quilt chest at its foot, then to the floor, and followed me out. I let her and Trapunto into the backyard, then tried to plan my day.

The fact that the quilts weren't insured had to make the thieves' plan unworkable, so they would either be forced to abandon their plan, or to improvise. Because the heist appeared to accomplish their objectives—they'd escaped with the quilts, and no one in pursuit knew where the quilts or the thieves were—the perpetrators would likely improvise. Their position was still too strong to abandon their plan when they found out the $15 million wouldn't be delivered by the museum's insurance company—Kentucky United Insurance, Robby had told Sheila. But could they be naïve enough to believe that the National Quilt Museum, local industries, and private citizens could raise $15 million by Monday at 5 p.m.? The likelihood of that happening was slightly lower than it was of me becoming a mime who plays the accordion.

Full disclosure: In the third grade I broke out in hives when, at the birthday party of eight-year-old Cecilia Jenkins, a mime mimed playing the accordion. Something about that silent combination creeped me out, and the skin on my neck and shoulders blotched so badly I looked like a pepperoni pizza. Mrs. Jenkins pulled on nitrile gloves before applying calamine lotion. Oddly, I wasn't invited to Cecilia's ninth birthday. This was before the absurdity proliferated of entire classes having to be invited to birthday parties.

For the record, I never said I was well-adjusted.

And, for the record, years later I found out I am allergic to hazelnuts, some of which had been in Cecilia's birthday cake. But that doesn't mean I'm not also allergic to accordion-playing mimes.

The city of Paducah had claimed poverty while negotiating my settlement with my lawyer, Mike Weiss. City officials cited the poor state of the city's sidewalks, its underfunded schools, and its strained tax base while suggesting I settle for a number to which a kindergartner would be proud to be able to count. Mike fought hard for me by suggesting that further numerical insults would be met by a subpoena to open the city's books. His negotiating skill eventually led to both sides reaching a settlement that allowed me to make a down payment on my askew bungalow and to launch *Paducah Pulse* (but only if I rented the *Chronicle*'s press because buying one was out of the question). My settlement wasn't within telescopic view—or even on the same continent—as $15 million.

So, the size of the ransom worried me. No one can squeeze blood from a stone or a turnip, and no one can extort more money from an account than is in it. Where would the $15 million come from? And when the powers that be didn't deliver the ransom money to whichever place and at whichever time the crooks demanded, how would the crooks react?

I let the dogs in and thought about how to cover the recent developments on the *Pulse* website and in Wednesday's edition, which would go to press on Tuesday night. Ash woke up, and I made her breakfast. While she ate, I filled her in on everything that had happened since Brandon and I left on our date the night before. She said she'd heard what she thought were fireworks, didn't think they were out of the ordinary because Barbecue on the River was coming to an end, and went back to sleep. She seemed lethargic in a way that said "depressed" more than "tired." I was not a therapist, but I understood loss and sadness, maybe even depression, although for me the condition didn't last long.

At the risk of making Ash's morning worse, I said, "When I lost Matt, then got beaten up, I was in a very bad place, and I needed help. I was really lucky to find a kind, skilled therapist, Dr. Elaine Bourget, and I'd be happy to set up an appointment for you as soon as she has an opening."

She set her coffee mug down (the one that said, "When life gives you scraps, make a quilt" on it—a gift from Jenny). Ash petted Chica's head for a few seconds, and said, "You think I'm crazy? Am I really that bad?" She looked at me, and I saw tears welling in her eyes.

"Not at all, Ash. I didn't say that. You've suffered the loss of your grandmother and your friend. Your mom is useless and is, in effect, another loss, and your dad, as mine is, is long gone. As difficult as it may be to believe that I understand what you're going through, I think I do, albeit everyone grieves differently, and 'every unhappy family is unhappy in its own way,' to quote Tolstoy. So, I'm saying that when I needed help, Elaine provided it to me. I'll pay for your sessions, so don't let money factor into your decision."

"Thanks, but I'm thinking I won't call her. I'm hoping I can forget all this stuff for a while when I write my paper. I'll either concentrate on psych and not think about this, or I'll not concentrate on psych, get an F on my paper, then I'll need to see your doctor."

She took a swig of coffee, then a bite of her oatmeal, which she'd doctored by creating a one-to-one ratio of oats to brown sugar, with a dollop of milk added for aesthetics, it seemed.

"Your choice," I said. She nodded, and I left her with Chica and Trapunto.

I rode my bike to the *Pulse* office and pulled up the *Paducah Chronicle's* website on my desktop. The lead article was about Baahir Ali's murder, which happened on Friday night. The *Chronicle* published more frequently than *Paducah Pulse*—seven days a week to our one—but our stories had more depth, and we updated our website many times every day, as opposed to the *Chronicle*'s website, which was only a digital version of the static newspaper, put out once a day. Their print deadline was 11 p.m., although the newsroom was usually empty by 10, and the website went live at midnight, then sat untouched for twenty-four hours.

I read Benny Washington's story about Baahir Ali's murder and counted the edits I would have made. Her bad journalism didn't surprise me because I'd worked at that atrocious publication for more than five years. What did surprise me, however, were the following sentences: "A source at Murray PD said Ali's murder was drug-related, based on evidence found at the scene, including two ounces of marijuana found on Ali's bed. MPD is looking into connections Ali was known to have with certain figures in the local drug scene."

If MPD really found two ounces of marijuana on scene, why hadn't Sergeant Vazquez mentioned that to Dan? And, if I accepted the forensic evidence that appeared to be verified by Sergeant Vazquez as accurate, then why would Durrell Mahan, the one whose prints were on the bloody knife stuck into a tree near the dormitory, kill Baahir? If Baahir was a drug dealer, had he sold drugs to Mahan before Mahan decided for no obvious reason to stab Baahir? Or, if Baahir owed money for drugs to Mahan, his theoretical supplier, then why wouldn't Baahir, when threatened with death, not return the two ounces of marijuana that he presumably hadn't paid for, rather than allowing himself to be killed? And the marijuana was said to be found on the bed, in the open? Why wouldn't Mahan grab it before he left? After all, he had enough time to carve four twenty in a tree, so he couldn't have hurried. Something didn't add up.

I called Dan. After saying hello, I said, "I assume Sergeant Vazquez didn't mention the two ounces of marijuana supposedly found in Baahir's dorm room, or you would have included that in your story."

"Of course not. He said the search didn't turn up anything unusual."

"Could he have spoken prematurely, before the investigation was complete?"

"Yeah, but he's a pro. Better than anyone I've worked with at PPD, except maybe Detective Green, and I don't say that because, you know—"

"Yes."

"Vazquez would've called me back to let me know if there'd been drugs on scene. Where'd you get that info?"

"Benny Washington."

"Well, there's your answer."

"What's that mean?"

"You've read her stuff, right?"

"Yes. It's awful. But you're saying it's also inaccurate?"

"What I'm saying is, I heard she didn't get her job legitimately. It's a nepotism thing, I heard. Friend of Greg's or something."

"I hadn't heard that. I just thought they hired someone in a hurry after I left. They were too cheap to hire a dedicated A&E reporter, then threw her to the wolves by burdening her occasionally with the cops beat, as well. Covering any one beat thoroughly can be more than a full-time job, so I was giving her the benefit of the doubt. But that doesn't stop me from wincing while I read her stories."

"Yeah, she's bad, worse than Matt was on that beat. Darn, I'm sorry. Shouldn't've said that."

"It's fine. Don't worry about it. Matt was lousy on A&E, but he proved to be a better cops reporter than any of us knew. He almost solved the Quilt City Murders."

"Yes. I have to track down Vazquez to see what's what." We said goodbye.

Because I was too wound up to concentrate during Mass, I decided to skip church. Instead, I got on my bike, intending to learn whatever I could learn while I rode around town. I wanted to burn some nervous energy as well as the non-nervous kind, so I fastened my helmet, rode to the river, dashed the length of the Greenway Trail, reversed course, then returned to the river. The vibe in the air felt weird. On my usual Sunday-morning rides, I would pass at least a dozen people walking along the trail, some of them pushing strollers, and at least half of those would be cyclists (or at least bicyclists—the distinction being the cost of their bikes and the amount of Lycra they wore).

But that morning, I passed exactly one person along my more than ten-mile ride. His face was dirty and unshaven, and he wore a tattered, heavily soiled, brown trench coat buttoned to the neck. He pushed a store buggy filled with what I guessed were his possessions, covered with a blue tarp. He saw me riding toward him and moved his buggy and himself to the side. As I approached, he gave me a military salute. I returned his salute, and, as I passed him, he smiled.

The unusual vibe I felt while riding the trail made me want to see if downtown was as empty as the trail was. Sunday mornings are usually slow downtown, with most of the businesses being closed. But, in pleasant weather, I always saw tourists wandering Broadway or locals running errands or walking for exercise. I stopped and pulled my phone out of my tracksuit pocket to check the time: 9:05. Still early, but not too early for anyone to be on the streets. My guess was that word of the attack at Barbecue on the River and the ransom request had grape-vined through town, and no one wanted to head into whatever madness was about to happen next unless they had to. But I kind of had to because heading toward trouble was my job.

FIFTEEN

A PERFECT RECORD

I wasn't a first responder, so I didn't run into burning buildings or pull wounded people from wrecked vehicles, but I owned a newspaper that covered the best and the worst of humanity—and many of the average human endeavors in between. *Pulse* reporters and I had to show up at disaster scenes so we could let our readers know what was going on.

I passed the *Chronicle* building and saw the black Cadillac that editor Greg Wurt drove. It was once a top-of-the-line vehicle, but it looked as haggard as I felt that morning. A significant ding—actually, more of a *dang!*—dented the front panel on the passenger's side, and the layer of dirt covering the car made me wonder whether Greg had moved from his large, beautiful home in West Paducah to a house along a dusty country road. That seemed possible, considering that his wife, Wendy, learned of Greg's affair with Missy Wendland as the Quilt City Murders were frightening Paducahans. It takes a special kind of woman to stand by her cheating man, although I hadn't heard that Greg and Wendy had officially split.

I leaned my bike against the *Chronicle* building, called Greg's cell, and asked him if he had a few minutes to talk. He said yes.

Because I rented the press to print *Pulse*, I had a key to the building. I headed upstairs, through the empty newsroom, to his office, which was filled with pictures of clowns. About three dozen framed photos of men and women with creepy, exaggerated features slathered on their faces with greasepaint hung on the four walls. Greg had hired the models, coordinated their attire, perhaps helped them slip into their comically oversized shoes, then posed them for his Nikon.

He offered me coffee, which I declined with a snicker that he probably didn't understand. Greg and I didn't see much of the world the same way—the man considered Sanka to be coffee, for heaven's sake, and have I mentioned the clowns? We'd grown accustomed to being at odds with each other. In fact, I used our opposing viewpoints to measure whether I fully understood a topic: If I agreed with Greg, I must have misunderstood or misconstrued whatever issue we'd agreed upon.

His sweater was tomato red that day. For four years, every day I worked for him (he arrived at the *Chronicle* about a year after I did), he wore a sweater, almost always a single, solid color. Nothing is inherently wrong with wearing a sweater every day (other than the fact that slogging through summer days in Paducah is like sitting in a Jacuzzi inside a sauna). But the combination of his short, squat, overdeveloped musculature and those solid colors made him look like a tomato one day (that one), a pumpkin the next, a lemon the next, etc., especially while sitting behind his desk, so I couldn't see his legs, as he was that morning. The red clown's nose that he kept on his desk was still there.

We had had more than our share of arguments (I had a 71-0 record, by my count). He resented me for various actions I'd taken, or he believed I had (which included bringing his affair with Missy to light), so I didn't expect a lot of pleasant reminiscing while I sat in the seat in front of his desk.

"So, Hadley, the candidate I will not be voting for, what can I do you for?"

"How have you been, Greg? I've been getting a kick out of your editorials."

"Well, it's good to know they're being read, even by our competition. As you know, the country has lost its way entirely. It's wandering aimlessly through the woods, and it's our job to inform the public how to right the ship."

"Mixed metaphors aside, I thought it was our job to report on the policymakers whose job it is to right the ship. Expressing opinions on editorial pages is a minor aspect of our job compared to our obligation to report news as objectively as possible. After all, they're called *news*papers."

"We have never seen eye-to-eye, Hadley"—which was true because I was five inches taller than Greg—"so let's agree to disagree on that front. What did you want to talk about?"

"Your reporter Benny Washington wrote that Murray PD found two ounces of marijuana at the murder scene of Baahir Ali. Dan couldn't verify that information. How solid a reporter is Benny?"

"I'm not sure what you mean." My discomfort caused by being in his clown-filled office began to morph into the frustration-bordering-on-anger I'd felt nearly every time I'd interacted with Greg.

"Are her stories factually sound?" I asked. "Has anyone caught her cooking info?"

"I don't like either your tone or your insinuation."

"Greg, I'm simply asking if her reporting is solid."

"As far as I'm concerned, she was as good a hire as any other."

"That's an odd way to put it. You didn't say she was as good a *reporter* as the others."

"Now you're editing my speech? I thought twice about answering the phone."

"You sound defensive, and I'm not sure why. Was there something unusual about Benny's hiring process?"

"I don't have to sit here and answer your questions. I've been more than cordial."

"You've offered me a cup of Sanka and evaded my questions."

"We're finished here."

"Do you think I won't dig up what you're hiding? I'm a tenacious reporter."

"Yes, I'll admit that much. I don't mind for a minute you wasting your time trying to figure out why I hired ... Benny. In fact, I'd get a chuckle out of it. But tell me why the marijuana info is bad, and I'll tell you why I hired her."

"A reliable source at Murray PD was forthright with Dan, and the source said nothing about drugs being found on scene. If Baahir Ali was a drug dealer, as the two ounces suggest, then why would the guy who stabbed him to death not steal the stash once Baahir was out of the way? If Baahir was the buyer and owed money to the guy who murdered him, why wouldn't Baahir have offered up the weed as at least partial payment? The motive for the killing makes no sense if drugs were there."

"Killer could've not known they were there, and the victim could've bluffed. But the killer called his bluff."

"Benny's article said the marijuana was found on Baahir's bed. And I'm pretty sure if I were bluffing, I'd lose my resolve and blab whatever I was concealing just before the knife plunged into me the first time."

"Possibly. With luck, you'll never know. I have things to do, so you should get going."

"You didn't tell me about hiring Benny."

"No, I didn't."

"We had an agreement."

"I was bluffing."

Getting into a shouting match with an unprincipled tomato didn't seem like a great way to spend my time, so I stood up and started to walk toward the door. However, I was incapable of biting my tongue, and my perfect record against Greg was on the line, so I slowly perused the clown photos, trying to get under Greg's skin by not leaving. I struggled to think of a clever, devastating response, and I started to worry that my mind was going because winning an argument with Greg was no more difficult than winning a chess match with Trapunto.

The third photo I looked at had not hung on the wall when I was last in Greg's office, about seventeen months before. The photo featured Benny Washington. I'd run into her at various media functions and while covering events around town, and her picture was on the *Chronicle*'s website. In the photo, she wore gaudy purple-and-orange oversized pants festooned with large pink polka dots. Her top was a white T-shirt with multi-colored handprints dappled throughout. She wore an orange traffic cone on her head and blue swim flippers on her feet. Her makeup appeared to have been applied by Tammy Faye Baker while galloping through a minefield on a three-legged horse.

The overall effect was disconcerting, but two aspects of the photo struck me as significant: One, Greg had asked a current employee of his to pose for one of his clown photos; and, two, Benny's right hand was held at her side, near her waist, and her ring finger and pinkie were sticking out, with the rest of her hand closed. The gesture was subtle—not an overt salute—and many people would likely overlook it in the midst of that profusion of color. But the gesture looked familiar, although I couldn't place where I'd seen it. The gesture was similar to the OK sign, but with only two fingers sticking out and the circle collapsed.

Because I was studying the photos slowly, delaying my departure, Greg became uncomfortable with my lingering. I sensed him walk up behind me. I heard him twice inhale deeply and let his breath out slowly, as if trying to calm himself.

"I did my homework before I came in here, Greg. I'm a professional. I wanted to see if you'd own up to the truth, but you've once again obfuscated and dissembled. Benny's your illegitimate daughter."

"What? That's ridiculous. You've gotten the facts wrong."

"I interviewed her this morning, Greg. She admitted it."

"That's impossible. She wouldn't say that."

I pulled a reporter's notebook from my purse, flipped through the pages until I found what I was looking for, and said the following: "I said to her, 'I couldn't find your journalism credentials, Benny. What is the true nature of your relationship with Greg?' She said, 'He's my boss.' I said, 'I understand that, but how did you get the job? I've done the research, and I have two sources who went on record saying you're Greg's daughter.' She said, 'I don't know how to respond.' I said, 'When in doubt, go with the truth.' She said, 'Okay, you got me. He's my dad.'"

"Preposterous. Utterly preposterous. Why would she say that? I'm her uncle, forgoodnesssake."

"Thanks, Greg," I said, turning the notebook toward him to reveal a blank page. "I was bluffing."

The red of his sweater seeped up through the muscled stump of his neck onto his fireball face. I almost offered to retrieve the red nose from his desk to complete the look. He clenched his fists at his side, said, "But ... but ... I ... you women," then went back to his desk and sat down.

"It's been fun," I said. "Next time, let's talk about your wardrobe."

72-0.

SIXTEEN
OUT OF ORDER

I rode five blocks to the *Pulse* office. The building used to house a quilting emporium, Paducah Patterns, similar to but smaller than Hancock's of Paducah, the *ne plus ultra* of quilting stores in the Quilt Capital of the World. The building had been abandoned for a decade when I bought it, so I did a ton of cleaning before bringing in an inspector to ensure the plumbing and electric were up to code. The new HVAC system cost about half as much as I paid for the building.

The space was larger than *Pulse* needed, at least for the size of its staff back then. I had the option to rent out as many as three of the offices in the south section of the building if the advertising dollars didn't continue to increase. Potential tenants could access those offices easily through the south entrance, but I asked the staff to stay out of that section so the maintenance people didn't have to clean it as often. I also asked the staff to use the south exit only in an emergency.

As I locked my bike to the rack in front of the building, I debated whether to call a meeting so the reporters and I could coordinate our coverage of the unprecedented mayhem that was happening in Paducah. In order to run a successful newspaper and website and to prove

how essential *Pulse* was to the public—and, by extension, to adver-
tisers—I should have called the meeting. But I didn't want to be the
kind of boss who interrupted employees' days off. They all worked
hard, and they deserved down time or family time or whichever kind
of time they wanted.

I was supposed to cover most weekend events so the reporters
could work Monday-through-Friday schedules almost every week,
although their hours only occasionally were nine-to-five. The two
employees in the ad department worked traditional hours, but the
reporters, depending on their beats, worked whichever hours their
stories required, then turned in their digital timecards every two
weeks. Our sports reporter, Mickey Lyle, worked the most inconsis-
tent schedule. He was a thirty-two-year-old bachelor who grew up in
Paducah, lettered in basketball, baseball, and football at Tilghman
High School his senior year, only wore sports jerseys, collected sports
figurines, and took his job very seriously. In truth, I worried about his
obsession to find eternal truths in high school volleyball matches. But
he turned in clean copy and met his deadlines, so who was I to act as
his therapist?

I decided not to call a meeting. As I passed the lunchroom, I
smelled coffee. Before I reached the newsroom, I heard typing, and
when I entered the large room, known as the bullpen, through which
I had to walk to reach my office, I saw Dan Eidie, Sheila Hatcher, and
Teresa Land at their desks, clacking away on their keyboards.

"Y'all know it's Sunday, right?" I asked from the doorway.

"Heard a rumor to that effect," Dan said, continuing to type.

"And your point is?" Sheila asked. She laughed.

"Yes, we know what day it is, but we're journalists," Teresa said,
"and breaking news, murders, hostage situations, and ransoms are
why we entered the profession."

"Really?" Sheila asked. "I did it for the riches and respect."

I set my purse in my office and returned to the bullpen. Mickey
wasn't at his desk, and the three other desks on that side of the room
hadn't had reporters assigned to them. I'd purchased most of the

office supplies from a law firm liquidation sale, including the extra desks that I hoped to fill soon. The money I saved on those purchases paid a smidgen of a sliver of the cost of the iMacs the reporters and I used. An Apple salesman had tried to convince me to buy a thirty-two-inch Pro Display XDR to improve my ability to build layouts in InDesign each week, but I couldn't justify the extreme cost (more than I'd ever paid for a used car), so I set up an off-brand monitor next to my desktop iMac.

"Not to be a spoilsport, you guys," Teresa said, "but we have serious stuff going on, so joking about it seems inappropriate."

"Gallows humor," Dan said, as Sheila said, "Just letting off steam. We're taking this seriously, believe me."

"You're all here on Sunday," I said, "so you don't have to convince me of your dedication or your belief in the importance of what we do." I leaned against the door frame and asked, "What are you working on?"

"Still trying to figure out what's up with Benny's claim that Murray PD found marijuana on Baahir's bed," Dan said. "It doesn't make sense that Sergeant Vazquez wouldn't have mentioned it. He went out on a limb by giving me what he gave me, so why wouldn't he provide that significant fact?" He took a sip from his teal coffee tumbler.

"I learned a relevant fact from Greg Wurt," I said. "Benny is his niece."

"Really?" Dan said. "I knew there had to be something."

"You were right," I said. "Under other circumstances, I'd give the benefit of the doubt to nepotism hires. After all, someone who is qualified shouldn't be eliminated from the job pool *because* she or he happens to be related to the person hiring. That's also a form of discrimination. But we've read her stuff. It's awful, so she was exclusively a nepotistic hire. It's true that Greg can't distinguish between decent writing and a poodle, but he probably received applications from dozens, if not hundreds, of qualified, experienced journalists. The collapse of so many newspapers over the last decade almost ensured he did. I know Greg has the authority to hire whomever he wants, but you'd think he'd have to justify hiring his niece to Ed and the other owners, wouldn't you? Of course, I'm ascribing morals and principles to an organization that has proven it doesn't even know what those are, let alone abide by them. Benny's stories read like parodies, so I suspect something's fishy. If none of you wants to look into her background, I will."

"It's all yours," Sheila said. "I have my hands full. I'm trying to pin down what happened at the museum. Why did the robbers take the quilts they took? What's the significance of them having been made by BIPOC members?"

"Wait, what's BIPOC?" Teresa asked.

"Black, Indigenous People of Color," Sheila said.

"Got it," Teresa said. I'd hired her away from *The Chronicle-News* in Trinidad, Colorado, to cover the city beat. She was younger than the other reporters, twenty-five. Her clips were excellent and her references superlative. She'd been raised in the tiny town of Aguilar, twenty miles north of Trinidad, and she let me know occasionally how lacking in diversity and inclusion southern Colorado was. However, she covered her beat well, and the insightful, thorough stories she wrote made me glad I'd hired her. After all, none of us has a comprehensive knowledge of all subjects. For example, I know nothing about hockey. Perhaps I shouldn't take as much pride in that fact as I do, but there you have it.

Teresa's desk phone rang. She answered it as Sheila continued speaking, turning toward me again and saying, "You and I both think they had help on the inside. Who was it? Why would an employee of the museum help rob it if not for part of the ransom? And I think it's weird the ransom demand only mentioned the fifteen million, not what their objectives are, or who they are. I mean, when the infamous terrorist groups make their demands, they almost always let the world know who they are and why they're demanding what they're demanding. But I guess if money is the sole objective, it makes sense to remain anonymous. I'd gladly stay out of the limelight, beneath the radar, and never see my name in another byline for fifteen million bucks."

"Be careful. Someone could interpret that statement as motive," I said, then smiled. "Keep digging. You'll find something."

Into her receiver, Teresa said, "That's big news, Liz. Thank you, and I'll keep you out of it. Take care."

She hung up, looked at me, and said, "The four city commissioners, plus Mayor Lewy, Robby Golden, and Ed Colapinto just met secretly."

"Meaning illegally," I said.

"Yes. Liz is the mayor's administrative assistant. We bonded in the gardening section of Lowe's a few months ago. We're friends now. She thought it was weird Mayor Lewy called her in today, especially when she realized they were breaking the law. Now she thinks they brought her in so she'll be implicated if and when this stuff all goes public. They needed her to take notes, transcribe the recording, whatever, but why couldn't they do that themselves?"

"Maybe something more nefarious than a violation of the public-meetings laws is going on," Dan said, "and maybe Liz has inadvertently been dragged into whatever that is. They called her in today so she knows she's now broken the law, too. She'll be less likely to blow the whistle on whatever crimes she's inadvertently been dragged into."

"With a conniving mind like that, you should be the cops reporter," Sheila said.

Dan smiled and said, "Did Liz say what the meeting was about?"

"They talked about the museum's insurance not covering theft" Teresa said. "Golden was, to use Liz's word, 'apoplectic.' The guy lives and breathes the museum. I mean, do you know how big an economic driver that place is for Paducah? It's huge. The commissioners discussed for about three seconds how to raise funds to meet the ransom, Liz said, but they quickly pointed the finger at Golden and basically said he was on his own. This is really bad."

"Yes, but why would Colapinto be there? Because he was

included, I should have been included because we're both newspaper publishers. Of course, I wouldn't have attended, and they know that, which means they know I would have reported on the illegal meeting. So, now we know why I wasn't invited."

"But not why Colapinto was," Teresa said. "Which is what I now have to find out. Obviously no one in that room, other than Liz off the record, will talk to me, so how do I write the story?"

"That's a great question," I said. "You could use her as an anonymous source because she's not anonymous to us. But everyone else there would know she spoke to us, and we can't cost her her job, especially not for what will ultimately be a meaningless story. No one will go to jail for holding an illegal meeting, but public officials covering up something illegal in an illegal meeting is a different story. It's our job to keep the powers that be in check, but if nothing will come of our story because the D.A. wouldn't bother to bring charges—not with dozens of felonies raining down on her—then we can't risk getting Liz fired. Of course, if she's fired for reporting an illegal meeting that her boss participated in, she could have a wrongful-termination suit. But, trust me, unless she likes being a pariah and has tough skin, she should think twice before filing a lawsuit."

I thought for a few seconds, then said, "For now, Teresa, try calling everyone who was in the meeting without revealing that you know the meeting took place. Say you're simply writing a story about the shooting and robbery and what the city is doing about them, which is a true statement. Maybe one of them will slip and mention the meeting. You'll know how to tease something from them if they do. If they don't, and you can tell the conversations are ending, you may want to say something like, 'I would have guessed the city would hold an emergency meeting in such a dire situation,' and maybe one of them will take the bait."

"That's good. I'll try that," she said, and turned toward her computer.

"I'll consider who owes me a favor and whether I have leverage on any of the commissioners," I said. "I know Commissioner Nettles secretly rebels against his wife's draconian dietary restrictions by visiting Munal's Donut Shop regularly. But who am I to destroy the relationship between a man and his cinnamon twists when I have frequented that establishment to scarf down a raspberry-filled donut followed by a strawberry one in the privacy of my truck. Once—and I admit this here off the record and will deny it in a court of law—I went in a second time so I could eat a strawberry one first to see if the order made a difference. Despite diligently employing the scientific method, I could not discern whether raspberry-strawberry or strawberry-raspberry provided the greater satisfaction. I did, however, feel sick for the next three hours and hated myself for the next twenty-four."

"You're definitely the best boss I've ever had," Sheila said. She, Teresa, and I laughed.

"Well, you're definitely *one* of the bosses I've had," Dan said, and we all laughed.

"Send me your stories before you post," I said. "I'll be juggling ads, Wednesday's budget, payroll, and thinking about layouts. And I hope to look into Benny's background. But I'd like to check that your stories don't duplicate each other. Be sure to include this overtime on your time sheets, and email me your Café de Fae lunch orders. And, what the heck, let me know which two, three, or fourteen kinds of donuts you want from Munal's. For some reason, I have a hankering."

SEVENTEEN

GATHERINGS

"I'm upset, but do you think Janet would have wanted us to skip the favorite part of our week?" asked Dakota at that Sunday's Paducah Quilters Quorum in her mansion.

Vivian Franey set a macaroni casserole on Dakota's kitchen counter between the large salad Cindy Baron had brought and the platter of peanut butter cookies I had. In the past, whichever PQQ member hosted that week had made or purchased desserts for everyone. But because the members had devoured my peanut butter cookies, lemon bars, Russian tea cakes, peanut butter brownies, spice cake, olive oil cake, and panna cotta in the past (and had asked for the recipes—*yeah, right!* I'm generous, but I'm no fool), I'd become the designated provider of desserts. Because the baking process soothed me, I was honored and pleased to provide the desserts each week.

In the kitchen, Vivian said, "Dakota, you and I both know Janet would have wanted us to hold PQQ. All I said was, 'You don't exactly look like someone in mourning.' I meant it as a compliment."

"Of course, you did," Evelyn Lewy said. "Heck, we probably all look like yesterday's ice cream, but none of us looks as bad as Robby Golden. The poor thing's a total wreck, but who can blame him? I mean, twenty-six irreplaceable quilts stolen on his watch. Not a great look for a CEO. On the hook for fifteen million. Can you imagine the stress he's under?"

Technically, I was not at work. I was supposed to be enjoying PQQ. Gathering with my friends and fellow quilters nearly every week for years had gone a long way toward making up for my not having had a real family. Some of the members had changed over time, but the group itself had remained supportive, vibrant, and productive. But as much as I wanted to lose myself in the cama-raderie, the quilting, and the food before we had to plan Janet's funeral, I couldn't let Evelyn's comments go uninvestigated.

"Of course, Robby's a wreck," I said. "The ransom is due by 5 tomorrow, but the museum isn't covered for theft, so anyone in his position would look, feel, and be worse than awful. But how do you know how many quilts have gone missing?" She could've read it in one of Sheila's stories on the *Pulse* website, but I wouldn't have bet on that.

"Richard told me," Evelyn said. Richard, as in Mayor Lewy, her brother.

"He learned that at the meeting with the commissioners today?" I asked.

"Yes." She didn't react for a second, but then her face looked as though she'd just emailed her social security number to every pris-oner in Leavenworth. I was not an excellent poker player, but if I played against people who were as easily bluffed as Evelyn was, I would make a fortune.

"I, um ...," Evelyn said. "Maybe I'm misremembering. Richard probably called Robby."

"Evelyn, a *Pulse* reporter has confirmed that an illegal meeting took place. You haven't broken any confidence," I said, "so you don't have to lie. But what you said makes me wonder if Richard mentioned the significance of twenty-six quilts having been taken."

"He didn't, but I'd really prefer not to discuss this, Hadley. I shouldn't have said anything."

Dakota said, "We should probably get started. The others should arrive any minute." We followed her from the kitchen down one of the three cavernous halls that led to the voluminous atrium, and then down a second hall past the two rooms she used to store her quilting supplies (one of which also contained a large easel and enough oil paints to slather a thick coat on the Pentagon). We entered one of three "living rooms," where we sat at the long, finely crafted oak table on which lay the quilt we were in the middle of creating: a Celtic Log Cabin in seafoam green and coral.

Tasha Wilson, the newest PQQ member who had grown up in Paducah, as Dakota and I had, was a decade older than I was (six years older than Dakota), but Tasha wore her fifty-two years as though they were thirty-seven. She rushed into the room saying, "Sorry I'm late," although my phone said it was only 2:01.

"I lost track of time reading the *Pulse* website," Tasha said. "Your reporters are resourceful and quick, Hadley. What weird stuff. It's all frightening."

I agreed and thanked her. She sat between me and the seat that Donna Ackerman usually sat in, two seats to my right. Since the murder of her son, Matt, Donna had been mired in a depression so deep that when she failed to show up to PQQ, which happened about half of the time, I wasn't the only one who wondered whether we might never see her again. Whenever she hadn't arrived by 2:30, one of us would call her, usually me, to check on her. She would say something along the lines of, "I can't muster the energy. I know that happens when we get old, but it's more than that, I think." Yes, it was more than that.

No parents should have to bury their offspring, especially if the deaths were caused by murder. Each of the other PQQ members had tried to convince Donna to get psychological help, and I had even orchestrated an accidental-on purpose encounter with my therapist, Elaine Bourget, in Kirchhoff's Bakery. But Donna, time and again, insisted she wasn't crazy, saying, "only crazy people go to shrinks." Sadly, according to Elaine, the people most in need of mental-health assistance almost never seek it. Thankfully, I'd sought it when I'd needed it, and it was essential to me righting the ship. So, I subtly touted the benefits of therapy to Donna every so often.

We started quilting, and within five minutes Donna walked in and sat down between Tasha and me. She kissed us both on the cheek and said, "Feel horrible and didn't want to get out of bed, but I couldn't miss this session, not with us needing to plan Janet's funeral."

Unlike almost every other session, the one that day wasn't filled with laughter, teasing, and minor complaints about our lives. Instead, it was a somber slog, with each of us failing to bring lightness and levity to a day fraught with sadness, uncertainty, and fear. Despite managing a few times to talk about our usual subjects—quilting, food, clothes, movies, binge watching, books, men, and our aches and pains —we kept returning to the murders, the theft of the quilts, and the ransom demand.

"I'm most worried about the racial aspect, being a woman of color," Tasha said after we'd finished eating and started to quilt again. "They're obviously targeting non-whites, so it makes sense that I should be more worried than I usually am, and that's a lot, as y'all know."

"Not to discount what you said, Tasha, but I think we all have reason to be nervous," Cindy said. "No one's gonna lose sleep over the dead terrorist, probably not even his family, but no one knows why the student was killed. What's his name?"

"Baahir Ali," I said.

"Yes, thank you," Cindy said. "No one knows why he was killed, although the *Chronicle* said it was drug related."

"Murray PD couldn't corroborate the drug angle," I said. "In fact, Baahir's girlfriend, Kelly Sprague, said he didn't even drink, let alone do or sell drugs."

"Wait," Vivian said. "Kelly Sprague was dating Baahir? You know who she's the niece of, right?"

"No," the rest of us said at the same time.

"I know her mother, Iris Sprague, through our volunteer work at Paducah Cooperative Ministry. One day she introduced me to her daughter, Kelly. Nice girl. Pretty."

"Vivian, darn it, who's her uncle?" Cindy asked.

"Nick Stoddard, the louse."

"Hold on," I said. "That's a fact?"

"Sure," Vivian said. "I mean why would Iris lie and tell me she *was* Nick's sister? A million reasons to tell me she wasn't, but I can't think why anyone would claim an association with that family if it wasn't real. I don't like Iris. She's dim. But guess that makes sense 'cause she's a Stoddard."

"I don't know if Kelly being Nick's niece means anything," Dakota said. "We can't choose our relatives, and guilt-by-association doesn't wash in the legal profession."

"True," I said, "but where there's smoke, there's fire, and the Stoddards emit more of both than a wildfire."

"You ain't exactly unbiased, Hads," Donna said. "You and Nick got a history."

"True, but practically everyone in town has a history with that family, and not a pleasant, remember-when kind of history. I am professional enough to put my opinions aside. I'll pull on this loose thread until something unravels. I'll have Dan interview Kelly again, but this time armed with the Stoddard connection."

"I don't see why you're accusing this poor girl of something just because she's related to Nick," Dakota said.

"I'm not accusing her of anything, D. Trust me, I will not allow Dan to grill her. She's grieving. I understand that, but I also believe she wants to know why her boyfriend was murdered. And Dan's a pro. He'll treat her respectfully, empathically, even if I don't remind him of her circumstances. He's in a hard-edged, thankless beat, but he's perceptive and considerate. He'll do fine.

"And I have a grieving eighteen-year-old living with me who just lost her grandmother and her friend, so I'm not about to be heartless in pursuit of a story. However, people are being killed, so I'll pursue whatever angles my staff and I need to pursue until this madness ends. If our stories are instrumental in bringing about that conclusion, great. However, we won't trample people so we can increase our circulation. The day I run *Paducah Pulse* the way Ed Colapinto and Greg Wurt run the *Chronicle* is the day I fold up shop and open a bakery."

"I didn't mean to upset you, Hads," Dakota said. "I'm just thinking about that poor girl, losing her boyfriend that way."

"I am, too," Donna said, "but that doesn't mean I'm against Hadley opening a bakery." We all laughed, and I took Donna's ability to make a joke as an encouraging sign.

After we'd cleaned up and put away the quilt, we planned Janet's funeral. While making the arrangements and doling out responsibilities, we managed to remember Janet fondly by recounting funny or poignant anecdotes, but we all spent most of that hour feeling miserable.

The funeral would take place at 9 a.m. Friday at Broadway United Methodist, per Janet's wishes, according to Ashley, if that schedule worked for the church. No one answered when I'd called the church, so I would call again on Monday. We made a phone tree so everyone who should be invited would be invited. I called Ash but got her voicemail. I left a message asking if Grammie J had mentioned any casket preferences, which wasn't likely because Janet hadn't planned to die at sixty. Cindy took charge of arranging the catering, and Dakota offered her home for the reception.

We all hugged goodbye, said we'd be in touch, and headed to our vehicles. I took the quilt because PQQ would take place at my house next Sunday. Before I drove home, I called Dan.

"Guess who Kelly Sprague's uncle is?" I said when he answered.

"Nick Stoddard."

"Wait, how'd you know?"

"She called me about an hour ago. Said she wonders if Baahir's race and religion had something to do with his murder. She said, and I quote"—he paused while he flipped through his notes—"'I'm as sure he had nothing to do with drugs as I am I exist, and I know I exist because I'm in a whole lotta pain.' She rambled for a little after that, but when I asked her for a second time if she was sure he didn't have any enemies, she said, 'Enemies, no. Nothing like that, but my mom walked out of the kitchen a few months ago when I told her Baahir loved me and I loved him. She said something mean and racist under her breath.' I asked what that was, and she said, 'I'm not going to repeat it, but it was very ugly.' She said she tried to confront her mom about it, but her mom stomped to her room and slammed the door."

"You are an excellent reporter, Dan. Really. I got a scoop from a friend, but you beat me there. Great job. I can at least provide a confirmation. Evelyn Lewy inadvertently confirmed that Richard, Robby, Colapinto, and the commissioners met this morning."

"On the record?"

"Not really. She slipped and spoke the truth, the bane of the politician. Or, in this case, the politician's sister. I don't want to ruin a friendship, so maybe Teresa can write the story without getting her friend Liz Bibby involved. By the time Evelyn gets home, she'll prob-ably have called four people to tell them she shouldn't have told me what she told me. Have you reached out to Iris Sprague to get her take on Baahir, his murder, and Kelly's claim that Iris made a racist remark? By the way, she must be a *much* younger sister to Nick, right?"

"Right. I just looked her up. She's sixteen years younger, forty-two to his fifty-eight. An oops baby, most likely."

"My guess is every one of that brood was an accident, or at least the parents tried to disown them when they saw who they'd become."

"You know that's bunk, boss. At least three generations of crooks, criminals, and ne'er-do-wells have stolen from, assaulted, or otherwise abused Paducahans."

"You're right. Just trying to be clever. I'm off my game today. A total lack of sleep and too much stress are weighing on me, but so is something else."

"What?"

"Sworn to secrecy?"

"Yes. What is it?"

"I tell you this as a friend, not as your boss."

"Jeez, now I don't want to know. Kidding. I promise. What is it?"

"I have a second date with Brandon in a couple of hours."

"Why would you think I should be sworn to secrecy about that? The whole world can see you two kissing on at least five different social-media platforms, and everyone in Paducah has watched it at least once. Have you seen the mash-up of you and Brandon alongside Peabo Bryson and Regina Belle singing 'A Whole New World'? It's hilarious."

"You're kidding, right?"

"No. There's also one using deep-fake technology to make you appear to be doing more than kissing, but you probably shouldn't watch that one."

"Seriously? That's really bad. I guess my attempt to act coy failed."

"But if you'd been going for foolish and needy, you'd've nailed it."

"Thanks for your support. You're fired."

"Thank you. I was getting tired of being paid far above industry standard to do what I love."

"Glad I could help."

"Good luck on your date. You'll be fine. You both obviously like each other a lot. Just don't try to act coy."

"And if he really likes foolish and needy?"

"Then invite me to the wedding."

EIGHTEEN
FULL DISCLOSURE

I should have gone home, taken a relaxing bath, primped just enough to impress Brandon but not enough to make me seem desperate, then impatiently waited for 7 o'clock to arrive. But, no, I had to poke into Benny Washington's past, which led me down a rabbit hole, so when I finally managed to scramble to the surface, it was 6:23. I'd intended to ride my bike to Brandon's house on Washington Street, about two blocks from Midtown Market. I hadn't realized it at the time, but his house was only a block away from Keiler Park, where he and I had discussed the Quilt City Murders on the day they were solved.

But, that night, making myself look presentable and riding my bike to Brandon's wouldn't be possible with time so tight, so I slipped into my favorite jeans, buttoned up the white silk blouse that Dakota had given me for my birthday three years before, and wasted three minutes trying to figure out which shoes to wear. I'm not the kind of woman who has a closet full of shoes, but I have enough to enable me to wear the proper pair for various occasions. However, I didn't remember having read which shoes to wear on a second date with a man who had kissed me passionately just after bullets had zipped over our heads. Would heels say I appreciated his first kiss and hoped for another? Would the flats I'd worn on our first date indicate I did not consider this second date to be special enough for me to break out a new outfit? Or would my new Saucony running shoes tell him I subconsciously was ready to flee? I chose the latter, hoping that sometimes shoes are just shoes.

I arrived at his door, with my peanut butter cookies in a tin, at 7:02, which I considered to be rude because punctuality was a point of pride with me. However, I fought the urge to apologize to him when he opened the door because I didn't want to wear my neuroses like a corsage. He was smart and astute, so he would soon spot the reasons why he should politely reject me, but that didn't mean I should advertise my damaged psyche.

"Sorry I'm late," I said when he opened the door to his modest brick home. I handed him the tin. He accepted it, smiled, looked at his watch, laughed, and said, "I have 7 on the nose. Thank you for being punctual. It's kind of a thing with me."

I kissed him on the cheek and gave him a hug. He wore a light-blue dress shirt, jeans, and Asics running shoes.

"Really?" I asked. "You're not just saying that because it's obviously a thing with me?"

He shook his head and ushered me in. I was surprised that a man lived in the house alone. If someone had offered me a thousand dollars to find a speck of dust in the well-appointed living room, I would have had to humiliate myself by kneeling on the hardwood floor and reaching under the leather couch, and I probably still wouldn't have earned the grand. The various men I'd dated had left apple cores in ashtrays, depleted toilet-paper rolls on holders, and soiled socks everywhere. I once found a crescent wrench covered in what appeared to be congealed butterscotch in Matt's jeans drawer. I never mentioned my discovery and never put his laundry away again.

I complimented Brandon's house and his décor. The house looked as though a man lived in it, but a man who wouldn't ever want a man-cave—one who grew up among females, in other words.

He offered me an assortment of drinks. I accepted ice water, he poured a Diet Coke into a glass for himself, and we sat next to each other on the couch.

"I've prepped dinner, and I'll start cooking whenever you'd like me to, but first I'd like to establish something. You and I like each other. Wait, let me only speak for myself. I like you and have waited for you because I felt a connection immediately, even when there shouldn't have been one at what we thought was the first murder scene in Noble. So, I'd like to make it clear to you that I have no reason to mislead you, to misrepresent myself, to try to impress you only to disappoint you when you learn who I really am. You seemed truly surprised when I didn't lose my mind over Dakota after she and I went on our date. Yes, she's a world-class beauty. She's kind, generous, athletic, and smart as a whip, as my dad used to say. But I could tell she was putting on an act, behaving as she thought she should behave on a date, rather than being herself. And, in the name of complete disclosure, I thought she was hiding something."

"You were correct," I said. He nodded and continued.

"You, however, appear to be Hadley at all times, or at least who you believe Hadley to be in the moment. Another woman would've either not been bothered by being on time or wouldn't have wanted to seem weird by apologizing for being late, although she was on time."

"But I tried not to say anything, so you didn't think I was neurotic."

"We're all neurotic to varying degrees. My clothes are color-coordinated in the closet, my books are organized by author, I don't ever put a single unmatched sock in my sock drawer. If I can't find its match, I throw it away or use it as a rag, although that rarely happens because I almost never lose anything. My mom gave me a matching pen and mechanical pencil set the day I entered the sixth grade. That set sits on my desk now. So, yes, apologizing for being late, although you were on time, is unusual, but it shows you're considerate and conscientious."

"And neurotic."

"If you insist. But what I'm trying to say is that I'm forthright and have no reason to lie to you. If you don't like the man I am, I'll learn to live with that. I'm not about to become a different man so you can fall for someone who doesn't exist, or at least who isn't me."

I looked into his eyes and leaned in to give him a gentle kiss on the lips. What I wanted to say sounded mushy and overwrought and far too early, so I said, "Thank you for expressing yourself so well and so honestly. I promise to do my best to do the same, but I didn't grow up in your home—"

"Please stop if you're about to knock yourself. Neither of us is perfect, and, for the record, I'll remind you my father accidentally-on-purpose killed himself by drunkenly wrapping the Corvette he and I had restored around a telephone pole. But we are who we are now, so—"

"Okay, I hear you. May we continue this discussion while you cook?"

"Yes." He led me into the small kitchen. He turned the burner under the large pot of water to high. On the counter next to the sink, chopped parsley sat next to chopped garlic on a checkerboard wooden cutting board. Two opened cans of chopped clams sat next to an unopened bottle of clam juice, two medium-sized lemons, and a yellow, plastic lemon squeezer. He slipped a canvas apron over his head, then turned to me to reveal the phrase "Kiss the Cook" scripted across it.

"Subtle," I said, then heeded the command, delivering a real kiss this time. When we finally stepped apart, I said, "I'm nothing if not obedient."

"Why don't I believe that?"

"You calling me a liar?" I smiled.

"I'm saying you're Hadley Carroll, a woman as constrained by conventional expectations as water is by a sieve." He poured three tablespoons of olive oil into the large frying pan and set the burner to low.

"You obviously don't think so, but I'm a follower of rules and laws. I never park illegally, don't speed, rarely J-walk, don't cheat on my taxes, and do my best to treat people fairly. Okay, for a while I deposited newspapers into the river, but I was under extreme duress at the time, and have you read the *Chronicle?*"

He scraped garlic into the pan with the back of a chef's knife, then distributed it throughout the pan with a wooden spoon.

"I guess what I meant was you're not passive, not a follower, not a woman who suffers indignities easily."

"No, I'm not, and I'm less charitable than I should be toward others who allow themselves to be treated like dishrags. It's a problem I have. I'm working on it. People have to find ways to live with themselves, and I understand that everyone has hidden pains and troubles. I have to work on not judging people who don't fight back, who allow themselves to be pushed around. I fought back. Jenny didn't, and I think she's paying a bigger price than I am. But I know we all have different skill sets. Obviously, I couldn't fight back against Officer Williams, especially with Kramer standing next to us, guarding the door. I might not have made it out of the room alive if I had. But, when I got the chance, I fought back how I could: legally. As I understand how the universe works, we only live once. I hope I'm wrong, but that's the way I view our existence. I intend to give everything I have to whatever I pursue."

He slipped the linguine from the box into the boiling water, eased the protruding ends beneath the surface with the wooden spoon, and looked at his watch. He poured the clams and half of the bottle of clam juice into the frying pan, added a pinch of salt, plenty of pepper, a dash of red-pepper flakes, and about half of the chopped parsley, then turned up the heat. The kitchen smelled amazing, and I started to worry about how fast I was falling.

Matt's idea of cooking was buying a pizza. A guy I dated in college caught his ponytail on fire while trying to make us French toast. He'd already managed to dip it in batter, so I'd thought his kitchen mishaps were over. But no. Neither of us saw the flames right away, but the smell of burning hair made me turn to him, grab his ponytail above the flaming section, and shove the burning end into the batter. I ate cereal that morning.

In other words, I was not accustomed to a man who was comfortable doing anything in the kitchen other than opening a beer or microwaving a Salisbury steak TV dinner.

Eventually, Brandon and I sat at the wooden table in the corner of his kitchen. We ate his delicious linguine and clams, and a simple spinach and tomato salad, accompanied by slices of Italian bread, which he'd baked. We drank an excellent white Bordeaux, but I started to feel uncomfortable. I attributed my discomfort to what I'd discovered about Benny Washington and to the fact I was not at that moment working to solve the murders of Janet and Baahir and the theft of the quilts.

"Do you mind if we talk about work?" I asked, after we'd discussed our younger sisters (my one; his four).

"Of course not. We're in each other's lives now, and I hope that doesn't change."

I had swallowed my bite of linguine before I asked the question, but I swallowed hard again. Had he just said that, and was it true? We were in the middle of our second date, and we'd shared two exceptional kisses, but did that make us in each other's lives? Was he putting the cart before the horse, or had I chosen to wear my running shoes for a reason? I felt myself flush and my heart race. Didn't his comment confirm that we shared the same objective—to be in a meaningful, supportive, loving relationship? If so, then why was my throat as dry as the Atacama Desert?

I said, "Just before I left tonight, I looked up Benny Washington, the cops reporter for the *Chronicle*."

"I've met her. The kindest way I can describe her abilities is, she's a little raw."

"Exactly, which is why when our cops reporter, Dan, said something was fishy about her, I confronted Greg Wurt, a pompous pretense of an editor. After I tricked him—"

"Because you're a rules follower and nothing if not obedient."

"Hush, you. He slipped and let me know she's his niece."

"Ah-ha. Nepotism's alive and well."

"Why would a company hire someone so unqualified? When I posted on JournalismJobs.com to fill positions at *Paducah Pulse*, I received so many résumés from journalists whose experience ran rings around mine that I got sad, then stopped considering anyone who wasn't among the first one hundred applicants I received. I could have hired any of three-dozen grizzled veteran reporters and editors who had worked at the *New York Times*, the *Washington Post*, *Esquire*, and dozens of other major publications. That's how tough it is out there lately. I decided to offer the jobs to younger, hungrier reporters with potential whose careers were still ascending and who hadn't turned cynical yet. I worried and lost a ton of sleep, but I believe I hired excellent employees. So, why would a daily news-paper that has been around for a hundred years, rather than a weekly startup, have to settle for the incompetent niece of the paper's editor?"

"As you said, nepotism. Why does it have to be more than that?"

"Because wouldn't Ed Colapinto, the publisher, Greg's boss, put the nix on that, if only for the sake of appearances?"

"Do publishers generally have a say in hiring? I'd guess that a veteran editor would have some autonomy in hiring decisions."

"Good point. Under most regimes, I wouldn't give it much thought. An editor hires a reporter for whatever reasons and has to justify the hire to no one. But when I asked Greg if Benny was a good reporter, he said she was as good a hire as any other. That clanged in my ear, so I poked him until he admitted she was his niece."

"Why is that significant, other than proving nepotism?" Seeing that I'd placed my fork and knife at an angle across my plate, he stood, took the tin from the counter, opened the lid, and presented the large cookies to me. I'd eaten one at PQQ that day, so I really shouldn't have eaten another. Ultimately, I ate two more.

"You're right. These are excellent," he said after snapping off one quarter and biting it in half.

"Thank you. I think they're best if you let them dissolve in your mouth." He heeded my advice with his next bite. After ten seconds he said, "Right again. Thanks."

"Here's the thing: Benny isn't her real name. At one point I thought I heard Greg hesitate before saying her name. At the time I didn't give it any thought, but I noticed it. Now, I think he started to say the name she was born with, the one he would have called her until she changed it: Cassie."

"Cassie Washington."

"Yes. Greg is from Roseburg, Oregon. I jumped from his Facebook page to that of Gina Washington, his younger sister. She had two children, Benny and Cassie. I didn't find the rest of this on Facebook, but I poked around until I learned that Benny was murdered by a drug dealer and multiple-murderer named Dennis Edwards."

"You've been sitting on this while we talked about this and that? No wonder you seem nervous."

"Do I?"

"Nervous may not be right. Maybe uncomfortable."

"Kind of the definition of nervous, isn't it?"

"Not really. You can't say, 'This couch is lumpy and nervous.'"

"Oh, I could say that."

"Yes, but you wouldn't, not the woman who's as exacting about her speech and writing as she is about her peanut butter cookies."

"Good point."

"Do you think she adopted her brother's name as a tribute?"

"Possibly. I hadn't gotten very far before I had to get ready for our date."

"Sounds like you learned plenty."

"If I have time tomorrow, I'll continue poking around or pass what I've learned to Dan and have him continue."

"Speaking of continuing, would you like to watch a movie, or play Scrabble, Boggle, or chess?"

"Are those the only options?"

"Are you being coy?"

"No. I was advised not to be coy. In fact, I was ordered not to do so."

"You have a dating coach?"

"A friend who is my employee, which means he shouldn't be my friend—Dan."

"And he said what, exactly?"

"Don't be coy."

"Okay, then what else might you want to do?"

"Could we take a walk?"

"Sounds great." He stood, and I started to clear the dishes. "Please, let me clean up later. Nothing has to be put up now."

"Okay."

We walked two blocks to Jefferson, crossed to the grass median, turned right, then walked between the two one-way sections of Jefferson on the grass. Only a few cars passed us as we walked, holding hands. I had eighty-seven thoughts running through my head, but none of them turned into words. I didn't know what he was thinking, and he didn't say anything for a block. When we'd crossed the cross-street, he said, "You're scared, and I understand."

"It's that obvious? I've been forcing myself not to think about you for, what, seventeen months? The few times we bumped into each other, you were in my thoughts for days, and there wouldn't have been anything wrong with that, except I knew I wasn't ready. I had been engaged to Matt, and only after he was killed did I realize how flawed our relationship had been. Yes, we'd loved each other, and we got along okay most of the time. It's not as though we argued a lot, and we had hobbies and activities in common. But I will not say we really got each other, that we communicated well, or that we were soulmates. And now I know that assessment is accurate, and I probably knew it then. We weren't soulmates. So, why did I accept his proposal?"

He stopped and gently turned me toward him. "Hadley, I haven't proposed. We're on our second date. We all have pasts we're not proud of, embarrassing mistakes that cost us sleep, humiliations at work or in relationships that make us beat ourselves up. I spent years trying to figure out how I could have prevented my dad from killing himself. And, yes, I believe his accident was deliberate. No one jumps a curb in a Corvette on dry pavement doing ninety without intending to.

"After his death, I wondered whether my refusal to go to law school, his dislike of the woman I was dating at the time, and whether my ambivalence toward his church contributed to his suicide. I wasted far too much time and energy on a man who basically spent his time and energy on himself, not on his five kids or his wife. You probably would have liked him. He was smart and personable and funny, but he wasn't a good man, and he was only an okay father. He obviously wasn't happy.

"So, this is me trying to say that you seem to have control issues. That's not unusual, I know, especially for kids raised in alcoholic homes. Expecting perfection, demanding the most of yourself, never cutting yourself any slack. If pursued in moderation, those can lead to success, to accomplishments. But trying to rewrite the past or trying to live life without making mistakes? That's not possible. You'd be the first person in history to do so. I probably sound condescending, but I'm not meaning to. I'm shooting for concerned and empathetic."

It took me at least ten seconds before I said, "Then you hit your target. I hear you. I really do, but I'm not ready. I'm going to screw this up. I'm already screwing it up. And I think I better go home before you don't want to see me again."

He sat on the grass, and I did, too, both of us facing the Broadway Church of Christ. A truck passed behind us.

"Hadley, do you think I haven't been borderline panicked? What if she hates my house, can't stand the way I dress, thinks my cooking is disgusting, or just doesn't feel any of the zing for me that I feel for her? That's called dating, which is part of the messy wonder of life. Everyone either risks rejection or lives a very lonely life. People talk about bravery all the time, mostly referring to cops, firefighters, and soldiers. But everyone who has ever found a soulmate has had to be brave, brave in a way that leaves them vulnerable and open to humiliation and feelings of inadequacy. Physical bravery is completely different, and less impressive, to be honest. Look at the millions of tough guys who could win a bar fight in four seconds but can't express their emotions to their partners."

I'd worried since dinner whether we were going to kiss again. For reasons I could not put into words, I didn't want to, despite almost swooning during both of our real kisses. But as I sat there next to an insightful, intelligent, self-aware, handsome, and seemingly unbroken man, I wanted nothing more than for him to take me in his arms, to look into my eyes, and to allow me to forget who I was as our lips met. I'd been "in the moment" during both of our kisses, and I'd almost felt whole, almost felt as though I had the right to be hopeful, to believe in a happy, fulfilling, loving future.

Almost.

"I'm not just scared I'll screw this up," I said. "I'm scared that I feel so much for you so soon. You're like an addiction. It can't be healthy."

"It may be very rare, but that doesn't make it unhealthy."

"Do you think you can demonstrate some of that messy wonder you mentioned?"

We leaned toward each other and lost ourselves for countless eternities in a kiss that changed who I thought I was and who I thought I could be. I believed in myself and believed in him and believed in happiness and believed in a hopeful future and heard bells and ... eventually realized I didn't hear bells. I transported myself back to the mundane realities of planet Earth when I admitted the ringing was coming from my phone.

Ungrateful for the intrusion, I thought about ignoring the call, but Ashley was now my responsibility, and she was alone with Chica and Trapunto in my house. She could need me, so I shucked off some of life's messy wonder and answered.

"Hadley," Dan said, "Chris Knudsen's dead."

It took me a few seconds for what he said to register. Who was

Chris Knudsen? Oh, the press operator at the *Chronicle* who recorded Brandon and me kissing with his phone.

"How?"

"Car wreck in Nashville. Sergeant Vazquez got a call from Nashville PD because Knudsen lived in Murray. A wreck out of state wouldn't necessarily warrant a call between jurisdictions, but Nashville PD said a witness saw a trash truck, which had been reported stolen, ram into the driver's-side door of Knudsen's Honda Civic. It looked intentional because the truck sped up before impact. According to the witness, the driver, dressed in black from head to toe, including a facemask, jumped from the truck and got into the passenger-side of a tan Ford Taurus following the truck. The Taurus raced off and turned up abandoned five blocks away. It had been stolen that morning. Nashville PD's calling the wreck a homicide."

NINETEEN
CURIOUSER AND CURIOUSER

I'd had dates go splat before, but never from such a high, swoon-inducing height. From bliss to yikes in a matter of seconds. Knudsen's murder seemed to be unrelated to the killings of Janet Loy, Baahir Ali, and Durrell Mahan, if I factored in the different modus operandi and jurisdictions. But if I listened to my gut, it was likely related to all of them. And what were the odds of the Nashville man-in-black (apologies to Johnny Cash) not having some relation to the men-in-black who wreaked havoc on a Paducah Walmart two days before? Slim to none, was my guess. Brandon, a trained officer of the law, corroborated my too-coincidental-to-be-a-coincidence hunch as we walked back to his house.

"Sure, wearing all black isn't a link that will convict anyone," he said, "but if this case fell to us, we'd work it under the assumption that the perp who killed Knudsen was among the Walmart perps."

"Ramming someone with a stolen trash truck seems like a weird way to kill someone. It speaks both to spontaneity and planning," I said.

"I know what you mean." We turned left on Thirtieth Street. "If someone happened to be driving a trash truck and saw his victim, he might think about ramming him. But stealing a truck big enough that would almost certainly kill Knudsen if the collision went as planned requires knowledge of Knudsen's schedule. The doer would have to know where Knudsen would be and when, meaning he'd have been aware of Knudsen's schedule, so stealing the truck would make sense. Although I understand what you mean about it seeming spontaneous, it wasn't."

"Doer? Really?"

"Sorry, but I *am* a cop." We walked past Keiler Park on Nahm Street.

"Yes, and maybe my falling for you proves I'm not anti-police, as many of Stoddard's campaign signs claim. True, I've gone on record as an opponent of police brutality, including when I'm on the receiving end of it, but I believe our kisses should put an end to any lingering doubts about my feelings toward members of your profession."

We turned left onto Washington and walked in silence until we arrived at my truck parked on the street in front of his house.

"Trust me," he said, "you and I feel the same way about police brutality and bad cops." He looked into my eyes. "But I wonder about the murder of the man who filmed our first kiss." We leaned against my truck, and I tried to look up to see the stars, but the light pollution was bad. I couldn't see many, so I turned to look at Brandon.

"Knudsen worked for the *Chronicle*," he said. "What was he doing in Nashville, how often did he go there, and who would have been interested in his schedule enough to follow him so they could kill him?"

"I only scratched the surface on Benny's research, and now I have to try to piece this together, so I have a long night ahead of me."

"Hadley, please listen." He turned to me, put his hands on my shoulders, and looked into my eyes. "You can't fix everything. Let's be honest: Your control issues flared up during the Quilt City Murders.

I'm not saying you weren't instrumental in helping to solve them, but they seemed to take a huge toll on you because you somehow felt it was your responsibility to solve them. That's a heck of a burden, and you already carry the world on your shoulders. Your sense of responsibility, your honor, your discipline—they all play into the way I feel for you. But seemingly random people are being murdered again, and we don't know why. Because no one has established a motive, anyone could be the next victim, and I can't emphasize this enough: I really, really don't want that victim to be you. So, please investigate by using your computer, asking questions, making calls, not by putting yourself in jeopardy. I understand newspapers have to fill their pages, keep the public informed, and hold authorities accountable. But last time I checked, law enforcement is tasked with solving murders and preventing thieves from receiving their ransoms."

I smiled and wrapped my arms around him, leaning my head against his chest. "I appreciate your concern, I really do. I will be a journalist first, second, and third, not a crime-stopper, to the best of my abilities."

"You had to qualify it, didn't you?"

"Dear Brandon, as you have just made clear, I'm a flawed individual, so you shouldn't expect me to be perfect. Seriously, I might not have shown it, but I had a wonderful evening, despite our date once again being interrupted by death."

"Murder, actually. But, yes, I had a great time, too. In fact," he said, "I don't want this evening to end, but I know it has to. I want very much to kiss you again, but that could lead to distraction, and it sounds like you need to focus on pursuits other than osculation."

"Wow, you really are smarter than the average bear."

"Or have a better vocabulary."

I stepped back, looked into his eyes, kissed his lips gently, and said, "You truly are difficult to dislike."

"Again with the dislike. Before you go, I'd like to ask you something personal."

"Okay."

"Why did you turn down the second glass of wine?"

I hesitated for a few seconds while I tried to figure out how I wanted to respond. Earlier, he'd told me he would present the most real version of himself he could muster, hoping to establish a healthy, supportive relationship with me. I owed him at least that much. I must have hesitated too long because he asked, "Too personal?"

"No. I'm just trying to express myself without sounding glib. The easy answer is 'I don't want to become my mom or my sister.' But only occasionally is the easy answer the best one. It's not that I didn't trust myself around you with a second glass in me, if that's what you're wondering. I don't need alcohol in my system to find you attractive. You are indisputably hot. And I've never thrown myself at anyone. I turned the second glass down because I haven't drunk alcohol since a couple of weeks after Matt was killed. I felt the need to drink immediately afterward, but only once since, and that passed in a minute. Because you asked, and now that I've examined my motives, I guess I didn't trust how much I'd be affected by the second glass because I've lost my tolerance, and I didn't want to get sloppy or slurry or stupid. In other words, I really wanted you to like me, and I suspected you didn't have a thing for drunk women."

"Thank you for explaining. I appreciate it. I'm guessing your mom wasn't also valedictorian."

"No, she didn't graduate."

"So, she didn't excel in college as you did, or succeed at one newspaper after another, then start her own paper?"

"Okay, I get it. I'm not my mother."

"And you can stop worrying about me liking you. That ship has sailed."

"Were you on it?"

He laughed and shook his head. "Goodnight, Hadley. If you want to update me on your research, I'll welcome the interruption, at any hour."

"Goodnight, Brandon. You are tremendous. I never looked in your freezer to see who may be in there, but if it's nobody I know, we're good. Everyone needs a hobby."

"Pfffew. I was worried you'd judge me."

"Not for that. For loving Abba? Definitely."

TWENTY
THE BIG MAN RETURNS

I floated home, lifted by possibilities, held up by hope, and propelled by the thought of what tomorrow would bring.

Then I remembered what tomorrow would bring: the ransom deadline.

The insurance company for the National Quilt Museum wasn't going to come through with the $15 million. It had no obligation to come through at all. Based on what was discussed during the illegal meeting the commissioners held with Mayor Lewy, Ed Colapinto, and Robby Golden, the city didn't feel compelled to help Robby out, despite the millions in annual tourist dollars the museum generated for Paducah. Would private industry step up? Why would it? Might some of the major quilting retailers, Moda Fabrics or Janome, for example, kick money the museum's way? Maybe, but what would a few thousand dollars from a half-dozen manufacturers do?

I sat at my desk and was about to look into Chris Knudsen's life, but I knew I hadn't finished researching Benny Washington, formerly Cassie, and I hated to leave anything unfinished. I still had to complete every task I had to complete each week to put out the newspaper. I hadn't checked in with the ad department to see how this week's advertisements were looking. I hadn't discussed with the staff which stories would run in the paper and which would only be posted online. And I hadn't given thought to the layouts or to the art that would contribute to those layouts. Usually, I would have had most of these tasks fleshed out, if not completed, by early Saturday evening, so I was more than a day behind schedule. But I couldn't focus because I couldn't clear my head of two people: Benny Washington and Brandon Green.

I could do nothing about my preoccupation with Brandon. In fact, I indulged it, even though I knew I couldn't afford to fritter away my time like that. But is time spent in pursuit of love ever really frittered? No. So what I didn't do was fritter the next eight minutes contemplating the man whose kisses I could still taste.

Then I called Garrett Hunt. It was 10:34.

"Hello, Garrett. Is it too late?"

"Not at all. You didn't mistake me for a sleeper, did you?"

"Sadly, no. I suspected you were a fellow member of the Ignominious Insomnia Club."

"I'm a founding member. What can I do for you?"

"Any chance you can come over? I want to discuss something, but I'd rather do it in person. Or I can come to you, but I'll provide Maker's if you head my way. It's nothing nefarious, and, as far as I know, my phone isn't bugged, but I'd rather—"

"Be there in ten."

Garrett lived two blocks away in Lower Town. I'd kinda-sorta hired him as a private investigator to help solve the Quilt City Murders. He'd been far too expensive for me to pay him properly because the *Paducah Chronicle* paid about fourteen cents per hour more than I would have made working a McDonald's fry machine— but without the discounted food. Garrett had worked pro bono for me because his granddaughter, Rachelle Hunt, was "dating" Nick Stoddard, thirty-eight years her senior, and Nick appeared to be

tangled up with all of it, as he seemed to be with nearly every unsa-
vory act in the Jackson Purchase Region. Garrett didn't approve of
married Nick toying with young and naïve Rachelle. Sadly, that
dalliance was still in full bloom, as was Garrett's dismay, I was sure.

He showed up wearing basically the same outfit he'd worn whenever I'd seen him: a black leather jacket, a navy-blue golf shirt that
barely stretched over the beer-keg of his chest and belly, faded black
jeans, and black Nike running shoes. He used to be a boxer, and,
based on the nose that zigzagged between his eyes and the
pronounced and discolored scar tissue that encircled them, he'd
stopped plenty of punches with his face. But twin tragedies were the
primary cause of his Basset-hound visage and woebegone personality:
He'd lost his wife and one of his two daughters to breast cancer.

After I received my settlement, I gave Garrett what he determined to be far more money than his efforts on that case warranted.
I'd estimated the number of days he'd worked, multiplied that by his
$400-per-day rate, then doubled the total. He'd taken it upon himself
to help solve the case, confronted an intruder who was out to do me
harm, was attacked by said intruder, and surveilled suspects for many
hours. He deserved at least what I'd paid him, although he'd
protested when I presented the check to him. He agreed to cash it
only on the condition that I'd let him work for me again so he could
earn the generous bonus I'd given him. I'd agreed to his terms, but I
didn't feel good doing so. I wanted the extra money I'd given to him to
be a show of my appreciation, but he insisted on his terms.

I answered the door, said hello, gave him a hug, and led him to the
living room. I gestured to the bottle of Maker's Mark I'd set on the
coffee table, and he nodded as he sat on the couch. I poured two and
a half fingers into a rocks glass, handed it to him, and sat in one of the
two upholstered chairs across from the couch. He raised the glass in
my direction, said, "Here's to ya," and downed a third of it.

"What's going on, Hadley?"

"First, how are you?"

"Same as always. Breathing, but not well, and not all that happy about it. Hillary and Chantalle are still dead, I'm older today than yesterday, and fatter, and Rachelle's still dating that disgusting scumbag Stoddard."

His negativity likely bummed out most listeners, but I respected him for his honesty. He didn't go through life pretending it was what it wasn't, at least not for him. His endless pain had influenced the size of my payment to him.

"And you?" he asked.

"I have something great developing, but it doesn't seem appropriate to mention it."

"Do you think I'd rather everyone around me, or in the world, be miserable like me? Come on. I'd have to be a monster, and you know I'm not a monster."

"Not even close. That was presumptuous and reductive of me. I apologize. But because you asked, I've started seeing Brandon Green."

"Excellent. He's one of the good ones. Couldn't be happier for you two."

"Thank you. So far, it's been wonderful. But it's early."

"Don't do that. Don't look for the negative or the exit. Don't jinx things 'cause you're afraid to be hurt. The only way we can really be hurt is to truly love, to love totally and completely, and why the hell would anyone try to avoid that? Only broken cowards would settle for humdrum loneliness because they can't risk the pain of rejection or loss."

He downed the rest of his drink but held onto the glass, twirling it in his hand. "What Hillary and I had was special, magical, and I'm only miserable now because we were so great together. The depth of my despair today is proportional to the magic I felt daily when I was with her. Everything has a cost."

"Yes, it does. Hillary must have been wonderful. I'm sorry I didn't know her. Thank you for the lesson. I won't sabotage my relationship with Brandon, or I'll try not to."

"There you go again. Just don't do it. Opposite of the Nike

slogan." He raised his right running shoe with its white swoosh sewn across it, then laughed. It was a big, loud laugh, and I realized it was the first one he'd emitted in my presence.

"I'm glad you're here," I said. "I'm swamped, and I know you feel you have to earn the extra money I gave you. I've begun to research a woman who writes for the *Chronicle* named Benny Washington. That's her byline, anyway. Her real name is Cassie Washington. Benny was her brother, who was murdered by a man named Dennis Edwards, a drug dealer and multiple murderer who is serving life in Oregon State Penitentiary. Yes, I could eventually find out more about Cassie, aka Benny, her brother, their relatives, and Dennis Edwards, but I know you'll do an excellent job, and I don't like owing anybody anything."

"For a very smart woman, you're a dingbat. You don't owe me anything. I owe you about four days of my time, and that's if I charge you my going rate, which I'm not inclined to do because I like you and you're a good person, and you're running against that steaming pile of moral turpitude. To be honest, I made that rate high so I wouldn't have to work so much no more. If someone's willing to pay it, then I'll get my fat butt off the couch. For you, though, we'll work something out."

"Garrett, stop it. We're in the situation we're in because you worked for free, and I don't like accepting charity."

"How 'bout this," he said, reaching for the bottle and pouring himself three fingers of bourbon. "You allow me to work for you at whatever rate I think is fair, and you stop worrying so much about poor ol' sad-sack me. Deal?"

"That's heads-I-win, tails-you-lose, isn't it?"

"Maybe, but those are my terms. You in?"

"Yes."

"When should I start?"

"Now, if possible, but I'd like you to do your best not to let Benny know you're investigating her. Not yet. Oh, wait, I almost blew it. I forgot to tell you that Benny is Greg Wurt's niece, so any poking around the *Chronicle* is likely to get back to her. I'm not sure why I don't want her to know you're investigating her, but my gut tells me that's the way to play it."

"I understand. Believe me, with a gut as big as mine, I listen to it." He laughed, then drained his drink.

"You can do it however your gut and your experience tell you to, but I think you should visit Roseburg, Oregon. Benny and Greg are both from there. Greg's sister, Benny's mom, is probably also there, or from there, and maybe she or someone else in town can tell you or hint at how Greg managed to convince his boss, Ed Colapinto, the publisher, to hire Benny, Greg's totally unqualified niece. Ed is a pretty-boy egomaniac who makes satyrs look celibate, but none of that explains why he'd be willing to make a further laughingstock of his paper by plucking the least-qualified person out of what had to be a huge pool of qualified journalists. What would his angle have been?"

"Hadley, there are only ever a few possible angles: Sex, money, love, hate, and blackmail, and blackmail only results from the others. And hate is mostly love gone bad. Sure, people include revenge as a motive, but that's nothin' but a subset of hate. All I gotta do, really, is figure out which one motivated Ed to let Greg dictate the terms. Off the toppa my head, looks like Greg's got something on Ed, so Ed had to let Greg be the boss in this case."

"Greg is usually spineless, and the joke around the office was that Ed picked out the color of Greg's sweater every morning, so you understand why I'm confused by the reversal of the power dynamic."

"Or what looks like a reversal. Ed could still be calling the shots. What if he just threw Greg a bone because Greg is still under Ed's thumb, doing some kind of dirty work?"

"Like what?"

"I just got here. Don't know Ed Cola-whats-his-face from a hole in the ground. Give me time, I'll get whatever there is to get."

"I'll pay for expenses, of course."

He leaned forward and poured another three fingers into his

glass. "Okay," he said, "but I'll deduct the cost of this Makers." He pulled a small notebook and pen from his jacket pocket and asked, "What's the killer's name again?"

"Dennis Edwards." He wrote it down.

"And spell Ed's name."

"C-o-l-a-p-i-n-t-o."

He wrote it down and asked, "And where's he from?"

"Murray, or that's what he told me. His sickly parents are still there, last I heard."

"He's gonna have a connection to Roseburg, just you watch." He downed the last of his drink, set the glass on a coaster, and stood, struggling to stuff the notebook in his pocket because his thick-knuckled hand was so big.

"How do you know?"

He tapped the side of his temple with his right index finger. "Don't let the ugly fool you, kiddo. It's what's inside that counts."

"I know, but I'm really asking. Why do you think Colapinto is connected to Roseburg?"

"Because a sister took her murdered brother's name, and followed Greg to Paducah from Roseburg to take a job she's unqualified to do, all of which happened with the blessing of Ed. Am I remembering right? Didn't you tell me when you gave me the check Greg is horrible at his job, too?"

"Yes."

"Bingo." He tapped his temple again. "Sit back and watch the big man do his thing." We hugged, then we walked to the front door. I opened it and asked, "Was that your nickname in the ring, Big Man?"

He laughed, crossed the porch, and walked slowly down the steps.

"Not even close," he said as he closed the gate behind him and turned right on the sidewalk.

"Come on, Garrett. You can't just leave me hanging like that."

He stopped and wobbled a little. He turned, took two steps toward me, and stage whispered: "Off the record?"

"Yes."

"Just between the two of us?"

"Yes."

"I was known as Garrett Hunt." He laughed hard, turned, and lumbered home.

TWENTY-ONE
THE GRIEVING WIDOW

I was at my desk in the *Pulse* building by 6 a.m. I almost always exercised before work, but since everything else in Paducah was out of kilter, I figured that sticking to my routine didn't make sense. Or that's what I told myself when I woke up at 4 in a cold sweat, believing that I was the one who had to come up with $15 million by 5 p.m. Sure, I could have run along the river and up Jefferson that morning, but instead I chose to worry umpteen calories away. Who knew that panicking could be such an effective workout? Especially when combined with almost no sleep and borderline illegal quantities of coffee. My body was practically a furnace.

Because I'd delegated the research on Benny, ne Cassie, to Garrett, I had time to research Chris Knudsen. I delved into the usual sources, but nothing about his life seemed outside the realm of what most people would consider normal, other than the fact that he had five children, all now orphaned, and he'd been arrested for DUI two years ago. He graduated near the bottom of his class from Murray High School, worked at a few local retailers after graduating, and eventually landed a job working the press for the *Paducah Chronicle*, where he'd worked for nearly thirteen years. The *Chronicle* ran its press after 11 p.m., and Chris's commute to and from Murray would have been about fifty minutes. So, he hadn't kept traditional hours. My guess was that he probably slept while his wife and children ate breakfast, and he would see them during afternoons and evenings.

According to his Facebook page, he married Clover four years after they graduated high school together. They had twin boys and three girls in quick succession. He liked hunting, fishing, four-wheeling, football, and beer. His favorite team was the Pittsburgh Steelers, and his favorite beer was Bud. In many of the photos on his Facebook profile, his five young children were either hanging on him, gathered in front of him, or wrapped in his arms. They looked like a happy family. He was five days shy of his thirty-fifth birthday when the trash truck killed him in Nashville.

My tears began to flow when I saw the first picture of Chris hugging his kids. The twin boys were dressed similarly to their father in many of the photos, and they looked like miniature versions of him, including their mullets. Their smiles seemed to be filled with equal parts admiration for their father and joy. The boys appeared to be about twelve in the most-recent photos, and the three girls appeared to be one, two, and three years younger, respectively. The girls favored their mother, Clover—featuring long blond hair and blue eyes, as she did. The boys and Chris had brown eyes. Clover's FB page provided more sadness—in the form of many more photos of a happy, smiling family.

Trying to lessen my anguish at another life being cut short, leaving behind so many broken lives, I walked down the hall, went outside, and walked five laps around the building. I considered myself lucky not to have had an all-consuming passion to have children because I didn't feel as hollow and haunted by my lack of offspring as I would have felt if I'd had a burning need to have them. When I was young, I wanted and expected to have children, and I thought I had an outside chance not to be an atrocious mother—if I did the exact opposite of everything our mom did, I'd be off to a great start. But the opportunity never presented itself.

Although I'd said yes to Matt's proposal, I didn't feel comfortable enough in our relationship nor feel positive enough that we would last as a partnership to mention the prospect of us having children together. He joked about us doing so, as he did with most everything (there can be a fine line between humor and deflection). When Matt said, "We should have eight kids so we can play five-on-five basketball as a family," it sounded more like the premise of an absurdist play than family planning. However, despite my not feeling gutted by never having had children, I still felt gutted when I returned to the newsroom.

I entered and saw Dan and Sheila sitting at their desks, typing.

"It's 7:04," I said from the doorway.

"Sorry I'm late," Dan said as Sheila said, "I overslept." We all laughed. Every day I thanked my lucky stars for the excellent journalists I'd hired. But the *Pulse* staff hadn't had to tackle any major crises together yet. Nearly any journalist can handle routine assignments, but to cover disasters and catastrophes well, without getting overwhelmed or sidetracked, journalists have to be much stronger and more resilient than they do when covering city commissioner meetings, high school musicals, ballgames, and bake sales.

Dan stopped typing and swiveled his chair toward me. He said, "I'm not going to ask how your date went. But, based on how exhausted you look, I'm guessing it went well."

I shook my head. "I'm not going there, but thanks for your interest."

"Oh, no," Sheila said. "That means it didn't go well."

"No, it doesn't. The date was wonderful. *I* wasn't so wonderful, but the date was, at least until Dan called."

"Yeah, I'm sorry about that on about eight levels," he said. "It won't surprise you to know that I've been up most of the night pulling together a piece on Chris. He seemed like a good, ordinary guy."

"That's what I found out, too. No hint of anything that would get him murdered. And you obviously saw his adorable kids."

"Yes. It's awful. My piece is nearly there, but I need to see what else I can get from Nashville PD and from friends and coworkers. What's the latest on the ransom?"

"Other than the fact it won't be paid, nothing. Because you have Chris's story in hand, I'll reach out to Clover, assuming she's in any condition to answer questions. This is definitely the part of the job I hate the most—pestering the bereaved. Hazard of the profession."

"I hate that part, too," Dan said, "so thank you for taking that off my plate."

"You're welcome. After that, I'll look into what the museum and the city and private industry are doing, if anything, to deal with the robbers. Or is it murderers or quilt-nappers?"

"For our purposes," Sheila said, "let's go with vermin, but if you prefer scum, I can live with that. I've left four messages for Robby, but I don't expect to hear from him. The guy's destroyed, and who wouldn't be?"

"I'll call Ed Colapinto to ask about him being included in the illegal meeting," I said, "among other issues I need to pursue. Neither of you probably knows about Garrett Hunt, a local private eye. I've hired him to investigate Benny Washington, partly because we are nowhere near fully staffed yet and won't be until advertising picks up. So, we need the help. Off the top of his head, Garrett concluded that Ed—"

"Wait," Sheila said, "who's Ed?"

"Sorry. He's the publisher of the *Chronicle*. He hired Greg and allowed Greg to hire Benny. Or that's the way Garrett has me looking at it now. Garrett's heading to Roseburg, Oregon, where he expects to find some connection to Ed, despite Ed being from Murray."

"What makes him think that?" Dan asked.

I tapped my temple with my index finger as Garrett had. "He understands how the world works in ways the rest of us really don't want to know. His pain and suffering—both physical and psychological—help him see in total darkness. He's really good at what he does, but I don't envy his ability or his nightmares."

"Neither do I," Sheila said.

"Let's hope he finds something useful," Dan said. "But I don't see why you're having him look into Benny now. Wouldn't his ability to see in the dark be more useful here, trying to figure out who the robbers, terrorists, vermin are so the cops can catch them?"

"You may be right, but Benny's article saying that Baahir had two ounces of grass on his bed has stuck in my craw since I read it. I can't explain why, but I think her twisting of the truth is the key to what's going on, or at least one of the keys. There's no rational explanation for her to have included that inaccuracy. If she reported an accurate fact, then why didn't Sergeant Vazquez mention the marijuana to you?"

"Look, Boss," Dan said, "you don't have to justify your decisions to me. I hope you're right and Garrett solves all this garbage fast. If the ransom isn't met—"

"When it's not met," I said.

"Okay, when. Then what will happen?"

"Who knows? But we'll soon find out."

Because interviewing people in person is far more productive than doing so on the phone, I called Clover Knudsen and asked if she would answer a few questions in her home, at her convenience. "Got nothing else going on now," she said. "Kids about to be picked up for school, and I ain't even told them yet." She sniffed loudly, and her voice wavered when she said, "So, yeah, come on over."

I'd been to Murray about a dozen times to see shows at Murray State University and to visit the impressive art gallery, Gallery 109. The masterful works of owner and painter Jennifer Fairbanks filled the gallery when I'd visited, although I hadn't been there for a few years. I didn't know the city well, but GPS delivered me to the Knudsen's house on Woodlawn, near Murray Calloway County Hospital, a trip of about an hour.

The three-bedroom, one-bath ranch-style home featured a recently mown lawn and landscaping that someone had spent time maintaining. Three pink bikes sat on the grass to the right of the concrete walkway, with two blue ones to the left of it. A red Hyundai

Sonata sat in the driveway. Clover saw me approach because when I reached the front door, she opened it.

For a mother of five children whose world had just collapsed, she looked amazing. Sure, her eyes were red, but she'd taken the time to make herself presentable. Her expensive jeans fit snuggly, her floral blouse had been pressed, and her black cowboy boots gleamed. Her long blond hair framed her pretty face to great effect, and she'd taken the time to apply makeup well. Whether she was always so meticulous about her appearance I couldn't say, but I found her concern about her looks disconcerting after she learned hours before that her husband had been murdered.

"How you doing?" she asked after giving me a hug.

"I'm fine, but how you're doing is what's important."

She ushered me inside with a sweep of her arm and said, "How else I gonna be, a time like this? Like last-week's eggs, you want the truth. But sobbing ain't gonna bring Chris back or feed my kids, so what's the point? Please sit."

I sat on one side of a teal love seat that formed an L with a teal couch. At the edge of the gap formed by the two teal pieces sat a blood-red lounge chair. She sat in it and said, "Where's my manners? Already had my coffee so forgot to offer you some."

"No, thank you. I've had mine, too."

The bookshelves against two walls held only a few books but were otherwise filled with tchotchkes and souvenirs from the family's travels to Memphis, St. Louis, and Nashville, as well as framed photos of the family. I saw drawings the kids had created taped to the walls in the kitchen and stuck to the refrigerator with magnets.

I said, "I appreciate you taking the time to talk with me. This is an incredibly difficult time for you, so I'll understand if you want to stop, although I only have a few questions."

"Cops already asked more questions than I knew existed late last night and again this morning. At least they only called today, just after you hung up. 'Just double-checking my story' is why they called, or so they said. Sounds like they ain't believed me, you want the truth."

"I'm sorry. Being interviewed can be trying in the best of times. If Murray PD is anything like Paducah PD, then I'm guessing the cops didn't show you a lot of empathy."

"What's that mean?"

"Understanding for your situation."

"No, they acted like I had something to do with his death, and I was asleep when they knocked on my door to tell me."

"I'm sorry. I didn't realize you've been through the wringer this morning, but can you tell me why Chris was in Nashville?"

"On his off days at the *Chronicle* he runs the press at the *Tennessean*, Saturdays and Sundays. Ran."

"He worked seven days a week?"

"Yup. Got five kids, and I ain't been working, what with the kids being young and all. Maybe soon. The girls are nine, ten, and eleven, and the twins about to turn thirteen."

"I saw pictures of them online. You have a beautiful family."

"Well, beautiful kids. Chris ain't with us."

"Yes, I'm sorry."

"You're fine. What else you wanna know?"

"How long did Chris work for the *Tennessean*?"

"'Bout six months. We was lucky they needed someone the same days he had off."

I'd heard enough, so I said, "I have other questions but none that can't wait. I'll get going now, and I promise to tell our cops reporter not to bother you. I'll check in to see if you or the kids need anything, if you don't mind. I'm only an hour away."

"Don't even know me. Why would you do that?"

"No one should go through what you're going through, let alone go through it alone."

"Ain't alone. Got family and friends, but I understand what you mean and appreciate your kindness, truly." She stood, waited for me to rise, and gave me a hug.

"Be kind to yourself," I said. "The only advice I feel qualified to give is: There is no wrong way to grieve."

"I hear you, and thank you."

I pulled away from the curb, drove down the block, turned a corner, and parked. I pulled up the website for the *Tennessean* on my phone. The staff page didn't list the press workers, only the editorial staff. I read the breaking news story on the website about the fatal wreck that Nashville PD had ruled a homicide. The cops reporter didn't mention that Chris Knudsen had been a *Tennessean* employee, only that he'd worked for the *Chronicle*. I called the main switchboard and asked for HR.

After the female HR employee answered with, "HR, this is Dina," I said, "Hello, Dina. I was surprised to read on the website that Chris Knudsen, who was killed in a wreck that the cops are calling a homicide, wasn't said to be a *Tennessean* employee. Did the reporter accidentally leave that fact out? Or is this another example of a hack reporter bungling things?" It hurt me to throw a fellow journalist under the bus, but I was trying to put her on her heels so she would provide information she should probably have kept private.

"I'm sorry, ma'am, but our reporters are excellent and hardworking, and in today's climate of hostility toward members of the press, the editorial department triple checks every fact. Of course, when reporters are covering breaking news and under a severe time crunch, an error slips through now and again. On those occasions, we publish corrections. I'm looking at our directory, and I can assure you the reporter did not make a mistake. Good day, and thank you for being a reader."

She said the last sentence in the tone someone would use when saying, "Thank you for being an idiot." But I agreed with her opinion and would have responded with saltier language had I been in her position. I'd confirmed my suspicion and hadn't lied. I'd outmaneuvered her by asking questions that I'd been told the answer to only minutes before. Of course, if I'd believed Clover's statement about Chris's employment, I wouldn't have tried to verify it.

I've conducted thousands of interviews, and one of the skills I've mastered over the years is knowing when interviewees are lying. Occasionally, I've believed people, then been proven gullible when I couldn't verify what they'd presented as facts. But I'd say well above ninety percent of the time I've known when I was being lied to, and I either left the inaccurate information out of my stories or brought attention to its inaccuracies. Clover was lying to me, or Chris had been lying to her. I couldn't tell which, but her demeanor and makeup and lack of being a basket-case suggested that the Knudsens were not the happy family that their social media profiles made them appear to be.

TWENTY-TWO
SNEAKING AROUND

Something felt not just off but wrong. I learned long ago to trust my instincts, so I went around the block and parked a couple of houses down from the Knudsens' house. While watching their driveway, I called Dan to let him know I didn't find out anything from Clover that he could use in his story and said it didn't make sense for him to contact her. I didn't tell him that the pictures of the happy family on the Knudsens' Facebook pages may be deceiving because I didn't want to influence his reporting.

For the next five minutes, I alternated between believing that Clover had been lied to by Chris about working at the *Tennessean* and believing that Clover was lying to me when she'd told me he'd worked there. If she had simply believed her husband, then she was blameless. My guess was that Chris had told her he'd landed the job so he could cheat on her with someone in Nashville. If that was the case, Clover had been victimized repeatedly, and no one deserved the kind of pain and grief she must have been feeling.

Plus, I had to listen to my own advice to her: There is no wrong way to grieve. If she chose to present herself to a stranger only after making sure she was perfectly put together, then that was her right, and I shouldn't judge her.

But, a few minutes later, when she pulled out of her driveway, and I followed her from a distance to a mansion on Robertson Road on a corner lot, I began to judge her. As I drove by the mansion, I noted the address of the enormous new colonial, replete with two ionic columns on either side of the front entrance and a front lawn big enough to play a football game and a soccer match side by side.

I slowed down enough to watch Clover park her Sonata on the circular driveway behind a black Mercedes sedan that aspired to be a Rolls Royce. I drove out of that ritzy neighborhood and pulled into a gas station. I looked the address up on Zillow. The house had sold for $1.875 million three years earlier. I could find out who lived there by visiting the Calloway County Assessor, but I didn't know which clerk was related to which mucky-muck and didn't know which rich Murray residents might get upset—and become vindictive—if a journalist looked into their ownership records.

I had another option. I could call a former high school classmate of mine who worked for the DMV and ask her—okay, bribe her—to run the tag of the Mercedes. I hadn't asked for her assistance for a while, and the last time hadn't gone well, but I have never been timid, so I decided to go that route until it proved to be a dead end.

I drove back to the upscale neighborhood and parked half a block away on the side of the house that didn't include the main entrance. I wouldn't have been able to read the tag if I'd stood at the end of the driveway, or even if I'd walked up it, because the Mercedes was parked on the far side of the circular drive, perpendicular to the section of driveway that led to Robertson Road. I opened the glove box and pulled out binoculars, the good pair I'd purchased to go bird-watching. I'd watched birds once. I quickly determined that—as I hunkered among the thick foliage, careful not to touch the poison ivy that seemed to be growing very fast in my direction—time spent bird-watching was time better spent quilting.

I locked the car, and my phone rang. "Hello, Brandon. I'm glad you called."

"Hello, and why is that?"

"Because I'm in the middle of a stakeout, and that made me think of you."

"Wait, we have an agreement."

"Which is?"

"Remember, you're not good at being coy."

"Okay, I remember what our agreement is."

"Go ahead and say it out loud so we know we agree on what our agreement is."

"I will behave as reporters behave, not as cops do."

"Yet you're on a stakeout."

"Well, I may have exaggerated my current activity for dramatic effect, but I am about to use binoculars."

"I hope you're birdwatching."

"Some hopes must be dashed, I'm afraid. I'm surveilling a potential perp. Did I get the lingo right?"

"Are you endangering yourself or the case every law enforcement agency in the region is pursuing?"

"No. I'm just trying to see who lives in a particular home, or at least owns the Mercedes parked in front of it."

"Dare I ask?"

"How brave are you?"

"Brave enough to date you."

"Ouch, but I'll take that as a compliment."

"Seriously, what are you doing?"

"Clover Knudsen, the recent widow of Chris, told me she didn't work and said Chris worked at the *Tennessean* newspaper, which he did not. I'm about to prove that she either works at the house I'm standing near, or she isn't broken up about her husband's death because she's sleeping with the owner of this house."

"And you need the binoculars to see the tag?"

"Yes."

"Next, you'll ask me to compromise myself and my authority by looking up the owner of that tag."

"No, Mr. Self-Important, I intend to contact someone I know at the DMV and ask *her* to compromise herself ... never mind. I'll put away the binoculars and head to the assessor's office. My DMV insider probably wouldn't have helped me anyway, and all of this is unnecessary because I'm almost certain I know who owns this house. He happens to live in a similarly gaudy and gauche faux castle in West Paducah. And he once asked Dakota and me to play naked Twister with him."

"Did you win?"

"A lady never tells."

"You're not going to tell me who you think owns the house, are you?"

"I shouldn't until I confirm it, but you could confirm it a lot faster than I can. How about if I tell you who I think owns the house, and if I'm right, you say something coppish, or is it coppy, or copperish? That sounds metallic."

"You're on."

I gave him the address and said, "Edward Colapinto is the owner of the house and likely the owner of the car whose tag you dissuaded me from perusing."

He was quiet for twenty seconds, then he slowly said, "India Lima India Kilo Echo Yankee Oscar Uniform."

"Why, Detective Green, Iay ikelay ouyay, ootay."

"We're dorks, right?"

"At best. Probably dweebs."

"Good to know," he said. "What do you intend to do with the information I didn't confirm for you? And, for the record, I didn't access anything you couldn't access to find the information. I used an app called Land Grid."

"Really? It's hard to keep up with technology. I should've known about that. I searched for my first property so long ago, I just got in the habit of doing it the same way. I'll pass along the app name to the reporters, who probably already know about it. Thank you."

"You think Colapinto's involved in what, the theft of the quilts?"

"I know I'm guessing, but I think Clover is the daytime caretaker to Colapinto's ailing parents. He mentioned them more than once when I was at the *Chronicle*. If I were to call his office now, his assistant would tell me he's not in, and that's because he's in the house with Clover, although I won't speculate on what they may be doing. Any word from the kidnappers?"

"Not that I've heard. We have every officer on standby, and we'll have twice as many officers as usual on at seventeen hundred. Deputies in three counties have similarly deployed, and Kentucky State Police and the FBI have muscled in."

"It would have killed you to say 5 o'clock?"

"I've read the medical journals. Not worth the risk."

"Be serious for a second, please. What do you think will happen when they don't receive the insurance money?"

"No one knows. They'll probably name the drop location as close to five as possible, so we don't have time to set up on it. Our SWAT team will proceed as if everything is going to plan, delivering the satchel where and when the perps specify. If they suspect a setup, they could spook, and we'll lose our shot at them. Not necessarily literally. But our best chance is to make the drop as requested and have officers, deputies, KSP, or FBI pick them up when they think they've gotten far enough away so no one is following them."

"What are the odds of catching them?"

"Very few kidnappers or extortionists escape with their ransom demands fulfilled. In this case, unless something drastic happens in the next eight hours, we know they won't get the fifteen million. I like our chances to apprehend them, but if they suspect a setup—"

I heard his text chime through my phone, then my phone chimed. I looked at the text: *Know you aint got the ransom. Small town, big mouths. Huge mistake. Hope yall sleep good tonight.*

"Did you get it?" Brandon asked.

"Yes. What do you think?"

"We all would have been a lot better off if the museum hadn't let its policy lapse. I wouldn't have been broken to bits if a giant corporation had to pay out, rather than profiting from people's fears and misfortunes. Not a big fan of the insurance industry. Kentucky United Insurance is worth billions. I looked them up. Scraping up families' last nickels by stoking their fear of catastrophes. It just seems heartless. The company would've been out a small fraction of its profits, and we'd be able to get some sleep. But the darn policy lapsed."

"It's going to be bad?"

"Who knows? These guys aren't terrible crooks. They've made mistakes, but nothing disastrous because they're still out there, and they have us off balance. I'm not sure the murder of Durrell Mahan was a mistake. It could have been part of the plan. They messed up badly by overestimating the museum's coverage, but which of us would have thought a museum wouldn't protect itself in case of theft? From what I hear, twelve officers from three agencies are set up on the Mahan hovel in Mayfield, at a distance, of course. But only one woman, presumed to be one of the two sisters, has shown up.

"Despite having Durrell's body and matching his prints to the Baahir Ali murder scene, Murray PD, KSP, and the FBI don't want to descend on the house because doing so could force the BPs—I'm choosing to go with that name because you're right far more than you're wrong—to step up their timeline for whatever the perps' big plan is. The Feds think the theft of the quilts may not be about money, or at least the money isn't the ultimate objective."

"There's a racial component to the thefts, it seems. Only quilts produced by BIPOC members were stolen."

"Okay, so we have Durrell for the murder of Baahir and for being at the scene of the shooting, and, of course, his prints were on the rifle found under him. But Durrell's dead, so the only way, at least for now, to catch the others is to let whatever they have planned happen, or at least try to thwart their plan as it's happening. If law enforcement hits the Mahan house now, we aren't likely to find anything.

The Barrel Proofs have set up elsewhere, so we aren't close to knowing what their plans are, let alone preventing them from implementing those plans."

"Sometimes the burden of proof really is a burden."

"Now who's talking like a cop?"

TWENTY-THREE
SIGN OF THE TIMES

For the most part, the next few hours in the office played out normally, with all of us working quickly to post articles to the website to inform the public about the theft of the quilts, the dead body found at the scene, the ransom demand, the National Quilt Museum's inability to meet the ransom demand, and the city's unwillingness to pay the ransom on the museum's behalf.

However, we struggled to be timely and accurate while writing our articles because our office phones wouldn't stop ringing. Nearly every sentence we wrote was interrupted by a phone call from a concerned citizen wanting to know if the police had been notified, a county resident concerned about how the quilt thefts would affect his livestock, the director of a pioneer museum in the Rockies concerned that her insurance premiums would go up, a quilting collective in the Adirondacks wondering how its members could help, a conspiracy theorist who blamed "JFK and the like" for the thefts, a master's degree candidate in criminology at a west coast university offering her expertise, a bakery in Ventura, California, wanting to send us pumpkin muffins for no discernible reason, an east coast production crew declaring its intention to create a documentary "of the calamity to come," and dozens of other distracting calls from people who probably meant well but didn't appear to *be* well. And the phone calls were nothing compared to the onslaught of emails that the *Pulse* website received, many of them apparently written by ungulates high on peyote.

During a much-needed lull in the telephonic interruptions, after I stretched my legs, refilled my coffee mug, and checked to see if the reporters needed anything, I sat down at my desk, noted the time—11:03—and heard my cell ring.

"They decided not to wait," Brandon said without saying hello. "So far, three quilts have been reported burning—one thrown from a black truck onto the steps of City Hall, another in the parking lot of the southside Walmart, and the third behind the museum, which took guts or luck because we have squads rolling by there every ten minutes. All three were reported within two minutes of each other, so it was a coordinated effort. They weren't dumped by the same vehicle."

"That's awful. Total losses, I'm guessing."

"The first officers on scene at City Hall said the gas smell was significant. They tried to stomp out the fire. By the time PFD arrived, they didn't bother to put the fire out, just made sure it didn't spread."

"Witnesses?"

"No one saw anything more than a big black truck without tags at City Hall. Officers are talking to Walmart customers and employees now, and we have nothing from the museum."

"Not good. Now what?"

"We don't know. They've just burned three of their twenty-six quilts. If they keep that up, they'll lose whatever leverage they think they have."

"The quilts are irreplaceable," I said, "but how much value does each have?"

"They asked for fifteen million for twenty-six quilts, so they're valuing each at, what's that, a little less than six hundred thousand per, right?"

"About that."

"Why does it matter?"

"I'm not sure it does," I said. "I'm just trying to get a handle on any of this. They seem to know what they're doing: Both the gun heist and the quilt heist were ambitious and executed well. But they didn't know the museum didn't have theft insurance, and they direly miscalculated the worth of the quilts, it seems. Nearly every quilt in the museum is world-class, but many rich collectors buy quilts, and no one has ever paid anywhere near a million dollars for a quilt, as far as I know. When I worked A&E at the *Chronicle*, I looked up the most expensive quilt ever sold, and it sold for about $260,000. That sale was a long time ago, and the quilt has probably appreciated since then, but not that much—and that was a quilt from the Civil War, not one created by a modern quilt master. The historical aspect of it probably was responsible for most of that price, not the technical mastery."

"As I mentioned, the FBI thinks this is more than a money play. I can't say any more than that, and that's not for the public."

"I understand. The *Pulse* isn't in the habit of printing FBI hunches slathered in hearsay, no matter how kissable the lips that utter them."

"Good to know. Gotta go."

"Thanks for keeping me informed. Stay safe."

Because I didn't know what else to do, I dug deeper into the life and death of Chris Knudsen. I found links to his friends and family on Facebook, sent a few messages, scoured other social media sites without much success and decided to go to the source: the *Chronicle*.

Inside the press room, the huge red machine with thousands of moving pieces sat idle. When running, it could be deafening, a whirl of thunderous motion. I was always careful not to wear anything flowing or loose when I entered that room. That afternoon, I hoped I might run into one of the other press operators, even though they worked the night shift, except when filling special orders. I called out and poked my head into both offices but saw no one. I was about to leave when I thought to search the offices for information that might shed light on who Chris Knudsen was.

Other than smelling of oil and having numerous large slots where printing plates were stored, both offices contained the usual office supplies that didn't teach me anything. But in the second office, on a wall, partially obscured by a signed basketball encased in a Lucite box, hung a photo of Chris, Greg Wurt, and Ed Colapinto standing side by side with Cheshire Cat grins on their faces. They were less subtle about the hand gesture they each flashed with their right hands than Benny Washington had been in the photo I'd seen of her in clown attire in Greg's office. Their index and middle fingers made a collapsed OK sign, and their ring fingers and pinkies pointed outward. In the past, I'd glanced at the photo when I'd sat at the desk while *Pulse* was being printed. I knew when I saw Benny making the gesture in the photo in Greg's office that it seemed familiar, although I couldn't place where I'd seen it. I took a photo of the photo with my phone and left the office. I walked down the hall, went up the stairs, and heard a man's voice as I approached Greg's office. Ed Colapinto, the vain publisher who elevated primping to an art form, leaned across Greg's desk. The sheepish look on Greg's face and the angry expression on Ed's when he turned toward me made me think Ed had been berating Greg, who hunkered in his desk chair. Greg wore a purple sweater.

Ed stared at me. If he had been a fop in seventeenth century London, the outfit he was wearing would have been over-the-top. I would have guessed that no self-respecting tailor would create a peri-winkle-blue suit with visible, clunky black stitching along the lapels and outlining the buttonholes, but I would have been wrong. His pink dress shirt featured a collar that looked like a cross between a peter pan and a dog's. The double Windsor knot in his canary-yellow silk tie made him look like he was holding a grapefruit under his chin. A gold tie bar secured his tie below the grapefruit, and a gold clip secured it farther down. His cufflinks spelled out EC in what I hoped were faux diamonds, his gold pinkie rings would have embarrassed Liberace, his teal pocket square jutted upward in a three-point crown fold, and his burgundy shoes were the only element of his outfit that didn't scream I-me-mine. I wondered if he'd left his tricorn hat in the bedchamber of last night's scullery maid.

Ed said, "If it isn't the professional meddler."

"More than one of us exists, so your use of the definite article is incorrect."

"Always a retort," Greg said.

"I have to go," Ed said to Greg, adding, "Remember what I told you." Greg nodded. "I didn't hear you," Ed said.

"Yes, I'll remember what you told me." Ed nodded, turned toward me, and leered in a manner designed to make me undress. But I didn't even swoon.

Instead, I said to him, "Who holds your pinkie ring when you flash hand signs?" He looked confused, shook his head, and left. While I could still hear Ed's heels clacking in the hallway, Greg said, "I thought I made it clear you aren't welcome here." He wore a purple sweater.

"If I had a nickel for every time I've heard that ..."

"I'm serious. Don't make me call security."

"There is no security. You made it clear while I worked here that I wasn't welcome, and yet I showed up every day. So, I won't leave until you answer a few questions."

"This is my office, and I won't be bossed around in it."

"By me, you mean? Because Ed just treated you like a cranky toddler. Was Chris Knudsen one of your special hires? And what does the hand sign mean that you, Ed, Chris, and Benny have all been photographed making? I found photos online of white suprema-cists making a similar, although not identical, sign."

"As usual, Little Miss Reporter, you think you have all the

answers. I'd bet Matt wasn't murdered but killed himself to get away from you."

The floor wobbled under my feet, and I started to sway. Sweat instantly covered my face, and the room started to go dark, even though my eyes were open. I took a step toward a chair, steadied myself on it, and tried to slow my racing pulse by breathing deeply for five seconds.

I let go of the chair, glared at him, and said, "Everyone in the newsroom always thought you were an incompetent bozo, but for you to say something like that, you either have to be a monster or someone whose depravity I just exposed. Or both. You don't have the spine to be a monster. You're an assemblage of weaknesses dressed as a grape. So, once again you answered my questions indirectly."

He stood, put his hands on the blotter, and leaned toward me in a power pose designed to intimidate me. But his attempt at physical intimidation was betrayed by his quivering upper lip (not to mention the red clown nose by his right hand). He said, "We are members of a social club. The hand signal is part of that, like a fraternity hand-shake. Nothing more."

"Let me guess: The name of your social club is the Barrel Proofs."

His startled expression made me wonder whether the room was now spinning for him. He looked like he'd just fallen into a boiling cauldron of ugly truth. He retreated from his power pose and collapsed in his chair. Sweat flooded his face so badly that I wondered if he would pull off his sweater. But he just sat there, sweating and looking stunned.

"I'm going to give you a piece of advice," I said. "Don't take up poker. You're a horrible liar and couldn't keep a secret if you were gagged and unconscious. I took a shot. I didn't have a clue you were connected to the Barrel Proofs. I didn't even know if the Barrel Proofs existed, but your response proved they exist and proved you are involved with them. You look like you're burning up. Take your sweater off."

"Get out of my office."

"Okay. I found what I'd hoped to find."

"Hope you're satisfied because you just killed that horrible rag you call a newspaper. I'll tell Ed to cancel your contract for our press. And there goes the election, too."

"You invoke Ed's authority over you, but you appear to have blackmailed him into hiring Benny."

"Security," he yelled. "Security."

"You're in Cuckoo Land, Greg. Again, the Chronicle doesn't have security. It barely pays its reporters. Well, at least the reporters who aren't related to you. What arrangement you have with Benny, only you, Benny, Ed, and Beelzebub know."

Even though I had improved my record in arguments against Greg to 73-0, I was shaken by what I'd learned. I'd confirmed that BP stood for Barrel Proofs, and Greg, Ed, Chris, and Benny were connected by the photos of them flashing hand signs. So, I should have felt at least satisfied because I was making progress on the crimes or cases or stories or whatever we were all working on. But I felt agitated and disappointed because I'd discovered proof that yet another person in my life, one who had been my boss for four years, was a bad person. I didn't have evidence I could use in a story or that would stand up in court, but he was bad—and now I had to prove it.

Instead of walking back to the Pulse office, I turned off my phone and wandered around downtown, trying to think. I wanted to look at the shops and restaurants and art galleries with fresh eyes, as a tourist would. I walked along the Paducah Wall to Wall, the series of beautifully painted and well-maintained murals that decorate the floodwall designed to protect the city when the Ohio River floods.

I walked for twenty minutes and saw almost no one downtown. A few workers entered or exited businesses, but the tourists and locals who would usually keep downtown vibrant were absent. It didn't take an advanced degree to determine that the populace was spooked by the robbery at Walmart, the shooting and murder during Barbecue on the River, the theft of the quilts, the ransom demand, and the burning of the quilts.

I didn't think the public had connected Baahir Ali's murder at Murray State to the other mayhem, so his death didn't likely contribute to the empty streets. But I'd made that connection—however tenuous and invisible—and I was determined to end this crime spree and return Paducah to its tourist-friendly, artistic, productive ways. I actually spoke the words, "You can do it, Hadley."

TWENTY-FOUR
GETTING THE MESSAGE

I knew something was wrong as soon as I entered the newsroom. The four reporters—Dan, Sheila, Teresa, and our sportswriter, Mickey Lyle—sat at their desks staring at the doorway, waiting for me to walk through it. They'd obviously heard the outside door close behind me and knew I was only seconds away.

"What is it? What's wrong?" I asked. Dan looked at Sheila, and she looked at him. Neither of them wanted to break the news to me.

"Please tell me. I can handle it," I said. But I knew I couldn't, not if something horrible had happened to Dakota, or Jenny, or Brandon, or Ash.

"It's bad but not that bad," Sheila said. "It's weird because it falls right in the middle of both our beats." I made a "Yes, what is it?" gesture with my eyebrows and upraised palms.

"Robby Golden's been kidnapped," she said. "No one noticed he was missing because the museum's closed because of the robbery, and the only employee who showed up, Dashiell Clark, figured Robby was still upset and stayed home. He called his cell, got voicemail, and didn't think anything of it. But when he was going to lunch, he saw Robby's

Town Car in the parking lot. When he'd pulled in at 8 a.m. so he could go through all the files to see if the thieves stole anything other than quilts, the parking lot had been empty. When he saw Robby's car, he said he thought, 'Oh, Robby's fine. He's here but must be running an errand.' But when he came back from lunch and saw the car, and Robby wasn't in the museum, he knew something was wrong. He called Gillian, Robby's wife. She told him Robby left the house at 8:45."

"You called the police, right?" I asked.

"Yes," Dan said, "and Officer Deion Donner told me where I could stick my questions."

I said, "They won't tell us anything until the public information officer writes a press release that won't tell us anything. If only someone we knew had a contact in PPD." I smiled, pulled out my cell, turned it on, and walked toward my office. "Great job. I'll let you know what I find out."

I grabbed my water bottle and listened to a message from Brandon while I walked to the water cooler.

"Hello, Hadley. I hope you're safe and doing at least okay. The perps are nothing if not adaptable. The quilts didn't work as planned, so they grabbed Robby Golden, or it certainly looks like they did. They've made no demands yet, so we can't be sure, but we're proceeding as though he's been abducted. They already leveled the veiled threat in the text, so we're mobilizing the various forces so we can coordinate our pursuit. All we have are two witnesses who saw a large black truck without tags near the museum just before nine. No one saw Robby arrive or get grabbed, or at least no one we've spoken to. None of this is on the record. Your reporters can corroborate what I've given you in minutes. For some reason, I felt compelled to let you know what's going on. If you ask me what that reason is, I'll have no choice but to become sentimental. Talk soon." I checked what time he'd called. About twenty minutes earlier, just after I'd turned off my phone.

After I'd silently called myself a nincompoop for thinking I had a right to a few moments of peace during the largest crime spree Paducah had ever seen, I called Brandon.

"I'm sorry I missed your call," I said.

"Not a problem. It's nice to hear your voice. How are you?"

"Peachy. Everything's grand. Couldn't complain if I wanted to."

"Good to hear. Denial can be your friend. No, seriously, how are you?"

"Stressed, frustrated, and feeling helpless. Not that I've ever been to war or plan to go, but I feel like we're fighting a war on three or four fronts."

"Hadley, you own a newspaper. Your job is to cover the war, not to fight it."

"Yeah, yeah. If you man-splain me one more time, I won't kiss you more than eleven times a day."

"Well, did you know Paul McCartney was in a band before Wings?"

"Paul who?"

"You, too, are very hard to dislike."

"Thank you, but do you think we should talk about what's going on?"

"I told you nearly everything we know in the message. We'll receive their demands soon. Fifteen million, probably. They came up with that amount for a reason. The money didn't materialize, but the reason shouldn't have changed."

"But do you think they believe they can extract that much from the city, from businesses, from whomever, even though those entities intend to give them nothing for the quilts?"

He paused for a few seconds, then said, "I won't pretend to understand how their thought processes work. If this proves to be some white supremacist garbage, then, no, I can't get my mind to function as theirs apparently do. Or don't."

"I think I can understand their logic. A person should be far more valuable than a quilt, even if that quilt is one of a kind and irreplaceable. But there are, what, eight billion people now, so there are many, many more humans than quilts."

"Meaning they may have overestimated the value of Robby, too?"

"They seem to have kidnapped Robby because they blame him for failing to insure the quilts. If he hadn't let the policy lapse, they'd be a few hours away from collecting their money."

"Or trying to."

"Good point," I said. "But what I mean is that kidnappers choose their victims because the hostages have rich parents or because they work for rich corporations. Conglomerates take out kidnapping policies on key employees as a matter of course—part of the cost of doing business, and a tax write-off. What if Robby didn't accidentally let the policy lapse, but he did so for financial reasons? Maybe he has financial problems and pocketed the insurance premium. If so, the BPs may have grabbed a guy who not only isn't worth much to the museum but one who may also have been about to be fired."

"If we were in the same room, I'd give you a hug. Your mind fascinates me."

"Only my mind?"

"I invoke my Fifth Amendment rights, your honor."

"Coward. I have to go. Keep me in the loop, and I'll do the same."

"Sure thing. Stay safe."

"You, too."

"And Hadley?"

"Yes?"

"I'm the one wearing a gun. Your weapon is a keyboard."

"Just another man lording his machismo over a helpless woman."

"If you're helpless, I'm Doris Day."

"Nice to meet you, Doris."

～

Fifty-six minutes later, I heard the text chime on my cell. The text read: *you cost us a day. if we aint got 15 mil by 5 tuesday you gonna cost him his life. Tell you where. Dont test us!*

I was able to overlook the grammar and punctuation mistakes because the message itself caused my anxiety meter to smoke, then catch fire.

"Their demand's impossible, right?" I asked when I answered Brandon's call fifteen minutes later.

"They aren't likely to get it. I don't know much about finances, but the city probably couldn't come up with that much even if it wanted to. Private industries or wealthy individuals would have to pitch in. But if word gets out who these guys are and what they believe, who would donate money that ultimately would support their cause?"

"You'd be surprised. A lot of people are angry, and they blame their circumstances and failures on anyone who isn't just like them. If the kidnappers were savvy—I almost said smart—they'd flood the media with their beliefs and objectives, then wait for millions in donations to roll in."

"They pretty much just did that. They included you—and I'm guessing the *Chronicle* and the radio- and television stations—in the text so you'd spread their message."

"Oh, no. That didn't register. If we do our jobs and report what's going on, we could end up funding their cause. This can't be happening."

"I'm sorry. It is. But you can control the narrative. You can report on Robby's kidnapping and the ransom demand, but if you leave out their motivations, or what we believe are their motivations, you'll still be doing your job. You haven't proven they're the Barrel Proofs or they're motivated by white supremacy, right?"

"I've gathered evidence, and if I were a DA, I'd probably have enough to get a search warrant but not enough to bring an indictment. Benny Washington, Greg Wurt, Ed Colapinto, and Chris Knudsen have all posed flashing a sign that is similar to one that white supremacists have appropriated, a modified OK sign. I've seen the photos. When I challenged Greg about them, I surprised him with the name Barrel Proofs, and he almost swallowed his tongue. I probably would've saved him if he had, but, on principle, I would've counted to four, maybe five, before I intervened."

"You've made great progress. We should get this on the record. But it's your word against Greg's. Do you have any proof?"

"Give me a second." I sent him the photo of the photo of Greg, Ed, and Chris flashing the sign.

"Nice. It's a start," he said. "I won't ask you to come to the station, but why don't we meet at Keiler again?"

"I'd like to, but can it wait? I have to persuade my staff to do their jobs without fully doing their jobs. Yes, withholding information happens in nearly every story. But leaving out what someone is wearing during an interview and burying the motivations of hostage takers are worlds apart."

"I understand. But I think you're letting your contempt for racists influence your approach. You wouldn't publish a story that contained facts you hadn't verified—for various reasons, not the least of which is you could get sued. When you have proof that would win a libel suit, you'll include their motivations in your stories. Until then, I have faith you'll handle this situation properly. Don't over-think it."

"Okay, thank you. But I'm also worried about something else. During my confrontation with Greg, he threatened to have Ed cancel my contract to use the *Chronicle*'s press to print *Pulse*. If he does that, then *Pulse* will be finished, and we've only just started."

"Can he cancel the contract? How solid is it? Wouldn't he have to find a loophole?"

"Dakota drafted it, so it's more than solid—it's ironclad. Maybe Ed couldn't tear up the contract without subsequently being dragged through a lawsuit, but he could tell the press guys to sabotage *Pulse*. They could riddle it with errors, rewrite the editorials, wash out every photo. We'd be done."

"Don't get ahead of yourself. Why did Greg threaten you with that?"

"Because I hit him right where it hurts—in his Barrel Proofs."

"Then the best solution—if you permit me to float a plan without accusing me of man-splaining—"

"Jackass."

"—would be for PPD to solve these cases and for *Pulse* to report every development. If Greg and Ed are involved—and we know they had something more than a work relationship with Chris Knudsen—they'll topple, and the threat to you will disappear. Who knows what will happen to the *Chronicle* if Ed and Greg go to prison?"

"Now look who's getting ahead of himself. We don't know what they're involved in and have proven them guilty of nothing. So, please forgive me if for now I consider Greg's threat to be threatening."

"All valid points. I hate when people say, 'everything will be okay,' because no one knows that to be true. In this case, however, my gut tells me at least some things will be within shouting distance of being okay."

"I didn't realize I was dating such a fount of positivity."

TWENTY-FIVE

THE SURROGATE MOTHER

"I know I've been through worse. I understand that, but this feels like more than I can tolerate," I said in the small, well-appointed office of Dr. Elaine Bourget, the psychiatrist who had helped me process my troubled childhood and my subsequent traumas. I hadn't seen her in more than a year, but, after speaking with Brandon, I discovered that I was having trouble taking in a full breath. I called her and left a message. Two hours later, she returned my call.

She wore a matronly dress, blue with white polka dots, and black Mary Janes that I wouldn't have worn but that suited her and her temperament well. Her wavy light-brown hair touched her shoulders, and her brown eyes almost always conveyed empathy. During our previous sessions, I'd found her demeanor soothing, as though she was a concerned, wise grandmother, although she was eight years younger than I was, and I'd never met my grandmothers.

"What do you believe will happen if your current situation exceeds your level of tolerance?"

"I don't know what you mean."

"How will that intolerable stress level manifest itself? Do you think you'll have a heart attack or stroke?"

"No, probably not."

"Do you think you'll consider self-harm?"

"No. Okay, I get it. I can tolerate more than I think I can. But because you taught me how to examine my emotions and motivations more carefully than I used to, I'm admitting that the murders and robberies and Robby being kidnapped and the threat of not being allowed to print *Pulse* are a small part of my anxiety. I think I'm more frightened by how I feel about Brandon." She nodded. I wanted her to give me credit for self-awareness. All I received was the nod, so I continued.

"We've only been on two dates, but he's been in my head since the night we met in Noble Park. Not that I saw him as a romantic partner then. I didn't. I'd just lost Matt. But Brandon stood in such contrast to the other officers—sympathetic and a good listener—that eventually I started to question what Matt and I had had. Each time Brandon and I interacted, I started to see how different he was from every man I'd dated. Even though he was in a position of power—and wore a uniform to prove it—he didn't condescend to me, although I was half out of my mind with grief, stress, and a lack of sleep. He teased me, but he never made me feel less-than when we spoke."

I wanted her to tell me that what I was telling her was proof of perfect mental health, but she only nodded again.

"And now we're involved. And it feels like we're involved far more deeply than we should be after only two dates. My feelings for him frighten me."

She set her notepad and pen on the small table beside the upholstered chair she sat in. She clasped her hands in her lap and said, "I don't usually use myself as an example. I generally speak abstractly when illustrating a point. But this isn't a rule, just a tendency. The public has adopted certain dating strictures: Don't kiss on a first date, don't call too soon thereafter or you'll look desperate. Play hard to get and he'll want you more. The third date is the make-or-break date—the one many people consider the sleep-together date. This is garbage, every bit of it. Kiss him if you want, call him if you want, and if you don't want to sleep with him until he marries you, that's fine, too. What matters is how you feel. If you proceed honestly, examine your motives and your dating history, and if you're able to assess yourself and your past critically—trust me, you have no trouble there, Hadley—then do whatever feels right."

I nodded. After a few seconds I asked, "You were going to use yourself as an example."

"Right. Years ago, I went on a first date with Chad, and it was nothing like any of the many first dates I'd experienced. It was like we'd grown up together as neighbors, although we'd met at a party the night before. The date was so magical that I didn't leave his side for the next three days. We've been blissfully married for nine years. Most of those naysayers who give dating advice would condemn me for how I behaved. Most of them are afraid and repressed, so they mistake weakness and fear for morality. They impose their beliefs on others—and feel superior while doing so. I broke every rule, and I'd happily do so again. I've only seen one partnership that I believed to be in the same ballpark as the one Chad and I share. We owe our success to self-examination and the fact that we communicate, communicate, communicate."

"Congratulations. I'm glad you found each other. You're saying I should trust myself."

"Yes, trust yourself. Our time's up, but I have to say this: You aren't afraid of how amazing you feel around Brandon. You're afraid he'll disappear the way Matt did, and you'll fall back into darkness. But Matt's murder defied the odds. It was awful luck, and Brandon is a very different man, from what you've told me. You said he waited for a year and a half until you thought you were ready to date again. From what you've said about him, I feel comfortable declaring him a catch." She smiled. "I saw the video of the two of you kissing. From what I could see, neither of you appeared to be holding back, and that's not a criticism. He won't disappear on you, not after waiting that long, and not if you admit you are not your past. Disappointment, emotional abuse, violence, alcoholism, and neglect defined your childhood, but hope, satisfaction, and love can define your present and future."

"Thank you very much, Elaine. You're amazing. May I see you next week?"

"If this time works for you, it's yours."

"See you then."

As had been true when I'd seen Elaine in the past, I left her office feeling much better about myself and the world. For almost two minutes I believed I deserved to be in a healthy, supportive, fun, inspiring relationship. But then I did what was developing into a bad habit: I turned on my phone.

"Hadley," Teresa said in the voicemail she'd left me, "I'm letting you know I'm covering the protest at City Hall. It's big now and growing by the minute. I'm taking photos of the signs—some of which are funny, others scathing—but I'm not comfortable climbing a tree across the street the way that *Chronicle* photographer did the last time people protested like this. Maybe it's time we buy a drone. I'll keep you posted."

Teresa's message didn't convey horrible news, especially because she was only covering her beat, City Hall, and a protest there was news. But the reminder that the world could be ugly, frightening, and dangerous slapped me out of the happy-fuzzy state I'd been in.

I drove ten blocks from Elaine's office to City Hall but couldn't find parking. Every space in the city lot and on the surrounding streets was taken. I found a space three blocks away, walked to City Hall, and eased my way through the crowd of about five hundred people until I saw the oval of protesters holding signs moving back and forth across the lawn and the walkway. Some of the signs read:

Get FIRED UP in Paducah!
Pay the Ransom. Bring Robby Back!
Paducah's new slogan: Quilts Afire!
Fat Quarters, Applique and Kidnapping!
Just More Fake News. Everything's Fine!

Hey, Cops — Hire Hadley!
Paducah's Reputation Again Gets Burned
What's next? Pestilence, famine, feminism?

The protesters weren't showing a unified front, which was fine with me because the First Amendment was on full display. Eventually, I found Teresa and asked her to show me her photos. I had nothing against climbing a tree to get a good shot, but why risk ruining my outfit if at least one of Teresa's photos was publishable? She showed me eight great shots. I commended her for her efforts and headed to the office.

I checked my email, and among the eighty-three I'd received I found one that Brandon had sent from his home computer.

It read:

Hadley,

You probably would have preferred I didn't look into it, but I had to do something after you told me about the present left on your doorstep. I questioned most of the officers, and one of them let me know he was pretty sure Officer Shannon had something to do with it. He heard Shannon badmouthing you in the locker room. Shannon denied involvement when I confronted him. I talked to your neighbors and found two teenage boys, both sixteen, who admitted Stoddard paid them fifty dollars each to drop their pants on your porch. They said they felt obligated because he's about to be our next mayor. Suzanne Bigelow won't likely bring charges against him, although vandalism and encouraging the delinquency of minors would be on the table. I'd like your opinion about how to proceed. I'll let it go if you want me to. At a minimum, you should catalogue every act of vandalism and harassment, by

anyone, including PPD, so we have something actionable, if
you want to go that route. I'll give you the same advice I gave
Dakota: Security cameras work. They won't prevent problems
—although they can be deterrents—but they can help after the
fact. We didn't need more evidence the Stoddards are awful,
but now we have it if you want to use it. Please forgive me if I
overstepped.

Best,

Brandon

One mystery solved, and it was a relief, if not a surprise. The
Stoddards had proven for generations to be classless and less-than-
enthusiastic adherents to the law. At least Officer Shannon wasn't
responsible. I'd thought he might have been after our rocky conversation in the Walmart parking lot. He could've been having a bad day,
but my guess was that he had more issues with women than he
admitted to himself. Bad apples exist in every profession—the entire
barrel had apparently spoiled at the *Chronicle*—so I set out to prove
that plenty of good journalists existed by being one.

I'd known in my gut that Benny and Chris were the keys to what
was going on, even though I couldn't articulate why. I didn't know
how they played into the theft of the quilts or in Robby's kidnapping.
However, my instincts and my years of investigative journalism told
me they did, so I pulled again on the threads I'd pulled earlier—going
over my notes a third time, checking my inbox to see if I'd missed any
helpful emails, and visiting Facebook again. Jackpot.

In a message from a profile that Mark Zuckerberg and his
minions must have overlooked while ridding Facebook of fake
accounts, I read: *Look into Fiona Mahan. That's all I'm gonna say.
You're the reporter. Investigate.* The name on the account was Adee
Do, and the photo was of the actor in a television commercial for a

plumbing company that advertised in the Los Angeles area in the 1980s. I had to look up that information. I wondered what the pseudonym said about whomever sent me the message. That she or he was older than I was? From the West Coast? A fan of television? Of plumbing? Who knew?

The sender was less important than the tip, so I proceeded as though the tip was worth investigating. Could someone—a Stoddard or another of my growing number of enemies—be trying to distract me from the stories I was pursuing by feeding me a red herring? Possibly, but I couldn't afford to think that way, and I also had no idea what to do next.

Robby Golden could show up dead in just over twenty-four hours, or the Barrel Proofs could kill him sooner, then disappear. I had interacted two or three times with Robby when I worked A&E for the *Chronicle*, and he had been professional, personable, and likable, if a little uptight. I wouldn't have been crestfallen if the BPs had kidnapped Nick Stoddard or Ed Colapinto or Greg Wurt. Of course, I would've wanted these hostages to make it through the ordeal—but frightened, chastened, and significantly worse for wear.

I found a profile on Facebook for a Fiona Mahan who lived in Nashville. I messaged her but couldn't find a phone number. I used a trick I learned while watching "Who Wants to Be a Millionaire?" I phoned a friend.

I met Audrey Root while both of us were reporters for the *Daily Bruin*, UCLA's student newspaper. As I had, Audrey had taken a series of journalism jobs after she'd graduated. We'd made our way to bigger papers with each jump, and we shared a newsroom again in Nashville. But when my mom got sick, I did what every fiber of my being told me I shouldn't have done.

I hadn't spoken with my mom, Ellen Carroll, in twelve and a half years when I received a voicemail from her while I was reporting a story about a house fire. When I saw that she'd called, I broke out in a head-to-toe sweat, my pulse raced, my hands shook, and my head filled with panic.

I didn't listen to her message until I was at home at the end of the workday. I debated whether to delete it without listening to it. I knew my mother would only call for one of three reasons: She needed money, she was dying, or Jenny was in trouble again. I sat in the lounge chair and meditated for three minutes before listening to her message.

"Hey, Had. Been a while, hasn't it? How you been? I ain't been great. Ha, that's some understatement there. Get back to me soon." She slurred every S. I was triggered again, shivering this time as though freezing. It took me an hour before I got the courage to return her call. I was tempted to down two shots of Maker's Mark first, but then I'd be emulating her. Since the age of five I'd been determined not to behave as she did, speak as she did, or treat people as she did. She was a perfect inverse role model.

I returned her call, and our conversation was every bit as traumatic as my worst-case scenario imagined it would be. She had given me a hundred reasons not to communicate with her, and as I listened to her berate me, my lifestyle, my career choices, my failures as a sister and a daughter, and my dismal dating record, I wondered why I hadn't broken off communication with her many years earlier than I had. I knew she was building up to her big news. As she'd always done, she had to try to drag me down to her level before conveying it.

Eventually, she told me the second medical opinion confirmed her terminal cirrhosis diagnosis. I made it through the call, asked for an emergency leave of absence from the *Tennessean,* and moved into her hovel in Calvert City, Kentucky, as soon as I could.

She was supposed to have only a few months to live after hepatorenal syndrome (kidney failure) was added to her advanced decompensated liver disease. My mom was meaner than a rabid wildebeest and taught mules how to be stubborn, so she lasted eleven months. She filled every one of those days with acrimony, accusations, and ingratitude. My bottled-up responses sent my blood pressure soaring and made for sporadic sleep filled with nightmares. I had responded verbally to her taunts and insults when I was a girl, sometimes after she'd slugged me or thrown a bottle of Jim Beam at me, but mostly before she did. I'd said what needed to be said, knowing what was coming.

Despite the physical injuries I'd sustained, I believed that fighting back verbally, the only way I knew how, had served me well. At the least, doing so had sharpened my wit and bolstered my resolve. But, during those eleven months, I couldn't bring myself to argue with her, or even to disagree with her. I was her punching bag. I hated myself and was proud of myself for allowing her to continue to abuse me. The day before she died, she spoke her last words: "Thought you'd help me but guess not."

I had bitten my tongue for more than thirteen years, but as I watched her casket being lowered into the ground, I thought, "Your best wouldn't have been good enough, Mom, and you, Jenny, and I know you never even considered giving us your best. I'm glad you gave me life, but you gave us little more than pain and anguish after we were born, and we wear those wounds everywhere we go. Goodbye, Mom. May you be someone else in the afterlife."

I threw a handful of dirt on the casket and put a second handful in a baggie because Jenny asked me to. She didn't attend the funeral (only four people did, including the priest), but she wanted me to bring her a "souvenir." I didn't return to the *Tennessean*. Instead, I returned to Paducah for reasons I didn't understand. I eventually landed a job at the *Chronicle* as the city reporter before I became the education reporter, then worked A&E.

That Monday afternoon, with the BPs holding Robby Golden hostage and panic spreading through Paducah, Audrey Root and I caught up for a few minutes by phone (she'd just gotten engaged and was about to call to tell me the good news). While we chatted, she found Fiona Mahan's number in the newspaper's impressive database and gave it to me.

I called Fiona, who answered, "This Fiona, what you want?" Her voice sounded like a talking ashtray submerged in honey. Her

Tennessee accent was so thick that it made my western Kentucky twang seem like a ripple compared to her tidal wave.

"Hello, my name is Hadley Carroll, a reporter for *Paducah Pulse* in Kentucky."

"Where?"

"Paducah."

"'K. You callin' 'bout Chris, ain't you?" I didn't know why I was calling, but she just told me.

"Yes."

"What you wanna know?"

"How did you two know each other?"

"You bein' cute?"

"No, ma'am. I'm really asking."

"His wife sent you?"

"No, ma'am. I'm calling because Chris worked at the *Paducah Chronicle*, and he was killed in what Nashville PD have classified a homicide."

"Everyone know that, so I don't get why you's callin'."

"You brought up Clover Knudsen. Were you and Chris seeing each other romantically?"

"Ain't no romance 'bout it. Just animal attraction, like Daddy would call it."

"So, you're confirming on the record that you and Chris were intimate?"

"Intimate. Where you get this stuff? We were doing it, loud and every chance we got."

"Okay. Do you have any thoughts on his death?"

"Like is I sad and stuff?"

"No. Do you believe he was murdered? And, if so, do you have any suspicions about who could have killed him?"

"'Course he was murdered. Witness saw a guy jump from a truck into a getaway car."

"Okay. What about thoughts on who might have killed him?"

"How dumb you think I is?"

"Excuse me?"

"You heard me. You think 'cuz you call with your uptown accent you can call me stupid, and you ain't gonna get no backtalk?"

"I did not call you stupid or imply it. I asked if you have any idea who could have killed him."

"Same thing. You think if I knew who done it—ain't sayin' I do—I'd tell a reporter? That's a whole new kinda dumb. Us Mahans ain't got no education but got street-smarts for weeks. Bet you got the opposite. We done."

"I'm sorry—"

Click.

TWENTY-SIX
PAINT BY NUMBERS

"Well," Clover Knudsen said when she answered her door, "I didn't expect to see you again, but please come in."

It was 6:45 Monday evening. Because Fiona had hung up on me before she told me much, I'd decided to drive to Murray and hope that Clover was home, relying on my history of having had much more success when I interviewed people in person. It's a lot more difficult to usher someone out of your home than to cut short a phone conversation.

"Hello, Clover. I'm glad you're home. I only have a few questions. Is now a good time?"

"As good as any," she said. We sat where we had during our first interview, but this time I could hear her five kids playing/fighting in one of the bedrooms.

"Can I get you some sweet tea?"

"No, thank you. I'm fine. I'll be quick, but I have a few difficult questions to ask you."

"What, like math?" She laughed.

"Not quite. What is the nature of your relationship with Ed Colapinto?"

She smiled a smile that was half smirk. "All you reporters ain't morons, are you?"

"No. Some of us can even read."

"Cute. How much you know?"

"I followed you to the house he owns on Robertson. His Mercedes was there when you were. That's how much I know."

"Not much, then." She smile-smirked. She wore a multicolored, bedazzled sweatshirt featuring a unicorn at the end of a rainbow that made me grateful I had taste.

"I could stall or lie," she said, "or we could go round 'n' round, but I got stuff to do. I'll just tell you. I started out taking care of his parents. Both of 'em got dementia. Sad as all get out. Ed and me hit it off. What can I say? It happens. Living with Chris wasn't all moonbeams and chocolate."

"How long have you been having an affair?"

"Why's it matter?"

"I don't know that it does, but my job is to gather information, then analyze it and write informative stories. How did it start?"

"How does any relationship start? We liked how the other looked, started flirting, then, wham, it's on."

"And Chris knew about it?"

"He's why I let it happen. Never stepped out on him and never planned to, but one day I'm doing laundry and find a love note in the jacket he wears to work. The note had those stupid hearts dotting the i's, you know? Some tramp with worse penmanship than my youngest and the grammar of a chipmunk telling him she loves him and can't wait 'til they can be together for real. Made me sick. Really sick. Barely made it to the bathroom. I confronted him when he got home, and I'll give the rat credit: He didn't deny it. We got five kids, so what am I gonna do, leave him and take a second job at FiveStar on the nightshift so my kids grow up thieves and junkies? No. I figured, two can play that game, and I let Ed's flirting lead to something soon enough."

A loud crash, followed by screams, came from the bedroom.

Clover leaped from her chair and ran toward the door, which opened before she reached it. Two blond girls shouted, "Mom!" and Clover asked, "What happened?" One of them said, "The boys ruined our game," while the other said, "They're bad, Mom. I hate them." It took a few minutes for Clover to get the boys into their room and to settle down the girls, but eventually she returned and said, "Sorry. Never a dull moment, as Momma used to say. She had her hands full, too. Seven of us Mackeys back in the day."

"They must keep you busy. I only have a couple questions. Why did you lie to me about working for Ed? If you'd told me you look after his parents while your kids are at school, why would that matter?"

"Didn't want you going after Ed, now that Chris is dead. Didn't want you thinking Ed had anything to do with the murder. Chris told me Ed asked him to do something he didn't want to do, didn't feel comfortable doing, for a friend. But we needed money in a lot bigger way than I knew because apparently Chris was spending something fierce on that tramp. But he tells me, 'Took care a that problem like the smart husband I am,' and he closes my hand around a grand—ten hundreds."

"He did whatever he'd felt uncomfortable doing? That's how you're interpreting the cash?"

"Pretty much, but the way he said it sounded wrong. Didn't just say, 'I took care of it,' but added the part about being smart. Look, he wasn't dumb—he was great with machines and tools and cars and putting together cheap furniture—but in all the years we been together, ain't never heard him call himself smart. Not once. But when he hands me the grand, he says it. And I can't figure any situation that a man like Ed would ask Chris to do something that would require Chris to be smart. Fix something, drive someone somewhere, sure. But it just sounded wrong. Then he's murdered, so you see why I lied to you about Ed. Who's the first person cops look at when someone's murdered?"

"The spouse."

"Right, then the person the spouse is sleeping with. Didn't want to bring Ed into it."

"If you had been a better liar, you wouldn't have. But I knew you were lying, so I followed you to Ed's."

"Well, there's worse traits than being a bad liar, and I got mosta them." Her smirk this time had no smile in it. She batted her eyes and flipped her hair, and I thought she was trying to seduce me. Maybe she thought that doing so would keep me quiet. Despite her atrocious sweatshirt, I understood how men could find her alluring. At that moment, I was relieved that I wasn't a man who might swoon at an attractive woman batting her eyes at me because the woman who posed with her adorable family in Facebook pictures was bad news. Although she seemed to be forthright, my gut told me she was still lying.

I asked her another question: "How bad was Chris's drinking problem?"

"What made you ask that?"

"He got a DUI two years ago."

"Don't miss much, do you?"

"Try not to."

"He got real bad about three years ago. Don't know what set him off, but I'd smell it on him a lot, like at times when I wouldn't expect to. 'Course, he worked nights, so his schedule was screwy. I didn't mind at first. Daddy always smelled like beer, so I kinda liked it. But then he started yellin' a lot more at the kids. The stress of five kids ain't just a little more stress than four, and four ain't a little more than three. It's the difference between walking your dog and grabbing a greased pig. Anyway, I told him he had to stop. I'd had enough, but that didn't to it. Then the cops and court told him he had to stop."

"Did it work?"

"Yes. He went to AA, got a sponsor. Working the steps is what he called it. I mean, I think it worked. I never smelled it on him again. But who knows? Didn't know about that tramp 'til they were together a long time, and that tramp practically drained us dry."

She was lying, but I thanked her, said goodbye, and left. She'd uttered at least one tramp too many.

I drove to the office while resisting my impulse to call Brandon. I was learning that there was a fine line between enthusiasm and neediness. I could justify calling him because Paducah's streets were swarming with law enforcement officers from at least four agencies in pursuit of kidnappers and blackmailers who, in effect, were holding Paducah hostage. I had hardly seen any locals or tourists on my drives to and from Elaine's office, and the people brave enough to tempt fate by being outside during this madness were all protesting at City Hall. So, as a journalist whose job description included writing about stress-inducing developments, I could have called Brandon without anyone questioning my motives.

But I didn't call him. Instead, I dialed Dakota. She and I usually spoke every day, if only to say, "Hello. I miss you. No time to talk, but we will soon."

"I was just about to call you," she said when she answered. "As usual, we're simpatico. How are you?"

"I'm doing as well as can be expected amid the mayhem. How about you? Were you going to call for a reason?"

"I'm okay, I guess. Well, not really. I was going to call because I want to cry on your shoulder."

"Oh, no. What's wrong?"

"Can we get together?"

"You're scaring me, D. What's wrong?"

"Nothing catastrophic. It's Paul, but I want to discuss it in person."

"Of course. I have to complete a few tasks here, and Ash and Trapunto have probably forgotten who I am, so can we meet at my place in an hour?"

"See you then."

I asked the reporters if they'd like to go home. They declined, saying they intended to cover every aspect of the breaking stories thoroughly. I told them to include every second of overtime and commended them for their stellar work.

I spent the next forty-five minutes laying out pages as fast as I could. I was well behind my usual schedule, and we went to press every Tuesday night at 8. Our run had to be completed before 11 so the *Chronicle* could start its run. I'd discussed that week's advertisements with Astin Taylor, our young part-time ad director whom I hoped to train to become a reporter one day. I had taught her everything she needed to know about advertising, and she was doing a better than adequate job on the occasional writing assignments I gave her.

The ads dictated that we would have thirty-six pages that week. Because *Pulse* was still relatively new, it had a higher ratio of copy to advertising than it would if our ad base had been larger. That made for better reading but made it more difficult to fill our pages. As a result, we ran more photos on occasion than were warranted. Thankfully and unfortunately, the robberies, murders, kidnapping, ransom demands, and protests filled every column inch that wasn't filled by photos or ads. I improved upon the fastest designing pace I'd ever had, hoped I hadn't also broken my personal record for design errors, and called it an evening.

I said goodnight to Dan, the only reporter still working, and walked out the front door into the night. I walked across the parking lot to my truck, opened the door, and felt a powerful thud between my shoulder blades, followed immediately by another thud against the truck. I flinched in surprise as the pain, sound, and torrents of red confused and frightened me. Had I been shot? Within a second, I realized I was more startled than in pain, and I saw the red that dripped down the windows and mottled my hair for what it was: paint.

I turned around, hoping to see the throwers of the paint balloons, but I only saw two dark figures of medium size running around the far corner of the building. Such a weak identification would be meaningless.

After I calmed down and caught my breath, I opened the hatch on the back of the truck shell and grabbed two of the many towels I kept there to dry Trupunto. He'd shredded most of them, but they still proved to be semi-effective to wipe paint from my hair, neck, blouse, and truck. After smearing paint around for a while, I grabbed a sweatshirt covered in dog hair from the back, took off my blouse, pulled on the sweatshirt, and sat in the driver's seat, ready to do what I'd hoped to do about ten minutes earlier: head home.

But I noticed something stuck under the windshield wiper. I got out, removed the piece of printer paper, unfolded it, and read what was written in twenty-four-point Comic Sans: *Stop investigating now or this will be your last investigation!!!*

I thought the three exclamation points were unwarranted, and Comic Sans is used by easily distracted second graders, but I took the message for the death threat it was. What little calmness I'd managed to achieve after partly de-painting myself was replaced by my fight-or-flight response. Because I'd worked hard in therapy to eliminate flight from my choice of possible actions, I had no choice but to fight.

Of course, I couldn't physically confront a note, and I had no idea who'd printed it in a substandard font. I didn't know which of my enemies had left it, but I suspected that my mayoral opponent was responsible. He'd paid two teenagers to soil my porch, so I believed him capable of paying them to commit assault-by-paint balloon. But when I thought about the level of escalation from vandalism and fourth-degree assault (they could have put out my eye or eyes, after all) to a death threat, I started to wonder whether Stoddard, as corrupt and immoral as he was, had it in him to leave such a note. To my mental To-Do List, I added, "Buy security cameras for the house and office."

I set the note in the passenger seat, hoping I hadn't smudged any fingerprints that might have been left by the assailant or assailants. I admitted I couldn't fight an opponent I couldn't even identify. I was not as physically strong, as politically connected, or as morally bankrupt as the people who had been harassing me. But I was determined and tenacious, and I would put my intellect up against anyone's, at least anyone I knew, with the possible exception of Dakota. And maybe Brandon. So, I would fight the only way I knew how: by outthinking my opponents.

I made this bold and defiant decree while I drove home. I was so distracted while steeling my resolve that I took a wrong turn. I tried to chalk this mistake up to a moment of absent-mindedness and not to mental infirmity. But by the time I pulled into my driveway and parked next to Dakota's Range Rover, I thought I had only a thirty-percent chance to win the fight against my unknown opponents.

Fortunately, I've always liked being the underdog.

Unfortunately, Dakota's driver's-side rear tire was flat and had the wooden hilt of a knife sticking out of it.

TWENTY-SEVEN
INCH BY INCH

I must not have erased the concerned expression from my face as well as I thought I had because when Dakota saw me, she asked, "What's wrong, Hads?"

She sat in the chair I usually read in, across from Ashley, who lay on the couch, with Trapunto and Chica snuggled on the floor beneath her. Trapunto raised his head, looked at me, but stayed where he was. I petted them both.

"Just stressed," I said. I bent over to hug Ash, who scooted to an upright position so I could sit beside her. Dakota came to me, we hugged, and I sat beside Ash.

"What's in your hair?" Dakota asked.

"Paint. It ruined my blouse, which is why I'm wearing this dirty sweatshirt. How are you both?"

Dakota nodded at Ash, asking her to go first.

"Pretty bad, actually," Ash said. "I mean, the shock of Grammie's death kinda wore off, but now the grief and reality that she's really gone—and I have to go through my life without her—are worse. I thought it would get easier."

"It will. I promise you, but not soon. You may even feel worse than you do now. After I lost Matt, I thought I was making progress, but the floor fell out from under me. Eventually, though, I regained my footing. This probably sounds bad, or at least inappropriate, but I'm stronger now, more who I am meant to be, more the real me because I lost him and fought through the pain. One of the best pieces of advice I heard about grief came from my therapist. She said, 'The pain of losing someone you love will decrease over time, but you'll probably never be okay with the loss.'"

"That's good," Dakota said. "I'll try to remember that. Do you need to say anything else, Ash?"

"No. Oh, I talked to Kelly, and she told me something weird. She said she was crying about losing Baahir. Her mom, who usually is all about herself and encourages Kelly to deal with her stuff alone, gave her a hug. Her mom said quietly, 'Was only supposed to be a warning.' Kelly asked what she was talking about, and suddenly her mom turned back into the mom she usually is. 'Nothing. Just muttering. Enough bellyaching. Go do the dishes.' Or something like that."

I looked at Dakota, whose expression indicated she was as confused as I was. "What kind of warning?" I asked.

"That's what Kelly asked three times," Ash said. "Didn't get an answer, so she went ballistic and accused her mom of having something to do with Baahir's murder, or she knew about it in advance. Or something."

"That brings conspiracy into this mess," Dakota said. "That's a significant development. It means Kelly's mom ... what's her name?"

"Iris Sprague, Nick Stoddard's younger sister," I said.

"Okay, it means Iris Sprague somehow knew Mahan. What's his first name?"

"Durrell," I said.

"Iris Sprague somehow knew Durrell Mahan, or that's how it looks," Dakota said.

"And knew Baahir was only supposed to be warned, but we don't know about what," Ash said.

"Wait a second," I said. "What if she meant warned as in threatened? As in, 'I'm warning you.' If that's what she meant, then the most likely supposition is that Durrell was supposed to threaten Baahir, not kill him. Could that be what she meant?"

"Makes more sense than the nothing I've come up with," Dakota said.

"Do you think that means Durrell was supposed to tell Baahir to stop seeing Kelly?" Ash asked.

"That would be my guess," I said. "A lot of parents would object to their daughters dating someone from another race and religion. It's sad. In my experience, most people give us plenty of reasons to dislike them, so if we're looking for reasons to reject people, we don't have to use race, religion, gender, political party, where they're from, etcetera. We don't need more than the way they treat people, their contempt for the less fortunate, their inability to empathize—"

"Showing me their food when they chew," Dakota said. "Their lack of personal hygiene and grooming—"

"The way they treat their pets," Ash said. "Or the disgusting way they keep their cars. Come on, people, you're driving a trashcan."

"See," I said. "Plenty of reasons to dislike people but no reasons to generalize. I know I'm speculating, which I try to avoid doing as a journalist, but let's say that Iris didn't hate Baahir for his fashion sense but because he had the audacity to date her daughter. Where does that leave us?"

"It leaves us to conclude that she hired Durrell to threaten Baahir," Dakota said. "He said something like, 'Leave Kelly now, or you'll regret it.' But the threat turned deadly."

"That's awful," Ash said, "but sounds possible."

"I think it does, too," I said. "Iris is a Sprague by marriage, but she's a Stoddard by blood. I think that family must've been fed toxins instead of baby food. They are wrong on so many levels. I think it's safe to proceed as though our hunch about Iris's motivations is correct."

"Proceed how?" Ash asked.

"That's the salient question, isn't it?" Dakota asked.

None of the answers we came up with was definitive about which next steps we should take, but they all included some version of "we should poke around until we discover an actionable clue."

The discomfort I'd felt since I saw the knife in Dakota's tire had been piled on top of the panic I'd felt at being hit by a paint balloon and receiving a death threat. Dakota had asked to get together so she could talk about an issue she was having with Paul, and when I'd seen her sitting across from Ash, who was dealing with complex grief, I couldn't bring myself to mention the knife, the note, or the balloons. I'd been engaging in conversation, but I'd also been suppressing information that could be relevant to the crime spree.

I made tea and decided to prompt Dakota to discuss whatever was going on with Paul.

"I feel petty for bringing this up while all the madness is going on," Dakota said, "but it's significant to me and my future, so I'd like to hear what you think."

"Of course," Ash said.

"Always," I said.

"During my first date with Paul, I found myself thinking I could be on my last first date. And it continued to improve right through our kiss. And let's face it, no matter how well-established, kind, funny, and hot your date is, if kissing doesn't work, there is no relationship, right?"

"That's how I feel," Ash said, "even though I've only really kissed two boys. Truth or Dare doesn't count."

"No, it doesn't," I said. "A player on the UCLA basketball team asked me out. Every player there is a big deal. I was shocked, to be honest, because I figured he'd be with a cheerleader or someone else who was overtly gorgeous. I'm attractive, but not like that."

"You're beautiful," Ash said.

"Stop your nonsense, Hads," Dakota said. "False modesty is beneath you."

"Okay, if I'm gorgeous or beautiful, then which words should we use to describe you, D?"

"That's not fair. I hate being reduced—"

"I'm not reducing you. I never said you are *only* exquisite. Okay, that's the word we'll use. Go on, D, I shouldn't have interrupted you."

"Finish the story," Ash said.

"You knew the ending as soon as I started to tell the story: We hit it off well enough for me to allow him to kiss me at the end of the night. He stepped in, planted one on me, and his lips felt like a squid drenched in olive oil—but tasted much worse."

They laughed, and Dakota continued. "The second date went just as well as the first, up to a point. We were eating a delicious meal at Cynthia's. We'd shared a bottle of wine, and I felt more comfortable in my skin than I had in a long time. But then Paul said, after taking my hand in his across the table, something along the lines of, 'If we continue to progress as it feels we are progressing, and we take that final step, I'd want you to stay home and take care of Paulie. What are your thoughts?' I started to laugh because I didn't think that a man who had entertained me, intrigued me, and made me think I could be on my last first date could really be asking me to stop being a lawyer to become a stay-at-home mom. Not that there's anything wrong with that for anyone who chooses to make that choice. But for a man on a second date to assume that his antiquated worldview—at least from my perspective—would supersede my career, the one I've given decades of study and hard work to? I was dumbfounded. It felt like he'd shown me a sliver of who he really is. I'll admit I'm grateful I saw that glimpse of his domineering nature now, rather than on our wedding night, but I still feel devastated."

"I'm stunned," I said.

"I'm confused," Ash said. "I mean, I understand that was a pretty stupid thing for him to say, but you're going to throw away the magic you described because he made one unreasonable comment?"

Dakota said, "Momma isn't big on giving advice. She's more a fan of letting us learn from our mistakes, but when I was fifteen and boys started finding excuses to knock on our door, Momma sat me down and said, 'Remember this: When a man shows you or tells you who he is, always believe him. He might say or do a hundred nice things, make you laugh or buy you pretty things. But the minute he shows you he's cruel or vindictive or chronically lazy or a liar, or he steps out on you, walk away. Those traits don't deserve second chances. Your daddy and I have our problems like everyone else, but if he was any of those things, we wouldn't be us anymore. Do you understand what I'm telling you?' I told her I did, and I took her message to heart. The second I learned Freddie was delusional and lazy, I packed my bags."

"You're young, Ash," I said. "I know what I'm about to say may sound condescending, but none of us really knew who we were or would become at your age. Every one of us thought we did, and that's normal. We were still trying on different versions of ourselves. It's true that people can change, but if someone is inherently cruel, mean-spirited, or prone to lash out violently when he doesn't get his way, then it's always wise to steer clear permanently."

"I understand," Ash said.

"Thank you, Hadley," Dakota said. "I was pretty sure you would agree with me, although a big part of me wanted you to say I was overreacting."

"No one else wants you to find and keep love as much as I do," I said, "but I think if you spend more time with Paul, you'll learn he has other views that will make your head spin. I could be wrong, but that's what my gut tells me. I think you should consider explaining exactly why you're not going to give him a third date. I would."

"Yes, you're right," Dakota said. "I clammed up and gave him a peck on the cheek as we left the restaurant, so he had to know I was displeased. But he deserves an explanation."

I carried our empty teacups and saucers to the kitchen, set them in the sink, took a deep breath, and let it out slowly.

"I have to change the subject," I said after I'd sat beside Ash again. "I would rather not discuss this, but because remaining silent could endanger people, I have to tell you that I was hit by a balloon filled with paint in the office parking lot, and another that was meant for me hit the truck. I was hurt and stunned, but when I gathered myself, I saw two figures run around the corner of the building. I couldn't identify them further. Brandon told me that Nick Stoddard paid two teenage boys to squat on my porch, so I think it's reasonable to consider that they were paid to do more of Stoddard's bidding."

"Hads, I'm so sorry. That's awful," Dakota said. "Maybe running for mayor isn't worth it. To paraphrase Momma, Stoddard has shown you who he is, and he's dangerous. He probably considers what he's had those boys do to you to be pranks, but they're crimes—no two ways about it."

"You're right, and on the drive home I wondered whether continuing to run made sense. I was so distracted that I took a wrong turn. I understand your concern. But there's something else, something worse. I received a death threat."

"Oh, no," Ash said.

"No, no, no, no, no," Dakota said. "Why didn't you tell us immediately? You've called Brandon, right?"

"Not yet. All I seem to do is pile my crises on him, and I'm not dating him because I need help from a cop. I'm dating him because I like Brandon, who happens to be a cop. I wanted to calm down before I told you or called him. I wanted to let the latest developments percolate so I could try to figure them out on my own. And I think I have."

"Really? Tell us," Dakota said.

"I'm not saying I know who left the death threat, but I don't think Stoddard or his teenage minions did. Whoever made the threat also stuck a knife in your tire."

"What?"

"I'm sorry. Your driver's-side rear tire has a knife sticking out of it. I'll change it for you."

"You can't be serious," Dakota said.

"Why not?"

"You received a death threat, and my tire got slashed, and you're going to go outside to change my tire? What's wrong with you?"

"I'm fine. If someone had wanted to kill me, I wouldn't have received a death threat, and the tire wouldn't have been slashed. I'd be dead, or at least an attempt on my life would have been made. Instead, I was warned—"

"As Baahir was supposed to be, but he's dead," Dakota said.

"Good point, and I find it perceptive that you should bring up Mahan, however obliquely, because I think these death threats result from my interviews with Fiona Mahan and Clover Knudsen. Clover is sleeping with Ed Colapinto, the *Chronicle*'s publisher, and Fiona was sleeping with Chris Knudsen, who was murdered. Fiona is Durrell's sister, and Chris knew Ed and appeared to be involved in white supremacy, as Benny Washington seems to be. My job, after I change your tire, is to connect Durrell to Chris. I think I know where to begin my search."

"Where?"

"At an Alcoholics Anonymous meeting."

TWENTY-EIGHT
RETURN OF A HERO

"Mind if I come over?" Garrett Hunt asked when he called.

"You're back. Great. See you in a few."

I set the Maker's Mark and a glass where I'd set them during his last visit. His call had interrupted my meditation session, which I settled into after changing Dakota's tire, and saying goodbye to her and goodnight to Ash. Garrett arrived, dressed in black as usual, gave me a tentative hug, and lowered himself with a groan into a chair. He poured himself nearly a full rocks glass of bourbon, and I made note to buy another bottle because one more heavy pour like that would empty the one in front of him.

"How you been?" he asked.

"A ton has gone on, some of it awful, but do you mind if you tell me what you've learned before I tell you what's happened?"

"No problem." He drank a quarter of his drink, set the glass down, and pulled out a pocket notebook, the kind sold at every drugstore. He flipped the pages, found what he was looking for, and read for a few seconds. He said, "I was pretty sure I had it down, but at my age, I can't be sure of anything no more, especially my memory. Happens I got it right this time. Here's what I know." He leaned forward, downed another quarter of the bourbon, set down the glass, and said, "Learned a lot in Roseburg. Physically, it's a beautiful place. Lots of water and trees. But it seems to breed hate. Saw more Confederate flags there than I do here. That surprised me. When I think of Oregon, I think of trees and Portland. I tracked down Benny's story. Talked to her mom, Gina, Greg Wurt's younger sister. She didn't want to tell me a thing. Despite my gruff exterior, I have my charms, or at least an ability to extract information from unwilling communicators. But, no, I didn't use violence, in case you're wondering." He downed another quarter of his drink.

"Gina's house sits next to a green on the Roseburg Country Club, but she's haggard, foul-mouthed, and unsophisticated—says the ugly-as-sin ex-boxer-turned-P.I. She keeps the filthiest house I ever saw, or at least the filthiest nice one. She was probably a real looker once, but, like me, she knows far too much about loss and grief. She said Benny, the original male one, lost his way, got caught up in drugs, mostly meth, went downhill fast, and started dealing. He was found dead, shot in the chest, just off the parking lot of a health-food store up there, Sherm's Thunderbird Market. He had the stem of a red rose stuck down his shirt, so the rose was under his chin. I went to the scene for a sense of the place, but this happened four years ago, so I didn't learn anything." He finished his drink and emptied the bottle into his glass.

"Thing is, the prosecution of Dennis Edwards was ridiculous. Yes, he was a local drug dealer, one of many, and he dealt meth. But none of the meth he sold was found on Benny or in the dump of a trailer three people told me he squatted in. But a cop pulled over Dennis Edwards, caught him holding, and found a dozen roses in his apartment. He was pulled over on Feb. 15, and his girlfriend gave him a dozen roses for Valentine's Day. Somehow, twelve jurors managed to convict Dennis of that murder, along with three others he confessed to committing. Note that I said a dozen roses were found in his apartment, not eleven. I read the trial transcript, and his public defender might be a fine person, but how he graduated law school, I got no idea. I hustled hard and found the guy who sold Benny the Colt Cobra the cops found at his side. 'Course, the cops never found him. Think what happened was the cops and D.A. decided they could solve another murder by throwing this one in with the others they were charging Dennis with. Either that, or someone put pressure on them not to chalk Benny's death up to suicide. I found the original autopsy report."

He smiled broadly, and the sight of his shiny, perfect teeth amidst that broken face was shocking. He laughed and said, "Don't ask me how I got it. Plausible deniability and all that. But anyway, I got it, and the chief Douglas County Medical Examiner wrote 'self-inflicted gunshot wound' as the cause of death. Eight days later, he filed a different report, leaving out the gunshot residue he'd found on Benny's hands and arriving at a different conclusion, one the cops and D.A. used in Dennis's trail. I tracked down Dennis in prison and finagled my way in to see him. He's a bad dude, no question about it, and he deserves to be inside, but he wanted the facts out there."

He pulled the smallest voice recorder I'd seen out of a pocket in his leather jacket. "Here's Dennis Edwards, in his own words. The guards frisked me going in, but this ain't my first rodeo. At my weight, I got folds no one's gonna check closely, and when I found this beauty,"—he held up the recorder—"I knew it would come in handy."

He hit "play," and a deep male voice said, "Ain't gonna lie. I'm here for a reason, doing life 'cause I deserve it. Killed the others. But what do I gain saying I ain't done it if I did? Already got life without. Could tell you I killed Biggie and Tupac, ain't gonna matter none. Think that guy done hisself, but the family don't wanna face it. Look, I told you I'm in here for good reason, but I ain't killed that Benny dude."

"Got that first thing this morning," Garrett said. "Kept hustling, talked to two dozen people total, flew home, and called you."

"That's tremendous work. You're the greatest. Thank you. Are you suggesting that Cassie, to honor her brother, adopted his name and became involved in white supremacy because she believed Edwards killed Benny?"

He drank a quarter of his bourbon. "Can't say when she learned to hate based on skin color, but I'd guess it was long before Benny killed himself. The trailer park she grew up in had half a dozen visible Confederate flags in it. You ask me, Benny's death didn't introduce her to that way of thinking. It put her over the edge. Her mom still calls her Cassie, maybe because she's got a shrine to the original Benny beside the idiot box, even though that idiot box is the biggest flatscreen I ever saw, practically a movie screen. Only saw one picture of her late husband, Dirk Washington, who died less than two years ago in a car crash."

"This is all excellent information. I'll try to confront Benny with what appears to be true: She was the inside person at the museum who let the BPs know which quilts to steal. She's written stories about the museum, and she would be a familiar face there. No one would care if she wandered the halls unescorted. I assume she had to have entered rooms alone and maybe looked in file cabinets."

"Would be my guess. But guessing doesn't pin down much in our professions—just points us in directions, most of them wrong." I laughed. "Good to see you laugh, Hadley, because I got more news, and you could find it disturbing." In a move that reminded me of my mother, he emptied his glass, three quarters full, in one long drink.

I nodded. "But who knows? You might not give it a second thought," he said. "Depends on your interpretation. The two of us, we don't walk around thinking life is lollipops and party hats. We know how ugly it can be, and we both deal in information. My line of work, I can't have too much of it."

"Same with mine."

"Exactly. We sift through mounds of it 'til we find what helps our case, or story, for you. Maybe I misspoke. Maybe what I found will help instead of adding to your troubles."

"Neither of us will know unless you tell me." He smiled.

"Yup, you got me. Here goes. You might wanna take notes."

"Okay, hold on." I hustled to the office and grabbed one of my recorders, a reporter's notebook, and a pen. I returned, sat, flipped to a blank page, wrote Roseburg at the top, hit "record," and nodded.

"Ed didn't make his money the way he tells everyone he did, not most of it, anyway. He made a lot more money being a model than you and I ever have in our careers combined, and he invested well. Don't ask how I know that either. But he knows Greg from way back, like in the late eighties. Still not sure how, but if I had to guess, I'd say Ed met Greg when Greg attended Oregon State, maybe at a party, maybe some other way. Doesn't matter, but they go way back."

"Ed got an idea he could run a land scam. Probably read about a different one that didn't work, and he figured he could correct whatever exposed it. He's a pretty boy and a womanizer of the most disgusting kind, but he's got a head on his shoulders." He slurred the S's in the last word and most of those thereafter.

"He needs financing, and he brings in a local guy named Terry Lee, and another guy you're familiar with, Nick Stoddard."

I stared at him. "Really? When did this scam take place?"

"Early nineties. The shell companies, dummy corporations, tax-avoidance schemes, bankruptcies, and other financial shenanigans worked. What I'm gonna say simplifies it a lot. I spent the flight going through the paperwork, trying to understand the nitty-gritty. Don't think I really do, but I don't have to, not for our purposes. The fact is a talented accountant understood it, and his name was Dirk Washington, Benny and Cassie's dad, Gina's husband, and, significantly, the brother-in-law of Greg, long-time friend of Ed Colapinto, who hired Greg and, it turns out, Benny.

"Trust me, this is the easy version. I got most of this from public records. It was covered extensively in the *Roseburg News-Review* and the *Oregonian*. Ed, Greg, and Terry secured sixty million in financing from various sources, which maybe included Nick Stoddard. They coulda used him for his criminal knowhow. That family should be on the Mount Rushmore of Kentucky crime. The scam involved building an enormous resort and housing development on the edge of town, on the banks of the South Umpqua River. A Jack Nicklaus–designed golf course, a dozen tennis courts, an Olympic-size pool, three playgrounds with barbecue grills at the edges, a skateboard park, even a movie theater and a hotel. All of that weaving around ninety-nine McMansions.

"People from around the country couldn't wait to select lots for their dream homes. The ninety-nine sites were snatched up in just over six months. They broke ground on many of the features, and the golf course was almost completed, when out of nowhere the company that backed the loans, Roseburg Finance Company, declared bankruptcy. Turns out, the likeness and endorsement of one of the key players used to promote Destination Roseburg, Rick Guidry, a Portland real estate billionaire, was used without his permission. Lawsuits flew left and right, but Dirk Washington proved to be a financial magician, and Terry Lee is a brilliant but corrupt lawyer. He buried clauses deep in the boilerplate of the seventy-page contracts each homebuyer signed that exonerated the owners and operators of Destination Roseburg and said refunds wouldn't be issued for any reason, including malfeasance. But he said that in less-obvious legalese. Ed, Greg, Dirk, and Terry successfully fought off the lawsuits and walked away with who knows how much. I couldn't find a single reference to Stoddard in any of the paperwork. The guy's careful, if not smart. But I found two families swindled in the deal who mentioned a snake of a guy with, quote, 'a hillbilly accent,' who said he was from Kentucky. That could describe thousands of people, but when I called Gina, after I'd been to her place and told her I knew all about the Destination Roseburg scam—I fibbed a little—she tried to get the blame off her late husband and put it on Ed and 'that Stutterer guy, from Kentucky.' My guess is they used Stoddard's criminal expertise to write the contracts. I mean, they don't teach how to write fraudulent contracts in law school, so maybe Terry needed some pointers. Or Stoddard could've put up some back-end money to secure the loan from Roseburg Title Company. I only got so far, and I only got access to so many documents, many I didn't have no right to see."

I nodded and realized I'd believed Ed's version of how he'd made his money. The land scam likely made the sums he tallied modeling and investing seem like chump change.

"Any chance you got more booze?" Garrett asked.

"Beer or vodka?"

"Ain't picky, but vodka for now." I went to the kitchen, poured him three fingers in a fresh rocks glass, put the bottle away, and handed him the glass. The vodka was gone by the time I sat down and looked at him. Did he drink this way often? Nightly? Was he trying to commit suicide without admitting it to himself? I made a point to bring up his drinking when his teeth weren't already floating. If his problems were significant enough for him to drink this heavily in my presence, perhaps I shouldn't mention the paint balloons and the death threat to him. Even though it was nearly 11, I intended to call Brandon after Garrett left, so I decided not to mention my recent troubles to Garrett.

Instead, I said, "You made incredible progress. The world would be a much better place if everyone were half as good at their jobs as you are at yours. What relevance does what you discovered about Destination Roseburg have to what's going on here, other than to connect Stoddard to Ed and Greg long ago?"

He raised his empty glass. "More where this came from?"

"I'm sorry, but I don't feel comfortable giving you more. I have some left, but I'm concerned you may not make it into my truck so I can drive you home. If you can't, then I'd have to walk you home, but I shouldn't walk back alone at night."

"Come on, Hadley. You're braver than that. This ain't the bad neighborhood it used to be. Don't strike me as the cowering type."

"I'm not." I didn't want to tell him about the death threat, but he'd kind of forced my hand. Maybe he could provide insight into who might have left it, despite his present condition.

"Someone left a death threat on my truck and shoved a knife into Dakota's tire, so I am not being cowardly by not putting myself outside alone at night. I'm being cautious."

"I'm sorry, really, I am. I'm drunk and not picking up on clues. It's been a tough two days on almost zero sleep. Got a room up there but napped in the rental car for a bit, and only used the room to shower. I'm not on my game now, but what can you tell me about the threat?"

"Not much. A mental-health professional could provide some assessment of a person who would type a death threat in Comic Sans, but I have no clue if that means anything. Standard office paper, folded and tucked under my wiper. I'd bet no fingerprints were left on it. I should've brought it in from my truck but didn't want to touch it again, in case there are prints. And just before I found it, my truck and I were hit by paint-filled balloons. Red paint."

"I've been sitting here drinking nearly all your booze, and you been sitting on that the whole time? I'm an idiot, really. But maybe I can make it up to you."

"You don't need to make anything up to me. You've delivered far more than I expected. I was hoping for some background on Benny that Facebook and other sources couldn't provide. You've truly delivered, but I expect to receive all of your receipts—plane, car, room, food, gas, incidentals—in the next few days."

"Then maybe you won't be so happy with me. I know this sounds like a lie, but I was robbed on my way over here. All the guy wanted was my receipts." He laughed hard and slapped his knee with his right hand.

"You're one stubborn individual. We had an agreement." I wasn't angry, just disappointed. But I learned long ago that disappointment emanated from problem drinkers in direct proportion to the amount of alcohol they consumed. "I really would like those receipts."

"I know we agreed, but you made me feel alive again. This was different than spying on a wayward spouse. Far more important. Thank you. And here's the thing I haven't told you, the ace in the hole. I believe journalists call it burying the lede."

"Okay, I can make peace with you eating the expenses because you insist, but I don't think I can forgive you for burying the lede." I smiled.

"Terry Lee, sixty-four years old, the lawyer who wrote the bogus contracts for Destination Roseburg, moved to Paducah seven months ago. I had to bribe a teenager works for a moving company up there for that info—and, no, you can't reimburse me for that either. I give the kid credit for holding out. When the price was right, he gave me the address the trucks hauled the stuff to. You won't be surprised to learn Terry Lee lives just down the street from that ridiculous castle Ed lives in."

"They're doing it again."

"Wouldn't bet against it."

TWENTY-NINE
MESSAGE SENT

I looked in on Ash, Trapunto, and Chica, who were sleeping. I texted Brandon: *Too late to call?* A few seconds later, my cell rang. "I guess not," I said when I answered.

"Hello," he said. "I was about to call you, but I didn't know if it was too late. With everything you've been going through, thought you might be asleep."

"Any chance you can come over? But not like that."

"Didn't think so, and, yes, I'll be there soon."

When he arrived and hugged me, I needed his hug far more than I thought I did. If I could have melted into him, I would have. I felt so overwhelmed with stress, frustration, indecision, and information-overload that I thought being able to melt sounded great. I kissed him on the neck, then the mouth, and said, "Before we get carried away, I need to show you something." My tone must have revealed my tension because he looked at me with a concerned expression. He touched the paint in my hair.

"What's this?"

"I'll explain, but please give me time. I'm more than happy to see you. I truly needed to, as much as I try to convince myself I'm incapable of such need. I'm scared, and I'll show you why." I walked him to my truck and opened the passenger door. "You probably shouldn't touch it," I said as he leaned in to read the note. He turned toward me with a look on his face I'd never seen: a mixture of anger and disappointment.

"When did you find this?" He closed the door.

"About three hours ago, at work, just after I was hit with a paint balloon."

"Oh, Hadley. I'm sorry you've gone through this at all, let alone without me. But I'm also angry. You know better than to disturb a crime scene, and you should've called me immediately. What were you thinking?"

I felt wounded, unstable. We hadn't disagreed on anything of consequence, but now he was chastising me. But I knew he wasn't trying to belittle me. I also knew he was right because I'd acted inappropriately—but for what I considered a legitimate reason.

"I didn't want to appear to be as needy as these last few days have made me seem. I feel like all I've done is burden you with my problems. And I didn't want you to think I'm only interested in you because you're a cop. I can't keep compromising you and your profession, relying on you to save me. But I also can't seem to get out of harm's way." I started to cry—and so did he.

"Hadley," he said, folding me into his arms. "Please learn to trust that I am who I say I am. I've fallen for you. I know that would scare most women off, maybe even sound deranged, but you are not most women, and we're building something special. Do you believe me?"

"Yes. You wouldn't know this, but I am naturally trusting, or I used to be. But practically everything significant my mom told me proved to be a lie. I'm almost certain Jenny and I don't share the same father, and I have no idea who he is, even if we do. And Matt, a man I pledged to spend my life with, withheld his biggest secret from me. And I've had half a dozen other significant betrayals. So, if I start to believe what people say, I'd be going against the lessons my life has taught me. I'd be stupid, but I'm not stupid."

"Not even close." He let go of me, and we walked to the house, and I closed the door behind us.

"I'm not sure I put it together this way before," I said, "but I probably became a journalist so I could pin down the truth and hold liars accountable. My mom lied constantly. 'No, I'm not drunk.' 'I'll be home for dinner.' 'I swear I didn't steal your babysitting money.' 'I sent the check for your dance lessons.' It was ridiculous. Seems like I should have figured that out much earlier."

He nodded and looked around the room. He saw the two rocks glasses sitting side by side on the coffee table next to the empty bourbon bottle. He looked at the reporter's notebook, pen, and recorder on the couch, and asked, "Company?"

We sat together on the couch. "Garrett Hunt," I said. "He has a major drinking problem that I think is a slow suicide, but he's a magician of investigation. I have no idea how someone so large and so physically unusual manages to get people to open up to him as he does."

"Maybe pity. But I know him, and his mind is one of the most insightful I've ever known. If we were all given the same stack of information, he'd connect all the dots, pin down half the motivations of the parties involved, and be home watching football before we'd sorted the stack into piles. Provided he's not drunk."

"Or even if he is, it seems. Can I get you something? A drink. Leftovers? Or I could make you something. You've cooked for me, but I have yet to whip you up a plate of culinary incompetence."

"I'm fine, as I'm sure your cooking is. What's going on?"

I stood, took the glasses and the bottle to the kitchen, put the glasses in the dishwasher and the bottle in the recycling bin, took a deep breath, and let it out slowly. I returned, sat, and looked at him.

I described being hit by one balloon and missed by another, how I couldn't identify the fleeing suspects, and finding the death threat under the wiper and the knife in Dakota's tire. He asked the questions any cop would have asked, but he did so in a tone that told me he was not just any cop.

I told him what Garrett had told me about his trip to Roseburg. I referred to my notes twice because, as always, I needed to get the facts right. It took me a long time to make sure I told the story as accurately as I could. When I finished it was 12:35.

"That's a lot to process," he said. He stood and looked toward the hall. I said, "Second door on the right."

While he was gone, I wondered whether I'd just destroyed what we were building. He hadn't said a word during my long recitation, and I'd expected him to have expressed surprise at the information Garrett had uncovered. Had I prattled on so much that Brandon now saw me as the collection of wounds and insecurities I often believed myself to be? If he saw me as a wonderful, self-possessed, accomplished woman, then maybe he wasn't as perceptive as I believed him to be.

He returned, sat, looked at me, and said, "You're correct. Garrett is an investigative magician. You and I would avoid using his methods, but he once told me he justified his trips outside of legal territory because he's a good guy, through and through. I'll never forget the phrase he used: 'Laws are made by upper-crusters in ivory towers who don't gotta follow them for people who live in the dirt who gotta break laws just to eat.'"

"He's a poet, in his own way. What do you think of his discoveries?"

"Connecting Ed and Greg to Stoddard way back then is significant, however meaningless that connection is legally. Stoddard wouldn't be brought down by anything you told me. Finding out why Benny changed her name and that her brother likely committed suicide may be interesting, but I don't know how it helps us. That Ed, Greg, and Terry pulled off a successful land scam could amount to the same thing: interesting but unhelpful. Terry moving to Paducah could mean anything or nothing. But from the way you told the story, it seems you think Ed, Greg, Terry, and Nick, or some combination of them, have something to do with the gunfire we lived through, the quilt theft, and the ransom."

"I do. I've made connections I haven't told you about." I told him I thought Chris Knudsen and Durrell Mahan, two murder victims, probably knew each other. I told him I didn't have proof, but I had a plan to find it.

"Okay, but I don't understand what finding a connection between them will prove."

"I'm hesitant to tell you because I don't have proof—I'm only going with my gut—and because you may conclude that I'm insane." He laughed.

"Try me."

"Okay. I'm going to state the following as facts, without the needed speculation. Iris Sprague is a racist and a bigot who hated the fact that her daughter, Kelly, was dating a Muslim from Egypt, Baahir Ali. Iris expressed her anger at the situation to her older brother, Nick Stoddard. Nick and Ed go way back, we've learned, so Nick asks Ed if he knows anyone who would frighten Baahir into walking away from Kelly. In fact, Ed was the boss of just such a person, Chris Knudsen, a press operator, and they shared a dislike of people who don't look and think as they do. I've seen a photo of them posed together flashing what I interpret as a white supremacy sign. I can't prove but strongly suspect they have something to do with the Barrel Proofs. They may not be members, but Greg turned into a conniption personified when I mentioned the name to him. Ed, at the behest of Nick, hires Chris to scare Baahir. Or maybe Nick hires him directly after Ed points Nick in the right direction. For reasons unknown, Chris decides he can't go through with it. He needed money, and the sum offered was probably large enough for him to say yes initially. But he gets cold feet and hires Durrell Mahan to scare Baahir. And Durrell is a big, strong donkey who loves the idea of scaring a minority. But Durrell is the dumbest donkey in the stable, and for reasons I haven't pinned down, Durrell kills Baahir. Durrell's so pumped after the murder that, instead of running, he takes however much time it takes to carve four twenty into a nearby tree. Wait a second, hold on."

I jumped up and hurried to the office. I plugged four twenty into Google. I scrolled through pages of listings confirming that four twenty was a nearly universal shorthand for marijuana and marijuana use. But I wanted to find what I suspected, not what I knew. I kept scrolling. Nothing. I heard Brandon enter the room.

"It has to be here. I know it," I said. I added "white supremacy" to four twenty in the search. I kept searching, page after page of listings. Then I saw a listing for white supremacy symbols. I scrolled down the page past dozens of symbols that proclaimed various forms of hatred. And then I saw it: twenty four; 20/4. Europeans write dates differently than Americans. 20/4 translates to April 20, Adolf Hitler's birthday. Written as Americans would write it: 4/20 or four twenty.

"I found it. I knew it had to be here. Kelly insisted that Baahir didn't do or sell drugs, and Durrell taking time to carve four twenty into the tree makes no sense." Brandon looked over my shoulder at the screen.

"Unless it means something bigger, a cause," he said.

"Yes. Hatred is one thing, but this is an ideology, something worth dying for. This was the key." I paced back and forth across the office. "I have to calm down. Let's go back into the living room."

We did, and he sat. I paced a few times between the couch and the coffee table, and I said, "This ties them all together. Not legally, but otherwise. No marijuana was found in Baahir's dorm room. But Benny found the knife in the tree. Not because she had anything to do with the murder that I know of, but because she was asked to stop eavesdropping on Dan, our cops reporter. She saw the knife, so she had to have seen the four twenty. She didn't see four twenty the way nearly everyone else would, as a reference to marijuana. She saw it as the reference to Hitler that it was. Here's where I start to speculate wildly, but I haven't fallen from the high wire yet, so I'm sticking with the speculation. She sees four twenty and knows Durrell has made a mistake. Maybe she even knows the murder wasn't supposed to happen. That doesn't matter. If she knows Durrell has made a mistake by carving the tree, then she knows something bigger is going on, so she creates a diversion, or maybe a coverup, by including in her story about Baahir a fact not in evidence: marijuana at the murder scene. Sergeant Vazquez of Murray PD said nothing about it to Dan, and Vazquez has proven reliable time after time. So, Benny tried to throw people off the scent."

I sat next to Brandon and gave him a hug. Eventually, I let go and said, "I wish everything we're discovering weren't so terrible, but I feel great that we're making progress."

"You're making progress. I'm just sitting here admiring a brilliant mind at work."

"If Benny knew there was a bigger plan in the works, then she provided the information to the BPs about which quilts to steal from the museum. And if I'm right about any of this, I should find out what the big plan is from her."

"Hadley, you amaze me, but you scare me, too. You and Garrett have put nearly all of this together yourselves. It all has to be verified, and law enforcement can't act on much of what you've speculated about. But it isn't on you to solve this crime spree. I'll admit, if I listen as a layperson, everything you've said ties together, and you are directly responsible for coming to these conclusions because you hired Garrett.

"But various law enforcement agencies are compiling a ton of overtime trying to bring down these guys. You're armed with a fierce intellect and unmatched determination, but the BPs are murderers, so trying to subdue a gun with your brainpower isn't going to end well for you. I'm not going to issue some macho ultimatum, but you promised me you'd behave like a journalist, not a cop."

"Yes, I did. Other than the surveillance—and that's a gray area because journalists are allowed to use their eyes—what have I done that's been out of bounds?"

"I'm not saying you have. I'm saying I'm afraid you might. Confronting Benny will be dangerous because she'll let her bigger, badder higher-ups know you've confronted her."

"Maybe. But everything I've discovered since the Walmart heist on Friday, I've discovered through hustle, persistence, and thought. Trust me, Brandon, I don't even want to flirt with violence. I've lived through far more than my share, and I'm not so messed up that I would court it."

"I know. I'm sorry. I feel more protective of you than I have a right to. I could blame it on having four younger sisters, but I'd be lying. I'm emotionally involved more than I've ever been. I haven't told you this, but I lived with a woman, Janelle, for about three years. She wanted us to marry, and the idea didn't seem unreasonable to me. But that's the way I'd felt: That marriage didn't feel unreasonable. The prospect of it didn't thrill me and make me plan for a happy future. I broke it off when I was finally able to admit that lukewarm is not a good temperature for a bath or a marriage."

"Thank you for telling me that. What happened to Janelle?"

"She met someone, got married quickly. Based on her Facebook pics, she's happy."

"I think most people use Facebook pics to hide reality, or maybe even hide from it. But I hope she found what she was looking for. I'm exhausted, drained from the mental energy and hardly any sleep since Friday. If I were to ask you not to go home, would you take that the way I intend it?"

"What other way could you intend but for me to sleep near you because you've recently received a threat?" He smirked a smirk that made me rethink the nature of my invitation. My therapist had suggested I follow my feelings and do whatever felt right. If I wanted to disregard dating rules and societal expectations, I could because Dr. Elaine Bourget gave me permission to do so.

"Am I being unfair to you?" I asked. "It will be awkward."

"No, it won't. It'll be a messy wonder."

It was my turn to smirk.

We prepared for bed. He retrieved his gym bag from his truck, and I slipped into my blue pajamas with a sewing machine stenciled on the top. I opened a new toothbrush for him and set it by the sink in the upstairs bathroom, outside my bedroom. The only design element of the house that I didn't like was the lack of an en suite bathroom. One hundred and four aspects of the house didn't work, needed to be updated, or no longer had any application, such as the coal chute and the cistern. But, as the saying goes, the bones were good, except for the compound fracture of not having a bathroom connected to my bedroom.

We made more noise than we should have while getting ready for bed because Ash walked up the stairs to the landing and asked, "You okay, Hads? Thought I heard a man's voice."

I walked out of the bathroom to the top of the central staircase, looked down half a flight, and said, "I'm fine. You heard Brandon. Sorry we woke you." She smiled and gave me a thumbs-up. Did I want to correct her by letting her know he was spending the night because of the death threat? Did I care if she concluded that he and I were spending the night together for reasons other than safety? As difficult as it was for me to do, I opted for minimalism. I said, "Goodnight, Ash."

"Goodnight."

My heart raced as I pulled back the quilt, the blanket, and the top sheet.

"Which side do you want?" I asked. He wore a gray T-shirt that said SIUC on it in maroon letters and gray shorts. I'd never seen his legs, or even his arms in short sleeves. What I saw pleased me and indicated he hit the gym often. If his muscles could talk, they would say, "He takes care of himself," not "He's obsessed with himself." Looking at him as he climbed into bed, I thought that getting into bed with each other was a horrible idea. Or a great one.

I gave him my extra plug for his iPhone. We charged our phones, I turned out the light, and I said, "I think we'd better not kiss each other goodnight. I'm pretty sure we wouldn't stop."

"You *are* nervous. You just used two contractions in one sentence."

"Fine, mock me, but, yes, I'm nervous. I want you very much but don't think I'm ready. Ha. I did it again, so sue me."

"Not exactly what I want to do to you, but I understand. And agree. Not that you're not ready but that we're not. I don't even know your middle name."

"Darlene. I'm not a fan. My initials are HDC. Sounds like a brand of cassette tape from the eighties."

"You think that's bad? My middle name is Stephen, with a ph, making me B.S. Green. Not that I was ever teased about that in high school."

He rolled toward me, and I turned on my side, facing away from him. He draped his arm over me and said, "Goodnight, Hadley. I promise to behave." I hesitated a second, then said, "I almost said, 'That's what I'm worried about,' but I'll take you at your word, promise to do the same, and wish you goodnight."

I lay there for half an hour, unable to turn my brain off. Having his arm around me, feeling the warmth of his body, and knowing he believed in me and in us comforted me. But the paint-balloon attack and the death threat had rattled me more than I realized. I thought I was correct when I'd figured that if I were supposed to be dead, I would have been. But they could still try to kill me if I continued to investigate. And after I'd received the threat, I hadn't stopped. In fact, I'd made an essential connection, linking four twenty to white supremacy.

I lay there in the embrace of an amazing man whose breathing indicated he was sleeping, but I couldn't relax. I wondered what was wrong with me. Why couldn't I accept that good things happen occasionally? Healthy people accept happiness without questioning whether they're worthy of it, right?

I heard rattling, followed by a loud crash downstairs. It took me a second to realize what it was: the inside doorknob smashing against the hardwood floor. The doorknob had fallen into my hand a few days earlier when I was about to take Trapunto for a walk. I'd tight-ened the screw that held it on as I had done the other times it had come off in my hand. But it had never fallen of its own accord.

Trapunto, awakened by the crash, barked furiously, accompanied by Chica's piercing yaps.

"Brandon, wake up!" I shook him, and he awoke, startled.

"What's wrong?"

"Someone's trying to break in." He sprang from the bed, reached into his gym bag, pulled out his gun, said, "Don't move and don't argue," and sprinted downstairs.

THIRTY
MESSAGE RECEIVED

I heard glass shatter and Brandon yell, "Stop, police." The burglar broke the window next to the door so he could reach the deadbolt. Brandon must have flung the door open because I heard it strain against its hinges and more glass shatter.

"What's going on?" Ash yelled from behind her bedroom door, accompanied by ceaseless barks in two octaves. An engine roared and tires squealed as the assailant fled, probably in a black truck without plates.

I'd remained in my bedroom and was pacing when Brandon returned, barefoot, with his right little toe bleeding. He was breathing heavily and held the gun by his side in his right hand.

"Are you okay?" he asked.

"I am, but you don't appear to be. Let me see how bad that is," I said, pointing to his bleeding toe. He looked down.

"Sorry, I'm bleeding on your floor." He hobbled into the bathroom and came back with a towel wrapped around his foot. He sat in the chair and called the department to report the attack. After he told them what had happened, he listened for a few seconds and said, "This wasn't a threat. It was B&E with probable attempted homicide." He set the gun on the bedside table between the bed and the chair. He slowly said my address, listened, described the truck, listened, and said, "Yes, but the truck's more important. Find it. We won't turn up anything here. Thanks."

He walked on his left foot and right heel to the bathroom, where I verified that no glass was in his wound. I applied pressure, rinsed the wound, and secured a Band-Aid. I sat him down, wet a towel, and cleaned the stairs and the floor leading to the front door, which he'd closed. I retrieved the broom and dust bin from the pantry closet and swept up the glass in the entryway and on the front porch. I let Ash know the excitement was over, although I didn't mention what appeared to be the continuing danger. I walked upstairs, saw Brandon set his cell next to his gun, then I stepped into the hug he offered. I felt my heartbeat slow down while we held each other for a minute. We sat on the bed.

"Are you okay?" he asked.

"We sure picked the right night for you to stay over."

"I know you like to crack jokes, but they were here to kill you. I'm sure of it. They didn't expect me. Glad I parked on the street. Otherwise, more than one of them might have tried to come in. There were at least two. The guy I chased jumped into the bed as the driver pulled away. Like your balloon throwers, this guy was no more identifiable than 'above-average height, dark clothes, maybe muscled.'"

Brandon was excellent at his job and well respected by his colleagues. He said the assailants were here to kill me, and I believed him. But something didn't make sense.

"I know you're right, but only hours ago they left a death threat that said, 'Stop investigating now or this will be your last investigation.' If they'd wanted me dead then, they would have killed me at the office, instead of leaving the threat. But hours later, they were here to kill me, which can only mean one thing: They know I made the connection between four twenty and white supremacy, which ties everything and everyone together. The only way they could know that is if they hacked my computer. I couldn't begin to guess how one hacks a computer. I know how to run InDesign, Photoshop, and a few other programs, but that's it. I assume no one had to touch my computer to hack it. But then someone could have broken in."

He slipped his feet into white athletic socks, then Adidas running shoes, and tied the laces. "Most hackers work remotely, and you're right. They had to hack you to know you're still investigating. Even if they've been following you, and I didn't see anyone when I arrived, they wouldn't have known you'd made that connection. You struck a nerve while poking around, interviewing people, but that last connection hit a vein."

I heard a knock on the front door, followed by boots walking across hardwood. Brandon stood and walked to the door.

"Do what you have to do," I said. "What I can do is think. I'll be here." He nodded and went downstairs. Over the next forty minutes, I heard men talking, caught glimpses of flashlights outside, and heard car doors slam, engines start, and cars pull away. During all that, I lay on the bed and closed my eyes. I tried to organize the tasks I had to do so my theories about what was happening would hold up: connect Durrell Mahan to Chris Knudsen; determine whether Greg and Ed were active members of the BPs or only aware of the organization's existence; figure out how to pressure Benny into coming clean about her role in the current crime spree; and find a way to catch the guys who'd tried to kill me.

I realized that—if I wanted to be persnickety about these tasks—not all of them fell to me. But they felt as though they did, and, if bumper stickers really do dole out truths, then *Perception is Reality*. Paducah PD and other agencies were investigating, but I was ahead of the officers, having put the pieces together, as well as being the one most recently targeted for murder.

The clock said 2:11, so a considerate person wouldn't make a call at that hour. However, I could make a case that routine civilities took a backseat when the social contract was in flames. Also, the recipient of my call would be Missy Wendland, widely understood to be the world's worst quilter, or at least that's how her fellow Paducah quilters referred to her out of earshot, followed by "Bless her heart." She was a notorious insomniac who assaulted fabrics most enthusiastically in the wee hours. Matt had uncovered an affair she'd been having with Greg Wurt—an affair that could still have been ongoing. I didn't know whether he and Missy were still involved.

I called her.

"Don't usually answer the phone when I'm doing God's work, but what do you want?" I was never sure whether she played up her kookiness for attention, to entertain herself, or whether she was really that kooky. Because I had more important problems to solve, I skipped that dilemma and said, "Missy, it's Hadley Carroll. Sorry to bother you so late."

"Just about to begin a masterpiece, titled "Missy's Modern Masterpiece," certain to be known as *Three M's* for eternity."

"Good to know. I only have one question. Is Greg a racist?"

"Oh, sweetie. Of course. We all are. Everyone favors their own kind. That's just nature. Not human nature—nature. You think lions hang out with hyenas?"

"I understand your point. But I'd guess that lions don't blame hyenas for the problems of the jungle—drought, wildfire, deforestation. What I mean is, has Greg expressed opinions that the average person would consider racist?"

"Like I said, of course. You ever see his arms?"

"No. He only wears sweaters."

"Exactly."

"What's that mean?"

"Sweetie, you're stealing my creative time."

"I understand, and I apologize. Please answer my question, and I'll let you go."

"He got a HH tattoo on his left arm and 88, for the eighth letter of the alphabet, on his right. Redundant, you ask me, but it explains the sweaters."

"HH meaning Heil Hitler, right?"

"Honey, we're done. Ain't never agreed with a word you wrote, but I can't honestly say I ever thought you was dumb. You got what you wanted. Goodnight." She hung up before I could thank her.

Greg's tattoos explained his long sleeves but not his sweaters. Maybe he was always cold. Missy had answered the important question I had about Greg, so I told myself to let the sweater conundrum go.

I didn't know how computer hacks worked, but I suspected that the hackers had compromised my internet. If I didn't piggyback my cell on my WiFi connection, I assumed that using my phone would be safe. I could have been wrong, and, if so, I could add that to the increasingly long list of times that was true.

I looked up Alcoholics Anonymous meetings in and around Murray, pulled out a notebook, and wrote down the times and location of the two meetings that would take place later that day, Tuesday. I made a point to try to get to the first one at noon in suite J of the Southside Shopping Center.

I was overcome with exhaustion. I wasn't sure when I'd last slept, but I suspected it might have been never. I climbed into bed, fell asleep within a minute, and bolted upright in a cold sweat less than two hours later. I got out of bed, pulled on jeans, a top, a UCLA sweatshirt, and running shoes. I brewed a twelve-cup pot of coffee, poured a mug for Brandon, who sat at the kitchen table, and drank two mugs of coffee as we talked.

"I haven't doubted the seriousness of what's been going on," I said, "but this hit far too close to home." He sipped his coffee. He'd added cream and sugar. I tried not to judge.

He said, "Every available LEO is scouring McCracken County for that truck. My guess is we'll find it abandoned soon. Then we'll find it was stolen in Tennessee or Illinois or California. These guys aren't world-class criminals, but they aren't run-of-the-mill junkies knocking over FiveStars, either. I wouldn't walk up to the front door of a house in which I intended to murder someone. Of course, you don't have security cameras, and they learned that when they flattened Dakota's tire. They've fumbled, but they're still in possession and moving the ball. We're still playing defense."

"Do I have to continue the baseball metaphor?"

"You're—"

"Yes, I'm kidding. Just for fun, I'll continue the metaphor. We can force a turnover by blitzing, then march downfield and punch one in for the winning TD before time expires."

"Impressive, but how can you joke about this? Tonight has been extremely upsetting."

"I get flustered by everyday tasks. Being unable to find the right kind of period-appropriate light for the living room on eBay; not coming up with a zinger when the situation demands one; missing a stitch but not discovering my mistake until many hours later. But when real danger and trauma arrive—a car crash, a death threat—I'm usually calm, rational, and able to make smart decisions. I only fall apart afterward. Most people do the opposite, I've found. Growing up amid trauma has its advantages."

"I'm sorry. We have to get you out of here. Two officers are posted outside, but the perps could come back with an army. It's not likely because they know you could communicate what you found out about the BPs to a dozen people, or thousands of readers, and maybe already have. They probably realize they missed their opportunity. But now your front window's broken, so anyone could enter uninvited."

"But I don't know what good connecting four twenty to white supremacy does us," I said. "It means something, or they wouldn't have attacked. But we still don't know their big plan. They've made no more demands, and Robby is still missing. Do you think he's alive?"

"I do. They thought the quilts would get them the fifteen million, and they probably still think Robby will. And he might, but we've heard no chatter about the business community and the city combining forces to come up with the ransom. And no one has contacted law enforcement about coordinating the drop."

"I have to apologize to you. I failed to tease you earlier as I should have about your use of the phrase LEO. Apparently, you didn't have the energy to say law enforcement officers. Mockery was required, but I was off my game. So, I apologize."

"I'll do my best not to abbreviate, use acronyms, or even contractions. And, above all, I promise never to split an infinitive. Unless I can't help myself because a UFO makes me LOL while eating KFC. Now, please pack a bag."

As I packed, part of me hoped Ash would wake up again so I wouldn't have to wake her to tell her she had to pack. She'd come to my house to be comforted, not for excitement. After I'd packed, downed another mug of coffee, and eaten a bowl of Cheerios doused in cinnamon while Brandon ate toast that he dipped in olive oil, I roused Ash and the dogs. Groggily, she said she understood and packed her few belongings in two minutes.

While Ash brushed her teeth, Brandon said to me, "I warned the officers here, and told them to spread the word, that if they hassle you in the most minor of ways, they will have to deal with me."

"Think they were sufficiently scared?"

"Only two or three officers could be hassling you. The others understand the public scrutiny of policing. A few of us, including me, think it's long overdue. Cops aren't supposed to be bad, corrupt, or incompetent. Nearly all of us are embarrassed, if not horrified, by the crimes committed by the bad ones. I think Kane and Shannon are the likely two. They're spoiled morons, which has historically proven to be a terrible combination."

Ash stood in the doorway, with Chica cradled in one arm and her backpack and a satchel slung over her other shoulder. Trapunto stood next to them, looking confused at the early rousing.

"We're ready when you are," she said.

We walked past the officer posted at the front door, and I saw the other one turn the corner and walk toward us. I assumed he was walking laps around the house, and they would soon alternate roles. The five of us piled into Brandon's Ford Ranger—the two-door extended cab, not the four-door crew cab. I had to lift Trapunto into the back because he failed to grasp what was going on, and he was not about to climb into an unfamiliar truck for no good reason.

"You have a choice. I can drive evasively to ensure we're not being tailed, then take you to what we call the safe house—a suite at the Holiday Inn Express. Or we can go to my place, and I'll post two officers there."

I love the feeling of checking into a decent hotel: the plush linens that are always three or four levels of luxury higher than mine; having a nice meal in the downstairs restaurant; ordering from room service; and maybe swimming laps in a pool, so long as it is not infested with screaming children.

But Brandon was not presenting us with vacation options. Law enforcement was hiding us from potential murderers. I looked at Ash, who said, "I've never stayed there, and I hear it's nice, but I kinda think I'd feel safer at your house, Brandon. And isn't safety the whole point?"

Ash and the dogs quickly fell asleep after we reached Brandon's. He spoke by phone to various LEOs (sorry—couldn't help myself), and I thought until my thinking led me to Brandon's desktop. I investigated until I needed to think while not looking at a screen, thought for a while with my eyes closed, then repeated the process.

"They dumped the truck where they dumped the U-Haul," Brandon said. "It was stolen in Nashville—just after Chris was murdered there. We have the Mahan compound in Mayfield surrounded, but activity is minimal and nothing out of the ordinary."

"Thanks," I said. "I want to tell you my schedule for the day." He nodded. "I have to go to the office to prepare the paper to go to press tonight at 8. I'm days behind. We're going to be scrambling like crazy because who knows what is going to happen today at 5 when the BPs don't receive the ransom. They could kill Robby. That would be tragic, and it would also be breaking news that would require us to create on the fly. I want to go to Murray to ask a question of people attending a noon AA meeting. I want to attempt to talk to Ed Colapinto. And, assuming you think the rest of my plan makes sense and has an outside chance to work, I need to go back to my house."

"Sounds good. We can arrange all of that. What's your plan?"

I told him.

He said, "It's hard not to like you."

THIRTY-ONE

WHERE THERE'S SMOKE

I spent the morning in the *Pulse* building laying out pages, lightly editing the impressive stories that the reporters had written, and making sure that advertising's run sheet synced with editorial's. The reporters arrived, checked to see if I needed them to clarify anything or add facts to their stories, then started to work on articles for the website and for the next issue of the paper.

I left the building and asked the officer posted at the front door to let the officer posted at the back door know I had to go to Murray. He did, and they followed my truck in their squad car for about fifty minutes. I'd never attended an AA meeting, and I didn't plan to that day. My mom claimed to have attended a few meetings, but that was as likely as her having written a book about how to raise well-adjusted children.

I arrived at the Southside Shopping Center at 11:45 and wandered into suite J a few minutes later, followed by an officer. An elderly man sporting a gray beard and a gray newsboy cap set a metal folding chair next to another in what would become a circle. When he walked across the room to get another chair, I said, "Excuse me, sir." He looked at me, smiled, walked toward me, and extended his hand. We shook, and he said, "Welcome. I'm Tinsley. First time at this meeting?"

"Yes, but I'm not here to attend. Oh, sorry, I'm Hadley Carroll."

"No reason to apologize, Hadley. Help yourself to coffee or cookies. I won't hold you being a normie against you."

"Thank you. I'm trying to find out if two men who probably attended meetings here—under a court mandate because they both received a DUI—knew each other. The reason I'm asking is because they've both been murdered, and I think I know why. From the little bit of research I had time to do"—two men and a woman entered the room and nodded to us—"I believe AA meetings, or at least some of them, have call sheets that allow suffering members to call others in time of need. I understand the anonymous nature of the organization, but I'm not asking anyone to violate anyone else's anonymity."

"Hadley," he said, "the program as a whole and this chapter lose people now and again. They are what are known as 'unfortunates,' men and women who are constitutionally incapable of being honest with themselves. But what we don't have much of are people being murdered, but we've had two former members suffer that sad fate in quick succession. We both know who you're asking about. I haven't seen either of them since their court cards were filled, but if you want to know if they knew each other, I will say with certainty they did. I signed their cards one after the other more than once." Two men walked into the room, talking to each other.

"Thank you for your candor, Tinsley."

"Didn't like the big fellow at all. From what I hear, no one in that family had a chance. But that doesn't mean I wish for his murder to go unsolved. Something tells me that with you in pursuit, the murderers will be brought to justice."

"I hope so. Thank you for the vote of confidence and your time."

No one's privacy had been violated, and I'd met a man who I would have chosen to be one of my grandfathers. If he could believe in me based on little more than a hunch, then I could appoint him fantasy Grampa.

The drive back to the office was uneventful, as was the rest of the workday, at least until 5 o'clock. I worked as hard and as fast as I ever had laying out the remaining thirty-six pages.

At 3:12, Brandon called to tell me that three more quilts were burning around town. Two witnesses who were walking their dogs along the river saw a full-sized blue truck with no rear tag pull away from the boat ramp, where a quilt that would prove to be titled, "Seeking Justice" was on fire.

At 4, I received a text that said: *15 mil. One hour. Tell you where in 30. If you fail, he dies.*

"Yes, I read it," I said after I answered my cell.

"We have every available member of four agencies scouring McCracken," Brandon said. "We should be able to set up on the drop site within minutes, no matter where they choose."

"That's great, but no money will be at the drop, unless sources at the city have been lying to Teresa and me."

"Wouldn't be the first time. But that's not the point. The BPs don't know the briefcases won't have money in them."

"But they could know. It seems they have someone inside, or someone's leaking information to them, because they knew the first drop wouldn't happen. They could kill Robby."

"They could, but then they'd have no leverage. They thought the quilts would be enough, but, despite the economic engine that quilting is and the irreplaceable nature of the quilts, no one put their money where their cloth is. Sorry, that was bad. In a way, neither did Robby. If he'd valued the quilts enough not to let the policy lapse, his life wouldn't be on the line. We'd still have to try to catch them at the drop, but there'd be no chance he'd die in the process."

"This is seriously stressful, and I'm only a bystander. Can't imagine how you and the others on the frontline feel."

"We've gone through a lot of training for this. To be honest, many of us don't handle the stresses of the job well, which is true of people in every profession. But cops are visible, so our mistakes are scrutinized."

"True. Similar to journalists. Our mistakes are printed for thousands, if not millions, to see. If an accountant makes an error, his boss and the IRS may notice, but the public won't."

"Have you been outside lately?"

"Not since my entourage and I returned from Murray. Why?"

"Paducah's a ghost town. More people than I realized listen to news radio, read your website, or watch TV news."

"Maybe the fact that Paducah is panicking is a good thing. I made the mistake of looking at Facebook for a few seconds, and Chicken Little is a calm pragmatist compared to the doomsday prognostications people are posting."

"If panicking and posting nonsense keep them off the streets where they could interfere with the apprehension, I'm all for it. Prognosticate away. But I have to go."

"So do I."

"Good luck at your place."

"Thank you. Stay safe."

At 4:30, I received a text that read: *Having fun yet? Change of plans. Wait until dark.* Ten seconds later, Brandon texted to be sure I'd received the update.

At 6:33, I put what I hoped were the finishing touches on tomorrow's issue. Because the ransom drop hadn't happened at 5, and because we hadn't been informed about the status of Robby, the *Pulse* staff didn't have to scramble against a hard deadline to report on the drop or on Robby's murder or release. I added a tag suggesting that our print readers should check the *Pulse* website for updates. I needed a few minutes to unwind before I rounded up my police escort so we could go to my house. I hadn't looked at what the *Chronicle* considered to be a newspaper for a couple days, so I unwound by counting the typos and grammatical errors in the headlines and decks. But then I made the mistake of reading Greg's latest editorial. The headline read: The least we can do is listen. The entire editorial read:

By now you've all certainly read — hopefully in this esteemed periodical — about the theft of so many quilts from the National Quilt Museum, Paducah's national treasure — although I think the gyms in this town are more important. The point I'm emphatically making is that the thieves who stole these stitched-together pieces of fabric did so for a reason. We don't know at this moment in time and space what that reason is — or maybe they have more than one — but we should not rush to judgement, and certainly not condemn, these industrious individuals. It could not have been easy to smash down the back door and haul the quilts outside, so in an era defined by laziness and entitlement we should give credit where credit is due — to the men who were strong enough to act on their convictions, whatever they may be.

I know I'm not in charge of the National Quilt Museum, but Robby Golden, who is in charge, seems to have fallen asleep on the job, and no one knows where he is. That smacks of irresponsibility. It's a shame no one wants to work anymore.

Anyway, we must listen to the demands of the men who liberated the quilts from the museum because they very well could provide clarity and guidance in uncertain times. The city of Paducah and the residents thereof will be well served by meeting whatever their demands happen to be.

***

I wanted to pity Greg and chalk up his editorial to some form of dementia, but it seemed too calculated, too pointed to be anything but intentional.

I'd called a repairman from the office early in the day to replace my broken window. Brandon had instructed the officer posted at my house to make sure the repairman didn't go beyond the front door. When I arrived at the house, followed closely by an officer driving a squad car, the window looked as it had before the attempted break-in. I said hello to the officer posted at the door, and the one who'd followed me joined him on the front stairs.

While I'd designed pages, I'd mentally started to write the email that I now had to craft. But I hadn't finalized what I intended to say when I sat at the computer. I wanted my words to be effective, but I didn't have time to obsess over my phrasing. I had to arrive at the *Chronicle* office before 8 p.m., as I did for every *Paducah Pulse* press run.

I addressed the email to every member of the *Pulse* staff, including Astin in advertising. After two false starts, I settled on:

Hello, Everyone,

You have worked even harder and more efficiently than you usually do during this extremely difficult and unprecedented time, and I hope you know how pleased and impressed I am by your workload and efficiency.

Some of you know that law enforcement and I have made great progress on the murders, the theft of the quilts, and Robby Golden's kidnapping. And we owe a lot of that progress to your efforts. Thank you.

In fact, because we've presented her with what we can prove, one of the principal participants is about to confess to her role in misdirecting the public and police in regard to the murder of Baahir Ali. When I accused her of being the insider who let the Barrel Proofs know which quilts to steal, she looked shocked but didn't refute my accusation.

When she meets me tonight at about 9 in the *Chronicle* press room, she will reveal what the BPs' ultimate goal is in return for sentencing leniency. She insisted on meeting me alone, without the presence of law enforcement, so she can tell her side of the story without feeling intimidated. I made it clear I couldn't offer her immunity, and the D.A. is not likely to do so. But she assumed that if she described her troubled background and how she was lured into the BPs, the D.A. could go easy on her.

The D.A. and the police believe this assailant will corroborate our theory that the BPs murdered Durrell Mahan and Chris Knudsen because they were in danger of revealing the bigger plan, the one for which the BPs are demanding $15 million.

I will probably write the story while the press is running (despite the noise), so I can post it ASAP. If you need me, you know where I'll be.

All the best,

Hadley

I sent the email, locked the front door, nodded to my police escort, and drove to the *Chronicle* building, followed by the squad car. However, one block from the *Chronicle*, the squad car turned right as I went straight so I would arrive alone. I parked in the lot at 7:50, as I usually did. But, after entering the building, instead of walking to the nearest of the two offices in the press room, I went upstairs to the lunchroom and saw Brandon pour what smelled like burnt motor oil into a paper cup. I added "offenses against coffee" to the list of backwards practices and beliefs that the *Chronicle* not only clung to but also displayed with pride.

"Have you given up?" I asked.

"Was so busy with the task force I almost didn't get here on time, so I couldn't make or buy real coffee. If you feel half as tired as I do, I'm impressed with your resolve because I'm exhausted."

The room was small and spoke to how little the *Chronicle* cared about its employees. A water cooler stood next to a nearly empty vending machine. A filthy microwave sat next to the putative coffee machine, which sat next to a coffee can that had a note taped to it: Honor System— 75 cents a cup.

He took a sip, grimaced, and emptied the cup into the sink that was half full of dirty dishes and cutlery. I kissed him on the cheek and asked, "They had me covered, right? That last block was nerve-racking."

As he said the following, he turned off the machine, found a fresh filter, spooned coffee grounds into it, filled the reservoir, replaced the carafe, and turned on the power. "I won't give you the details, but I'll say with confidence that this building is the safest one in Paducah right now. I can't speak to the building's integrity."

He gave me a real kiss, and the building shook. As we kissed, we felt the vibration that occurred every time the press kicked on. The rumble of the press's engine reached us a split-second later.

"That's one powerful kiss, Detective."

"I was about to say the same to you."

"You were going to call me Detective?"

"You're lucky I like you."

"I am, indeed. Do you have any theories about how not to watch the clock for the next hour?"

"Do a crossword? You should try to relax. You laid out an effective plan. Command agreed to it almost to the letter. They're set up on Benny's place. If they go for her there, or if she takes off, we have four agencies in place that will take them down or follow her to them. They sent two to get you at your house, but only one came in. They won't make that mistake again. We have enough manpower in place that they won't reach the entrance. We all wish we knew how big their crew is, but they'll let us know when we apprehend them. The Feds will muscle in because that's what they do."

"And because kidnapping is federal."

"Sure, if you want to pick nits. I think it's safe for you to relax.

Pull out your laptop and play solitaire. If everything goes close to plan, this should all be over soon."

"Does anything ever go close to plan?"

"Yes. I once met a fascinating woman with a dog named Trapunto—"

His text chime sounded, followed quickly by mine. Our texts read: *Almost there. Its gonna be fun. Dont be late.*

"They haven't named a time or place. How can we not be late?" I asked.

"We needed you here for the plan to work, but you won't be at the drop site. That's policy. Neither will I. We'll stay here until this is resolved."

"I understand. Was that text meant to toy with us? It didn't tell us anything."

"Reminding us they're in control, making us their dancing puppets. I hope they believe that. Overconfidence has never served anyone well."

He answered his cell, listened, said thank you, hung up, then told me three more quilts were burning: in Noble Park, in the Texas Roadhouse parking lot, and outside the office of Market House Theatre downtown.

"They're doing this to thin us out," he said. "We have to investigate each incident. They don't know how many of us there are, but with the various prongs of this operation—in Mayfield, throughout McCracken, at Benny's, at your house, at mine, and here—we're already stretched very thin. If they know about us setting up here and at Benny's, they've seen through your email, and the plan has failed. They know we have no choice but to descend full force on the drop site, so they're thinning our resources to increase the odds they escape."

"But they've burned nine of the twenty-six quilts. They're losing what leverage they think they have."

"Maybe. They're probably gambling that the city and the museum and the residents of Paducah won't let twenty-six irreplaceable quilts burn without various agencies coming together to round up the ransom. They're overlooking the fact that if that were going to happen, it already would have. And now that I've put it like that, I get a bad feeling. If they're still trying to manipulate the powers that be to come up with the money, then they must know the drop tonight will be bogus. They might be hedging their bet, and that's what I'm hoping, but this could be bad."

"Robby?"

"Yes. The smart play would be for them to kill him and disappear. We don't have much to convict them unless someone talks. Everything's riding on your plan."

I wanted to look out a window to see what was happening outside, but I knew I could destroy the whole operation if the assailants who were coming to get Benny and me saw me at a window, rather than in the press room. We moved to the bullpen, where the roar of the press was a little quieter. Whichever reporter was supposed to work late that night wasn't there. Maybe on a break. Greg always left before 6. The designers usually arrived at 9, but I didn't know if they were in their office.

I sat in the chair I used to sit in when I'd been the A&E reporter. The reporter's notebook to the right of the desk phone indicated that Stephen Glaudini now sat at that desk and covered the city beat. I'd read about a dozen of his stories, and he was two or three cuts above the other *Chronicle* reporters.

Brandon paced, made calls, paced, and finally picked up a copy of the *Chronicle*, although he didn't sit down. He turned the pages, read for a few minutes, and said, "Did you see this? Greg practically confessed to being in league with the BPs."

"I did. And the worst part is, he thinks he's clever."

He looked at his watch, and I looked at mine: 9:07.

"Do you think they'll be here?"

"Hard to say, but they were willing to kill last night to keep you quiet. Can't see why their plans would change. If they saw through your email, this is a waste of resources that we should be deploying elsewhere. My guess is they're giving you and Benny time to get here."

He flipped pages, and I checked my newsfeed on my phone. My timing couldn't have been worse. A fourth journalist in Mexico had been murdered within days of the first. Reporting on corruption and criminality worldwide was more dangerous than ever. I didn't need to learn about these murders, especially not while waiting to see if the murderers who were determined to kill Benny and me would be apprehended before they accomplished their objective. My heart raced, so I closed my eyes to meditate. One minute later, Brandon's text chimed again, followed by mine. This text said: *Middle of the PAL yard flyover. 1 5 minutes. If moneys right, youll find him. If not* ...

THIRTY-TWO
LET'S MAKE A DEAL

About a dozen short sections of track split from the main rail line south of downtown. The spurs allow crews to link cars without impeding trains running the 223-mile route. The Paducah and Louisville Railway, PAL, runs between those two cities, with branch lines running from Paducah to Kevil and Mayfield and port connections on the Ohio and Tennessee rivers. The flyover is a track that runs above and perpendicular to the large railyard. I thought the BPs had chosen the drop site well because the railyard is both central and remote. It's only minutes from downtown but isn't easily accessible to bystanders, so the public wasn't likely to interfere with the money drop or impede an escape.

Matt had taken me to the railyard once. I'd thought it was far less fascinating than he had. But as I sat in the *Chronicle* building, with Brandon pacing nearby, both of us waiting to see if the assailants would pull into the parking lot with guns drawn, the railyard was the second most important location in the world to me—the *Chronicle's* bullpen being the first.

Over the rumble of the press, I heard, "Stop! Police," followed by sirens and at least five cars skidding on pavement, followed by shouting. I ran to the window and saw squad cars with flashing lights, a SWAT truck, and officers in flak jackets running toward the front door, which I couldn't see. Whoever had arrived to kill Benny and me were out of sight. In the excitement, I hadn't heard Brandon move to my side, but I felt his arm across my shoulders. He said, "I got you. You're safe."

A lot of pent-up emotion moved from my bunched shoulders, tight lower back, and knotted stomach into my tear ducts. I turned toward Brandon so we could wrap our arms around each other and said, "Words seem inadequate, but for now I'll say thank you from the bottom of my heart."

"You're welcome from all of mine. I hate to spoil the moment, but I should monitor what's happening at the railyard. I won't leave you, but ..." He turned up the volume on his radio and walked to the far side of the room. I composed myself and called Dan. I hadn't told the staff that the plan I'd laid out in the "bait" email had mostly been the real plan. I'd also failed to mention the huge law enforcement presence that would be essential to the plan's success. I'd told the reporters to be prepared to report and post to the website that evening.

"Already here," Dan said when he answered. "Followed the convoy at a distance from the station."

"Good job. We don't know if other BPs are willing to die trying to free their henchmen, so be careful. Staying alive is more important than any story."

"Got it. You, too."

I called the other reporters to see how they were doing, and they confirmed they were safe and hard at work. When Brandon saw me hang up, he pulled a chair from the desk behind the one I sat at, set it next to mine, sat, and asked, "You okay?"

"Alive and with you, so, better than that."

"Great. Want an update?"

"That you asked makes me think I won't like what you have to say."

"We'll see. The Feds left fifteen large briefcases at the middle of the flyway, stacked four, four, and seven. Only the one on top of the other six was unlocked. It had one million dollars in it, stacks of hundreds, weighing about twenty-two pounds. The money's real. The Feds have those kinds of resources. The locked briefcases weighed the same. The Feds made the drop, then appeared to leave. Had the BPs arrived by helicopter, they probably would've been shot down, but I would've given them credit for effort. Instead, a few minutes after the Feds retreated, two morons dressed in black from head to toe arrived from the west on a handcart. They opened the live briefcase, hopped around and gave each other three high-fives, loaded the cargo on the cart, and started to pump back the way they came. They made it less than fifty yards before the Feds and SWAT stopped them. Their buddies fired rounds from cover and hit a Fed in the back. His vest worked. He was stunned but fine. We returned fire but aren't sure yet if anyone was hit. Some probably escaped. We don't know how many there are total, but we rounded up four, and it's only a matter of time before one of them realizes that the first one to talk wins the best deal."

"Wow. I'm glad it's over, and I'm glad you were with me."

"I am, too, but I don't think it's over. If these guys are as ignorant as they seem to be, or are too loyal to talk, then we have a lot of loose ends. And we haven't found Robby. Because they didn't get away with the money, they haven't told us where he is. We're searching every car at the railyard, every building, and every inch of ground. It would make sense for them to have him near the drop, but I don't know if we should be using norms of rational thought while trying to figure these guys out."

From Brandon's radio came a male voice saying, "Detective, we got Benny Washington down here. Her detail brought her in voluntarily. Says she wants to talk to Hadley."

"Be right down," Brandon said, and left the room. Two minutes later, he returned with Benny. She wore a long multi-colored coat lined from top to bottom with fake whitish fur, a white button-down blouse, low-rider jeans, and knee-high brown boots. Her light-brown shoulder-length hair was unbrushed, and she didn't appear to be wearing makeup. She did, however, have a large purple bruise on her left cheek beneath a black eye. Brandon sat her in the chair he'd been sitting in, took four steps to the edge of the room, and leaned against the wall.

"Why'd you send them after me?" Benny asked.

"I didn't," I said. I pulled the voice recorder from my purse, hit "record," and took out a pen and notebook.

"You were surrounded by officers who would've stopped anyone trying to get to you," Brandon said. "Our objective was to catch them, not to put you in danger. That bruise isn't new, so don't blame us for that."

"I'm not. It's from initiation. Gotta show your loyalty to the BPs by letting one of them punch you in the face. Joined a few days ago."

A smart-aleck response ran through my head before I decided not to respond to her decision to join a group that subjected its members to assault and battery. I looked at Brandon and understood by the way he held his phone that he was capturing our conversation with a recording app.

"Why are you here?" I asked.

"It's gone bad. All of it, looks like. Thought if I come clean first, maybe I don't get locked up forever. 'Course, they could kill me for talking, but think I gotta take that chance, don't you? Got any water?"

Brandon went to the lunchroom and came back with a cup of water. He handed it to her, and she nodded to him. She chugged the water, emptying the cup.

"Why did you come to me instead of to the police or D.A.?"

"Been reading your stories. You're really smart, and I wanted to be a great journalist someday, really, but I don't have the talent or eye for it or something. And Uncle Greg hasn't taught me squat. Thought you'd at least write down what I said without mangling it. Can't say the cops or D.A. would do that."

"We don't have time to start at the beginning because some of the

BPs are still out there, and they could still implement their plan," I said.

"No, they can't. They needed the money. When I asked them what went down, the cops that drove me here said, 'The threat has been neutralized.' Means the exchange didn't happen, right?"

"Correct," I said. "Why did they need the money?"

"For their big plan. I thought it was the stupidest thing I ever heard first time Lawrence told me."

"Lawrence Mahan?"

"Yes. Our president and my boyfriend. Or at least he was. I don't know now."

"What was the plan?"

"To re-create the Confederacy, make it a land for whites only. The New Confederate States of America, they were gonna call it. They thought the money would be enough to bribe Congress and create ads that would inspire millions of others to donate millions and join the cause. Don't think they were way off reading the country, but I thought they would need billions, not millions. And there's no way Lawrence could be the leader. He's funny and has plenty of street smarts, but he ain't gonna talk people into changing their mind. Except me, I guess. He uses muscles and weapons, not words. They needed a celebrity. Who knows? Maybe they woulda got one."

"Okay, I think I understand the plan, such as it was, but why steal twenty-six quilts?"

"Twenty-six is more than half of fifty, the fifty states. It was symbolic. They figured if they could get twenty-six states to join the New Confederacy, they would succeed."

"And secede. But the Constitution doesn't work that way. Three quarters of the states have to agree before the Constitution can be amended. Thirty-eight states."

"Confirmation bias," Brandon said. "Because they think a certain way, they assume others do. Twenty-six made sense to them, so who needs facts?"

"Their ignorance of the Constitution doesn't really matter," I said, "because that plan would have fallen apart half a dozen ways even if they'd gotten away with the fifteen million."

"Maybe, maybe not," Benny said. "Could I get more water?" She held the cup out to Brandon, who filled it and returned it to her.

"I think I understand that quarter-baked plan," I said, "but I don't understand the land scam."

"What land scam?"

"In Roseburg, Ed Colapinto, Greg Wurt, Nick Stoddard, and Terry Lee ran a land scam called—"

"Destination Roseburg," she said. "That's why I'm here. My dad was their accountant. He figured out what they were doing and he—guess there's no nice way to say it—he blackmailed them. That's how Mom got that nice house, and Greg hired me as part of the deal. Wouldn't bet my life on it, but I don't think my dad really died in a wreck. I mean, he died in one, but I don't think it was a real wreck. I think Mom musta known something about it, and she kept up the blackmail. They can't kill everyone and get away with it."

"No, they can't. But I'm still confused. Were they running, or about to run, a land scam here?"

"Not really. Not the same as Roseburg. Ed bought a big chunk a land on the edge of Land Between the Lakes, something like three hundred fifty, four hundred acres. On the Kentucky side, not far from Aurora. The plan was to make that the capital of the New Confederate States of America. Lawrence, who's a lot smarter than his brothers and sisters, said if it all didn't work as planned, they could start a small new state. He said something a couple times about a lost state of ... something or other."

"Franklin. A bold idea and a short-lived failure," Brandon said.

"Yeah, that's it. We've been down there removing trees, clearing brush, building things."

"How many of you? And have Ed, Greg, Nick, and Terry been involved?"

"Twenty-five, give or take. Mosta the Mahans, their cousins, and friends. Never saw Ed there but Greg and Terry helped out. Don't think Nick has anything to do with us."

"Why did you guys go with Barrel Proofs instead of White Dogs? That would've covered the bourbon and the race angles."

"We started with White Dogs but found out it was already taken by skinheads in Tennessee. Lawrence said we had to have our own brand." I laughed, despite myself. We lived in a world in which even hate groups worried about branding. "But they kept the stupid 'woof' part 'cause they liked it," she said.

"I have to tell you something, then I'll ask you two more questions. After that, Detective Green will take over, and I'll call Suzanne Bigelow, the D.A."

"Okay."

"Dennis Edwards didn't murder your brother. He's serving life without parole for murders he admits he committed. He insists he had nothing to do with Benny's murder."

"Whatever. We all gotta believe what we gotta believe."

"But your misguided beliefs contributed to you getting involved in this ill-conceived criminal enterprise. We're all products of our environments, but we also have the power to make decisions that help or harm us."

"Too late now. Can't turn bacon back into a hog."

"The second part is true, but it's not too late. That's why you're here—to mitigate what you've done so you have a chance at a future. Do what you can to help yourself. Where's Robby?"

"Not sure, but I'd say he's at the Compound."

"That's what you call Ed's land?"

"Yeah. Well, the trailers there for now and the unfinished buildings."

Brandon left the room. I heard him speak but couldn't make out the words.

"Okay," I said. "Where's Lawrence?"

"Don't know."

"Suzanne could use your denial against you. Aiding and abetting. Impeding a police investigation."

"Said I don't know. Haven't been in contact since he punched me. Woody, one of the brothers, said he ain't at the Compound. Said he hasn't seen him for days." Brandon entered the room and leaned against the wall again.

"When did you speak with Woody?" I asked.

"He called about your email, seeing if I was gonna meet you here. Told him I didn't know. You guys are smarter than we are."

"Are the remaining quilts at the Compound?"

"I think so. In one of the sheds, I think."

"I said I'd only ask you two more questions, but I'm going to make a statement. You let me know if it's correct." She nodded. "Nick Stoddard hired Chris Knudsen through Ed Colapinto to rough up or scare off Baahir Ali. Chris subcontracted to Durrell, who messed up or improvised and killed Baahir because he could. He carved four twenty into a tree because he was keyed up on adrenaline and hatred, and you recognized it for what it was, a white-power symbol.

"You knew that if we recognized it for what it was, the Barrel Proofs' big plan would be in danger, so you threw us off the scent by writing that marijuana was found at the scene. Durrell, because he's as smart as a doorstop, bragged about having committed the murder. I'm confident my theories hold together up to here. I had a clue how the rest played out, but I think you just filled in the gaps. Let me know if I'm correct.

"Lawrence, fearing the whole operation was about to fail because Durrell was blabbing, broke Durrell's neck during the shooting at Barbecue on the River, then pushed him off the building."

Her eyes got wide, and her expression went from resigned to frightened. "Lawrence killed Chris in Nashville when Chris left Fiona's apartment because Chris had to know Durrell killed Baahir. After all, he'd been the one hired to scare him. With both of them dead, the big plan was on track, as far as Lawrence knew. The loose ends regarding

Baahir's murder were now tied up, other than Ed having put Nick in touch with Chris. But Lawrence couldn't kill Ed, the owner of the Compound, and Nick is running for mayor. If he were killed, the authorities would've come down full force, and the big plan would've fallen apart. Of course, Lawrence couldn't know if Durrell bragged about the murder to others. He'd covered the most obvious tracks and thought the BPs could proceed as planned. Murder, however, isn't a federal crime. Kidnapping and interstate extortion are. Big mistake. So are hate crimes, or they can be. His big plan ensured that the Feds would get involved, which they did—putting an end to all of it. How'd I do?"

She folded her arms in front of her, leaned forward, and rested her head on her hands. She sniffled, and I saw a tear run down her cheek. Quietly, as if to herself, she said, "Why, Benny? Why'd you have to die?"

After two minutes, she raised her head, looked at me, and said, "I was right to come to you. You know most of it. Impressive. We didn't even know the thing about three quarters of the states. We're idiots."

"I paid attention in school, and I still do homework every day, although I call it research. As I was recounting the events that led us here, it occurred to me that Ed Colapinto is not a moron. He's a narcissist who couldn't keep his zipper shut if it were Super Glued, but I think he has the usual number of functioning brain cells. And that means he had to know the big plan wouldn't work. If the BPs had managed to secure even part of the ransom, my guess is that Ed would've managed to separate them from it—whether to flee to an island or to finance another land scam, I can't say. And, of course, I'm just speculating. Regardless, you've been very cooperative, and I'll give this recording to Suzanne. Are you sure you don't know where Lawrence is?"

"Wish I did."

THIRTY-THREE
HIDE AND SEEK

"What do you want, Hadley?" Greg Wurt said when he answered my call. "It's late."

"Although I don't like you, and you were the worst boss I've had, you're a human being, and I don't believe you're inherently evil, despite your hateful tattoos."

"You've never seen my tattoos."

"Correct. I've never seen atoms either, but I know they exist. I'm calling to tell you something and to ask if you or Ed put pressure on Chris Knudsen to change the caption on the video he posted of Brandon and me kissing."

"It's Brandon and I, smarty-pants."

"No, it's not. Would you say, 'the video of I kissing'? Well, you probably would, so never mind. Did you?"

"Yes. The *Chronicle* has endorsed Nick Stoddard, and Chris worked for us. I put my foot down."

"Then Ed put his foot on yours, I'm guessing."

"What?"

"Forget it. I'm letting you know that I realize you're a dupe. You are not—and never will be—a mastermind, so don't let yourself become a patsy."

"What are you talking about? I'm hanging up."

"Which is it? It can't be both."

"Tell me."

"Four BPs were caught during the ransom drop, and they're certain to talk when they're threatened with federal time. To apply leverage, the Feds and local authorities will threaten to charge them with murder, or with aiding and abetting the murderers. Many people will go to prison for this crime spree, with Lawrence Mahan foremost. Y'all are guilty as all get-out, but I suggest you, specifically, pin everything you can on the biggest fish, Ed. Convicting him will be a feather in everyone's cap. He's gotten away with far too much for far too long—as you have, now that I say that. But you've always been a lackey. My guess is Nick will slip away like the greased snake he is. What I'm saying is, blame it all on Ed. Ignorance has always been your defining trait, so hide behind it."

Click.

I tried. I wasn't sure why I did, but I tried.

A little more than an hour later, Brandon heard that Murray SWAT found Robby tied up in a shed on the mostly raw swath of land that the BPs called the Compound. Robby was weak, hungry, and dehydrated. He'd been beaten, but not brutally. He would recover soon enough. Every available law enforcement officer in and around Western Kentucky was looking for Lawrence Mahan.

Because Lawrence and many of the other BPs were still on the loose, I asked Brandon if Ash and the dogs could stay at his place another night.

"Of course. What about you?"

"I'd like to deliver the papers. I forgot to do something I should have done days ago, but I can't remember what it was. It's important, I'm sure of it, but it escapes me. If I deliver the papers, keeping my mind occupied on a simple task, maybe it will come to me, the way things often do when I'm quilting."

"The shift I'm on is becoming endless," he said. "If I declare myself dangerously exhausted, would you mind if I join you?"

"Of course not. If you want to sleep while I drive, I'd like that."

When the *Pulse* print run was completed a few minutes later, I told the delivery drivers I'd pay them to go home. Brandon and I stuffed my truck with as many newspaper bundles as would fit. Based on the number of bundles, I'd probably have to make six trips because I'd tripled the print run. Brandon did his best to be good company while I left one bundle after another in racks around town, outside of various closed businesses, and inside many of the twenty-four-hour ones.

"What do you think will happen to these guys?" I asked while driving to the *Pulse* building to pick up our second load.

"Lower-downs will turn on higher-ups. That's how it always works. Suzanne will at least consider offering lighter sentences to the first ones to provide evidence that will lock up the bigger fishes."

"Ed being the biggest."

"Depends on how we look at it. Did Ed commit murder? Doubtful. Did he know Durrell would murder Baahir? Almost certainly not because Chris wasn't supposed to kill Baahir, and Chris subcontracted to Durrell. No one is likely to pay for Janet's death. No one can prove she wouldn't have died of a heart attack that afternoon at home, although we know the stress of the robbery caused her heart attack. If any of the underlings are smart enough to pin the extortion demands and the kidnapping on Ed, he could take a fall. I'm not well-versed in hate-crime laws, so I don't know how that stuff will play out. But when we find Lawrence, he's going to go away for a long time. If he's as savvy as he appears to be, he'll bring Ed down with him. Who am I forgetting?"

"Greg and Stoddard."

"If I had to guess, Greg will plead ignorance, which, based on his editorials, he can do credibly. But conspiracy charges are a certainty. With Stoddard, who knows? Benny said she never saw him at the

Compound and didn't think he had anything to do with the BPs, and
you said Garrett couldn't pin anything on him."

"So, once again, the Stoddards out-Stoddard the justice system."

"Maybe, but I'll bet you anything he'll lose an election soon."

"Do you expect me to bet against myself?"

"No. You bet on yourself more often than you realize."

He fell asleep a few minutes later. I liked having him beside me
as I worked. I felt much more comfortable with him than I'd felt with
anyone else, including Dakota. Despite loving each other and being
best friends for decades, she and I were more competitive than we
should have been. I didn't feel competitive with Brandon, and there
were no barbs behind our teasing of each other. We were amusing
ourselves and showing our affection.

Even so, I was disappointed in myself as we delivered the papers
because I couldn't remember what I knew I was supposed to
remember.

On my third run, I dropped a bundle at the front door of Etcetera
Coffeehouse on Sixth Street. I looked at the photo on the front page,
the one I'd looked at many times since late on Saturday night,
including every time I set a bundle down that night: the photo of
Durrell Mahan's body sprawled at the base of the River Discovery
Center on Water Street, surrounded by Paducah Police Department
officers. Dan had taken the photo. Compositionally, it was a little
busy, and I'd had to lighten it to allow viewers to see what was
depicted. I knew I'd receive hate mail for putting a picture of a dead
man in the paper at all, let alone on the front page. But the prevalent
misconception that local newspapers should present their communi-
ties as residents would like them to be, not as they are, was not on my
mind then. Instead, I silently asked myself, "Why haven't I looked up
what Lawrence looks like, especially after Benny confirmed he'd
killed Durrell? Why hadn't I found out what all of the Mahans
looked like when I first learned they were involved?"

I pulled out my phone and checked social media. Nothing on

Lawrence. I went to the Kentucky Online Offender Lookup site, typed in Lawrence Mahan, and realized I was a dunce.

I got in the truck and said, "Brandon? Brandon, wake up." He shook awake, took a second to realize where he was, and asked, "What is it?"

I showed him the picture of Lawrence, next to his statistics and above his arrest record, which was extensive and included two convictions for assault.

"Okay. What's that tell you?" he asked.

"I blew it. If I'd thought to look him up earlier, I might've prevented a lot of this from happening."

"Why? I don't understand."

"In his mugshot he isn't as dirty as he was on Sunday morning when I rode past him on the Greenway Trail. He saluted me, and I returned his salute. He smiled, and I thought nothing of our exchange. I saw him as someone who was unhoused, not as the president of the BPs."

"How could you have seen him as anything but what he appeared to be? You didn't even know about the BPs then, did you?"

"No, but still. What's important is that he was pushing a buggy full of stuff along the Greenway Trail, which, of course, grants easy access to the river. He could be hiding out there. He looked like he'd been sleeping outside. When the other shooters fled in vehicles, he could've walked the short distance to the end of the trail, then disappeared into the woods anywhere along it. Benny and his brother Woody haven't seen him for days. Maybe he's using the river as transportation, heading upriver to get to—or near—the Compound."

"I'll call it in."

Brandon and I slept in his queen bed, chastely, as we would've done the previous night in my house if someone hadn't tried to kill me.

When we woke at 10, I noticed that Ash had set her backpack and satchel by the front door with the small, burned quilt she'd made with Grammie J on top of the satchel. I hadn't realized she'd brought it with her from my house. With everything else I was juggling, I'd forgotten to ask her if she wanted to keep the quilt or to put it in the casket with Janet, whose funeral would take place in two days. I decided not to bring the subject up. She'd make her decision without my input.

Ash smiled as she poured us the coffee she'd made. Trapunto and Chica formed their familiar lowercase-c inside capital-C configuration on the rug under the kitchen table.

"Are you smiling at us?" I asked.

"Technically, but not like you think. I mean, I'm happy to see y'all together, but that's not why I'm smiling. I guess you haven't seen social media."

"No," I said.

"Do my best to avoid it," Brandon said.

"Want me to show you?"

"No, thank you. Tell us, please," I said.

"You've won the election!"

"What are you talking about? It's not until November." Brandon pulled out his phone and started scrolling.

"Doesn't matter. Nearly every post on every platform, except for a few obvious trolls, is screaming some version of 'Hadley did it again. She saved Paducah. Caught the murderers. Vote Hadley, Gladly.' And when I took the dogs for a walk earlier, I didn't see a single sign for Stoddard. People must've swiped them."

"Really? I guess that's good, but I'd prefer that people didn't steal on my behalf. And I haven't caught any murderers."

"Actually," Brandon said, "You pretty much have." He pulled out his cell and made a call. "Give me the broad strokes, Dave." He listened for two decades, and I didn't know if I'd die of impatience or old age. He asked a question, listened, asked another question, listened, and he seemed to take pleasure in my pacing. He said, "Got it. Thanks." Instead of telling us what he'd learned, he stood, smirked, poured himself a cup of coffee, and put a slice of bread in the toaster.

"If you think you're waiting for your toast before you talk, buster, you—"

"You're cute when you're ... Hadley. I mean, impatient." He sipped his coffee and said, "PPD found Lawrence's camp at five this morning and staked it out. He came downriver about an hour and a half later in a skiff with an outboard. We could've had a protracted manhunt on our hands. He's an avid hunter and ex-Army, albeit dishonorably discharged. He could've stayed out there a long time, but he came back for his stuff. Take a guess what it included."

"No idea," I said.

"A bottle of E.H. Taylor, which is what his ID said his name was."

"That's good and expensive bourbon," I said. "At least he didn't get himself caught for a bottle of Jim Beam."

"A photo of the entire Mahan clan posed on a front porch was also among his stuff," Brandon said.

"A sentimental murderer," Ash said. "How sweet." Brandon and I laughed.

My cell rang. It was the manager of the FiveStar on H.C. Mathis letting me know that every copy of *Pulse* was gone, and it was only 10:20. Over the next two hours, I received five similar calls. I should have at least quadrupled the press run. Obviously, the claim that "nobody reads anymore" was inaccurate.

"Maybe this isn't the best time to bring it up," Ash said, "but since we're going back to your house—"

"Yes, you can move in officially. Trapunto and I would love to have the two of you."

"Thank you very much. I can't face living in Grammie J's house alone. Not yet, anyway."

"It's your house now. I'll help you rent it or sell it, whichever you choose."

My cell rang. I saw who was calling and said, "Good morning,

Big Man. I've been thinking about calling you. Mind if I put you on speaker?"

"No. Good morning. Got another case for me already?"

"Thankfully, no. I need a long vacation or two before I can make it through anything like the last few days again. But because you and I both know I won't take a vacation anytime soon, I'll vacation in my quilting room, one stitch at a time."

"Whatever works. I was calling to congratulate you. You got the election sewn up. See what I did there? Wouldn't know it to look at me, but I'm not a stranger to social media, and you are a hero on every platform."

"Thank you, but you did the heavy lifting."

"Is that a crack about my weight? Kidding. It was you slighting yourself, which is refreshing in a public figure but ain't a good look on you. Take credit when you deserve it, which is often. Own up to your successes and welcome joy."

"Wait, what did you do with Garrett?"

"He's still here, but he's a tiny bit more hopeful. You made me feel useful, so I'm also calling to thank you."

"You're welcome. The reason I was going to call was because I received an anonymous message that helped me significantly. In fact, it was the key to everything that followed. You haven't told me if you've been to Los Angeles, but I suspect you were there long enough ago to see a certain series of television commercials."

He laughed long and hard. "You should take your hunches to Vegas—you'd clean up. Who knows how you'd do? Adee Do!"

"You amaze me. Why didn't you tell me what you knew about the Mahans and Chris Knudsen and everything else that was going on?"

"You needed me to point you in the right direction, not come to your rescue."

"How'd you know what was going on?"

"Can't say I am now, but a while ago I tried to get sober. Went to different meetings all over, looking for one that worked for me. Found the one in Murray. Went there a lot. Heard Chris share about the stresses he was under with all his kids. I read between the lines. He was already cheating or was about to step out. I heard Durrell share one day. Everything he said was bad news. Bragged about his criminal exploits but not a word about sobriety. Since then, I kept tabs on him and that dumpster-fire of a family. Started investigating for real as soon as I learned from the *Pulse* website Durrell was no longer among us."

"You're incredible, and I'll always be in your debt."

"You owe me nothing, but you know how to reach me if there's a next time."

We said goodbye, and Ash said, "Congratulations. How are you going to celebrate your victory?"

"I learned long ago not to count my chickens, but thank you for believing in me."

"Madam Mayor," Brandon said. "Or do you prefer Mayor Carroll? They have a nice ring to them, don't they? Speaking of rings and pistons, my tools and mechanic's creeper have been waiting patiently. Are you ever going to show me your MGA?"

"Is that a euphemism?" He and Ash laughed.

I looked at him and smiled. The look in his eyes filled me with hope and assurance. I felt safe, understood, and accepted when he was near me. Eventually, he could see me as the imposter I often believed myself to be. But right then, sitting in his kitchen with two people who appreciated and admired me, I felt at peace. No looming threats ate at me, and I couldn't think of a single murder I needed to solve.

The cloud I floated on that morning was made of self-acceptance and happiness—and something that felt exactly like love. I promised myself to let it flourish, unexamined. I vowed to trust myself and Brandon—and to admit that no one can control the future.

The election was five weeks away. I liked my chances.

Liked *our* chances.

The End

THE OPENING OF QUILT CITY:
MEASURE ONCE, CUT TWICE

"How's the cookbook coming along, Hadley?" Vivian Franey asked during Paducah Quilters Quorum, our weekly quilting group.

"Okay," I answered, "but the deadline's almost here, and I may not finish. I'm exhausted, and I haven't seen Brandon this week."

"The world won't end if you allow yourself some downtime," Cindy Baron said. "You could've said no."

"Yeah, right," Dakota Crowley said. "When has she ever said no to a challenge, especially if it involves overworking?" The pained expression on my best friend's face contradicted her playful teasing.

"I thought *Quilt City Cookbook* was a bad idea from the beginning," Donna Ackerman said. "I mean, with everything you're juggling, and you about to become mayor, why'd you agree to that deadline? Not that your panna cotta and biscotti aren't delicious. They sure as shootin' are."

Seven of us were seated around the dining table in my decrepit Arts & Crafts house in Lower Town on that November Saturday afternoon, instead of the usual Sunday because two members wouldn't have been able to attend the next day. We were putting together a crazy quilt that utilized one one-millionth of the scraps we had collectively accumulated in our stashes. Evelyn Lewy, the sister of the outgoing mayor whose seat I was almost certain to win in three days, had suggested we make a crazy quilt. The idea was fine, but the quilt we were creating was so chromatically and geometrically discordant that it made me queasy. Working on the quilt made me feel like I was on a sailboat in rough seas looking through a kaleidoscope.

Ashley Pope, the eighteen-year-old Murray State freshman who'd moved in with me after she'd suffered significant traumas six weeks before, shuffled from her room to the bathroom without acknowledging us.

"How's she doing?" Tasha Wilson asked.

"Better and worse days," I said.

"Like everyone else," Donna said. She understood depression in a way no one ever should: Her son, Matt Ackerman, my former fiancé, had been murdered. Donna had technically existed since I'd delivered the horrific news to her, but just barely. Her drinking had increased, and she'd put on a significant amount of weight by rarely eating anything other than Domino's pizzas and Oreos. She managed to fill her shifts at Michael's and to attend church occasionally, although I hadn't seen her at St. Francis de Sales the last two weeks. The only socializing she did was at PQQ, and she missed about one quarter of our sessions. In fact, I was surprised to see her that day because she'd called on Friday to say she likely wouldn't attend. "My friend from work, Luann, ain't doing good," Donna had said, "so I think maybe I'll visit her instead." I was glad Donna had changed her mind and joined us.

On her way back to her bedroom, Ashley lifted her hand in greeting, and said, "Hey, y'all." We said hello, and I said, "Ash, we're about to eat, so please join us, if you feel up to it."

"Maybe I'll grab something quick," she said. "Don't want to be a bother."

"Not even close to a bother," Vivian said. "It would be nice to gab a while."

"Maybe in a bit."

Ash had hardly interacted with me in days, so I took her "maybes" as a good sign, as I did Donna's presence at PQQ. But Dakota's expression concerned me.

"You okay, D?" I asked.

"Fine," she said. "My stomach's upset, but not enough to stop me from indulging. What's for dessert?"

"Paducah Cheesecake. Chocolate. It's my take on New York cheesecake, but less dense. It took me eight tries to get it right. Some recipes required more attempts."

"No wonder you're exhausted," Cindy said. "Well, I can't wait to dig in. It's that time, isn't it?"

We broke for lunch, and our potluck meal that day was as delicious as it usually was. Dakota surprised us all by preparing a dish herself, rather than buying one as she nearly always did. She'd made a simple spinach salad. My tastebuds said she'd under-seasoned it, but I ate my salad as she'd presented it so she didn't catch me salting and peppering it. I didn't want to discourage her culinary efforts.

While we ate, we joked and gently teased each other—as usual.

Evelyn said, "Bought me four yards of delightful Moda Berry Basket Blueberry at Fabrics & Notions yesterday. Not a clue what I'm gonna create with it, but sometimes fabric whispers, 'Buy me,' don't it?"

ACKNOWLEDGMENTS

I owe everything I have and most of who I am today to my wife, Sedonia. She believes in me and my writing when I lose confidence in both (usually near the middle of each novel I write). And her belief in me is nothing compared to the love she shows me daily. Thank you, Sedonia.

As they've been for each novel I've written, my beta readers were invaluable for this one. They pointed out my errors and let me know which aspects of the novel worked well for them. Thank you, Jessica Carroll, John and Carla Dodd, Biz Lyon, Jenny Raith, and, of course, Sedonia Sipes.

I want to thank the group of writers who have been through far too much together because we signed with the wrong publisher. However, we're resilient and are doing our best to thrive.

Once again, I owe a debt to Paducah, Kentucky, to its arts community, to its restaurants, and to its people. The National Quilt Museum, With Love, From Kentucky, and Pages Turned have been especially supportive. Thank you, Paducah.

Many Paducahans read, rated, and reviewed on various platforms the prequel to this novel, *Quilt City Murders*, the first Hadley Carroll Mystery. Their support for *QCM* enabled me to feel confident—most of the time—as I wrote *Quilt City: Panic in Paducah*.

I'd like to thank my mother, Barbara Leonard, my brother, Brett, my sister, Brigette, and my late father, Bruce Sr., as he occasionally called himself. I called him Pops. The funniest jokes were inspired by him.

Thank you for reading *Quilt City: Panic in Paducah*. The third Hadley Carroll Mystery, *Quilt City: Measure Once, Cut Twice*, is available, as is the fourth, *Quilt City: Proving a Negative*, as well as *Quilt City Cookbook*, a companion book narrated by Hadley at her funniest and most vulnerable. It contains dozens of sweet and savory recipes, as well as anecdotes, character backstories, and plenty of laughs.

If you enjoyed this novel, please leave a rating and/or a review wherever appropriate.

All of my books are available via my website: bruceleonard writer.com. While there, please sign up for my infrequent newsletters, which will keep you informed about upcoming book signings and new releases. I will also let you know when my novels that don't involve Hadley will be published.

I thank all of you (or all y'all) for supporting my efforts as a novelist. I promise to do my best to continue to deliver quality novels for you to enjoy.

Printed in Great Britain
by Amazon

41971148R00158